The Time Hunters and the Sword of Ages

Carl Ashmore

For Lisa and Alice

For Kath, Caitlin and Eleanor

For Athina

For Keith and Barbara

For Jane and Finn

In memory of Bernard Ashmore, Cameron Waugh, and John Lindenberger

CHAPTERS

ACKNOWLEDGMENTS

I would like to thank the following people for their unwavering support for the TH Books:

Mum, Anne & John, Aud & Rob, Mache, Liz and Isla, Gabe, Jane and Finn, Pat Owen, Gingerlily, Frenchie and the Fantastic Four, Kay, Vanessa, Kay, Tej, Amy, Sarah and Matthew Wise, Joo / Julie Stacey, Rob and Leah, Mike Eldred, Emma Sly, Emily Grantham, Dawn Hills, Jamie, Ann Astrop, Mark and Helen Marcia Donkin, Andy Taylor and the Stoke on Trent College Film crew of 1996, Isabel and Zac, Michael Fleming, Amanda Fleming, Velma Rasmussen, Caitlynn Clewlow, Phil Jones, Ben Peyton, Kathryn Marriott, Mark Baddeley, Mel Green and Isabella, Jen and Grady Adams, Heather B Moon Author, Fred and Ann Moyer McCann, Steph Weston, Dean and Ethan Yurke, Max Andrew, Lola and Emma Grace Roberts Dinsley, Daisy and Markus, Rachel and Henry, Louie and Evie McKay, Holly Beddow, Kelly Ann Inman, Lilly Ann Sidwell, Alex Rockeimer, Caralyn Beattie, Lily Thraves, Sarah Lily and Isaac, Wendy and Kira, Susan Watson, Lesley, Cheryl Ann, Shiloh, Austin, Wyatt and Dakota, Kayleigh and Archie, Simon Parker, Simon and Alexander McGovern, Sally Parsons, Rosie and Alex.

Cover Design: Dreamtime.com/Andreus

Thanks to Graham Worthington for audio support. Please check out www.autumnlungs.com

Thanks to Sean Cusack for assistance with cover design.

Thanks to Richard Litherland for the forthcoming Book Trailer.

Thanks to Giles Livesy for character art - www.pawcasso.co.uk

Carl Ashmore

Chapter 1

The Modern Prometheus

Darmstadt, Germany. 1714

Otto Kruger's eyes snapped open. At once, his senses were assaulted with information: the bitter scent of disinfectant; the sight of the rutted stone ceiling above; the purr of a machine humming softly to his left. Remaining still, he took a moment to process this new environment.

Where was he?

The last thing he remembered was being helped into a time machine outside a pirate tavern on Nassau, arriving at a Gerathnium facility somewhere in the Kamchatka Peninsula in Medieval Russia, before being transported, drifting in and out of consciousness, to an underground room. But more than the events, he remembered the pain, the unspeakable pain, as the blood spilled from his severed arm like an unstoppable tap.

His head blazed with fury as he recalled the swordfight that had resulted in the loss of his right arm – the clash with that insufferable groundsman, Will Shakelock. And then another memory joined the others, his last before this very point: he was lying on a rusty bed, barely large enough to cover his massive frame. An unseen syringe propelled the anaesthetic into his body, sending him into a merciful oblivion, as the words of his employer, Emerson Drake, met his ears.

'You will live, Otto. I told you, I reward those most loyal to me. I shall rebuild you, better than before, better than anyone that has come before. You will consider these events a blessing, I promise you ...'

But how long ago was that? He had no idea.

It was then he heard that same voice again. 'Welcome back, Otto.'

Kruger turned his head. Emerson Drake was standing there, a self-satisfied smile set on his thin lips.

'Thank you, sir.'

'How do you feel?'

Kruger took a second to answer. 'Good.'

Drake's eyes narrowed. 'Just ... good?'

Kruger sensed his employer had expected a different answer. And now he was fully conscious, he could understand why. Good didn't begin to describe it. He felt magnificent. The pain had gone, replaced by an innate raw power he'd never felt before.

Kruger pushed himself up. As he did, his icy green eyes fell on his right side. Grafted seamlessly to his elbow was a silver arm, identical in size and weight to the one he had lost.

'Do you approve?' Drake asked.

Kruger didn't answer. Instead, he raised his enormous silver hand and balled his fingers into a fist. The deep scar on his right cheek was cast in a silvery hue. Slowly, his mouth formed the following words, 'I do, sir.'

'Excellent,' Drake replied. 'The arm is made from a polynythene carbonite alloy, and attached via the somatosensory system, to the premotor cortex region of your brain. Essentially, it will feel and function precisely as your old arm did. With one notable exception, you can now punch a hole in a wall without feeling a thing.'

Kruger glanced at the wall opposite as if keen to try this out.

'And I trust that you won't mind I made a few other modifications whilst you were asleep – sensory and corporeal augmentations that make you unique.'

Kruger looked confused.

Drake responded with a smirk. 'You are now stronger, faster, more agile than any man alive.' He paused. 'In short, I've made you super-human…'

Kruger was about to respond when he noticed two men in the far corner of the room. The first, slim and elegantly dressed in a flowing robe, had a high forehead and thick black hair that spiralled down in tight curls. He was staring back at Kruger, mesmerised. His mouth was ajar, as if wishing to express words of approval but unable to find the confidence to do so. The second, a middle-aged man with a striking gold and white striped tie had a warm, generous face, but wore a very different expression - as pale as stone, he looked petrified.

'Ah, of course,' Drake said. 'Otto, may I introduce you to these two gentlemen?' He nodded at the curly haired man. 'This is Johann Konrad Dippel, our esteemed host. Indeed, we currently inhabit a room in the western tower of his magnificent castle. Mister Dippel has been an Associate of mine for some time now, and I consider him to possess one of the most deviant minds of the early eighteenth century.'

Dippel clearly considered this a great compliment. 'Danke schön, Mister Drake,' he said, before bowing at Kruger. 'My house is yours, Herr Kruger.'

Drake turned to the other man, who was making an effort

to contain his trembling body from the others. 'And this is Arthur Kingsley Porter – Professor at Harvard University, and without doubt one of the most eminent scholars of medieval architecture in the twentieth century.'

Porter looked too scared to respond.

Drake gave an ugly smile. 'I'm afraid Mister Porter had to be coerced into making the time-trip, but I did feel he should see this wonderful castle. After all, it is indisputably one of the most renowned specimens in history, there's no question about that. Have you found it interesting, Mister Porter?'

The man gave an anxious nod. 'Y-yes,' he replied in an American accent.

'I am glad,' Drake replied. 'Anyway, Otto, would you care to stand? I'm keen to see just how successful the surgery has been.'

With a swift turn, Kruger dropped his legs to the floor. He pushed himself on to his feet. At six foot five, he dwarfed everyone in the room.

'And do you feel fit enough to get back to work?' Drake asked. 'I have some thoughts on the fourth Eden Relic, and I think you might appreciate where the trail is leading.'

'I welcome it, sir.'

Drake gave a nod of satisfaction. 'Excellent. Then it seems our work here is done.' He turned to Dippel. 'Mister Dippel, thank you again for your hospitality.'

'You honour this house with your patronage, sire,' Dippel replied.

'And Mister Porter,' Drake said. 'I assume you wish to return to your time and your charming wife, Lucy?'

Hope flickered in Porter's eyes. 'Yes … please. Very much.'

Drake pondered this for a moment. 'I'm afraid that won't

be happening,' he said. 'You see … you're a friend of Percy Halifax, are you not?' He spat out the name like the words scorched his tongue.

Porter said nothing as if fearful of giving the wrong answer.

'I know you are,' Drake confirmed. 'But what you're not aware of is that Percy Halifax is a time traveller, just like me … or that a few months ago, I told him if he continued to try and thwart my activities, I would punish his friends and family.' Turning into the light, his face fell into silhouette. 'I'm afraid he didn't listen…'

A horrific realisation spread across Porter's face.

Drake glanced at Kruger. 'Otto, would you give Mister Porter a *hand* in showing the dangers of befriending Percy Halifax.'

Without hesitation, Kruger marched across the room. Before Porter could shout an objection, Kruger's silver hand seized his throat, crushing his windpipe, transforming his intended scream into a muffled, desperate wheeze.

Kruger hoisted Porter into the air.

Porter kicked wildly, his fingers clawing at Kruger's hand, but it was to no avail. Kruger's grip tightened like a vice, choking the air from his lungs.

Drake watched it all with a cold detachment. He looked uninterested, bored even. 'I could suggest you choose better friends in the future, Mister Porter,' he said. 'But then again … you have no future.' He nodded at Kruger.

Like a child throwing a ragdoll, Kruger hurled Porter at the far wall, ten feet away or so. Porter smashed into the stonework, before crashing to the ground, twisted and lifeless.

Drake looked at Kruger, who seemed shocked at his newfound strength. 'You seem to have made a full recovery,

13

Otto?'

'I think so, sir.'

'Then I suggest we leave this time zone,' Drake replied. 'I intend to be very busy in the coming months, so I'd like you to go on a time-trip for me, a very important trip.'

'As you wish.'

Drake smiled. 'You know, Otto, I've always appreciated your ability to follow orders. And you never question, you never ask for anything in return.'

'Ah, but this time there is something, sir.'

Drake looked surprised. 'Really? Continue …'

Kruger's voice fell to an ominous snarl. 'I want the groundsman. I want him to suffer like no other.'

'Of course you do.' Drake shrugged indifferently. 'Then Shakelock's fate is in your hands.' He turned to Dippel. 'I'll have to erase this tower from history, Dippel. I've left too much of a mark for it to continue to exist.'

'I will not object, sire,' Dippel replied.

'I know. Actually, in the future, some credit you with destroying this tower yourself in a failed experiment using nitroglycerine.'

'Nitroglycerine?' Dippel replied, puzzled. 'And what is that?'

'It's an explosive liquid,' Drake replied. 'However, as Ascanio Sobrero doesn't invent it until 1847, many considered this an impossible claim. Ironically, it's nitroglycerine I intend to use to blow this place to oblivion.' He chuckled. 'Isn't it fascinating how the actions of the time traveller today can influence the minds of tomorrow?'

'And, Otto, let me tell you another story, one that also intertwines the castle and the life of our host. I said earlier this castle was a renowned specimen – well, its name is Burg Frankenstein. Does that ring any bells?'

Kruger nodded. 'It certainly does, sir.'

'I thought it might. In a hundred years time a young woman, Mary Shelley, will visit Burg Frankenstein, and conceive an idea that will later become arguably the most famous horror novel of any age. And, furthermore, do you know whom many believe was the inspiration for Miss Shelley's protagonist, the scientist, Victor Frankenstein?' He nodded at Dippel. 'None other than Mister Dippel himself. Now isn't that amusing?'

Kruger remained stone-faced. 'Yes, sir.'

'But the real irony is, with my recent experiments at the castle, it's conceivably me who is the actual figure on which she based her tragic hero.' Drake laughed. 'And if that's the case you know what that makes you, don't you?'

For the first time since he had gained consciousness, Kruger's face was split with a smile. He glanced over at Porter's corpse before looking back at Drake.

'That would make me the monster, sir...'

Chapter 2

Cat on a Hot School Roof

Becky Mellor was fed up. She'd been sitting on a hard bench in a draughty corridor, staring at the clock opposite, which ticked so slowly she felt certain a spiteful teacher had rigged it deliberately to extend the school day.

Only an hour earlier, pupils had swarmed out of Coppenhill High School, desperate to start their Easter holidays. But not her. She was stuck here waiting for her brother, Joe, who had been given detention for fighting with an older boy. Granted, the fight had been with Steven 'The Mallet' Hallet, a notorious bully, and the only person she knew with a chin like a coconut, but that didn't alter the fact she had plans, and remaining at school one second longer than she had to wasn't one of them.

With a frown, she looked down at the coin in her hand. Well, if truth were told, it wasn't exactly in her hand - it hovered about an inch above it, spinning like a carousel, her shoulders hunched in an arc, shielding it from sight of any unwelcome witness. And this was one of the many astonishing things about Becky Mellor. She was telekinetic: she could move objects with her mind.

She had developed this gift the previous summer on a trip to Ancient Greece with her time travelling Uncle Percy, but, at the time, had no capacity to control where and when it occurred. Since then, however, she had learned to master it, and now it came as naturally as breathing.

As a rule, she avoided using these powers – the last thing she wanted was to draw attention to herself, but every now and again she couldn't resist. Only the previous week, in the school canteen, she overheard Debbie Crabtree telling her buck-toothed friend, Melinda Palmer, that Becky's hair looked like seaweed, until for some inexplicable reason, Debbie's plate of Spaghetti Bolognese rose off the table and slammed into her face like a custard pie, starting the rumour a poltergeist haunted the school. Another time, she discovered Joe had emptied her tub of moisturiser and replaced it with marmalade. In revenge, she sent a toilet brush flying into his bedroom to beat him round the head until he begged her forgiveness.

Becky glanced up at the clock again. She exhaled a despondent sigh. What made matters worse was that she knew Uncle Percy was in the visitors' car park, waiting to escort her and Joe to what promised to be another wonderful week at Bowen Hall. Furthermore, Uncle Percy had said something during a recent phone call that had intrigued her to the point of obsession. His words still reverberated in her head.

'I really can't wait for you to see what's happened. It's a sight to behold. In fact, if I may employ your vernacular for a moment, it's "totally awesome..."'

But when Becky pressed him for more information he refused to answer, insisting its true impact came from witnessing it first hand. She couldn't imagine what it might be. After all, everything at Bowen Hall was awesome as far as she was concerned – from the magnificent Jacobean building, to its array of remarkable inhabitants: Maria and Jacob, the housekeeper and butler; Will Shakelock, the groundsman; Milly and Sabian, the Sabre-tooth Tigers; and Gump and Peggy, the Triceratops and snow-white winged horse.

So what could make him react like that? She couldn't wait to find out.

Impatiently, she glanced down the dimly lit corridor hoping for Joe's athletic figure to appear. She looked back at the coin, concentrated hard and watched it spin faster and faster, until its edge blurred into a silvery cloud. Then, from her left, she heard an unfamiliar voice.

'Are you camping here for the night?'

Momentarily flustered, Becky let the coin fall into the palm of her hand, hoping the passer by hadn't noticed. Looking up, she saw a tall boy emerge from the gloom, a floppy black fringe framing his handsome face. He was wearing a tracksuit and carried a sports bag across his shoulders. She recognised him at once. Dan Hardman was in the year above her, a brilliant athlete, captain of his year's football team and widely accepted as the hottest boy in Year 10.

Becky was lost for words. 'Err, I - I'm waiting for someone,' she replied weakly.

'Your boyfriend?'

Becky gave an involuntary laugh that sounded like a pig. 'My brother, Joe,' she said. 'He's in detention.'

Dan revealed the kind of smile usually reserved for film stars or professional footballers. 'Joe Mellor. Yeah, he was fighting with that idiot, Steven Hallet. I hear he was winning, too, before Miss Canner split up the scrap. Not bad for a Year 8 kid.'

'I don't know about that.'

'I'll wait with you if you'd like.'

'Err, sure.'

Setting his bag on the bench, Dan sat down beside her. 'I'm Dan. Dan Hardman.'

'Becky Mellor.'

'I know who you are,' Dan said. 'I used to deliver newspapers to your house in Lindon Crescent. Your mum gave me a tenner tip last Christmas. That was well nice of her. She seems really nice.'

'She's all right.'

'I also saw those pics you posted of your uncle on Facebook. He's got that dead cool Rolls Royce, hasn't he?'

Becky couldn't believe he'd seen anything she'd posted on Facebook. 'It's a Silver Ghost.'

'It's wicked.'

'It is … yeah.'

'I wish I had an uncle like that,' Dan said. 'What's his name?'

'Uncle Percy. He's pretty cool.'

'And does he really live in that massive house?'

'It's called Bowen Hall,' Becky replied. 'It's well nice.'

Dan took a long, surprisingly deep breath. 'Listen, I don't normally do this, and say no if you want to, but would you fancy going for a coffee sometime?' He paused. 'With me…' he added as though he hadn't made himself clear.

It was then Becky realised his strange behaviour was due to something completely unexpected. He was nervous. Dan Hardman was asking her out. And he was nervous about it.

Becky didn't know how to respond. 'I don't know.'

It was Dan's turn to look embarrassed. 'I mean, forget it. It was just … I don't know … it might've been nice, but forget it.'

Becky's pulse was racing. 'No. I mean, yes, it might be nice. I'd like to go. But only if you would.'

'I wouldn't ask if I didn't.'

'I don't suppose you would.'

'It's a date then.'

Becky felt her stomach lurch. 'Okay.'

Dan looked relieved. 'I'll send you a message on Facebook and you can let me know when you want to go.'

'Cool,' Becky nodded.

Just then, another voice filled the corridor. 'Hey up.' Joe walked towards them, his school tie dangling loose around his neck, his shirt hanging out of his trousers.

Panicking, Becky cast him a surprisingly toothy smile. 'Hi, Joe,' she said in an overly cheerful voice. 'How are you?'

Joe knew at once something was wrong. 'I'm sound. Are you all right?'

'Yes,' Becky said. 'Why'd you ask?'

Joe studied her closely. 'Because you're as red as a beetroot.'

'I'm not.'

'You are,' Joe replied. 'You're sweating cobs, too. What's the matter - are you sick?'

'No,' Becky replied, trying desperately to stop her reply becoming a snarl.

Dan stood up hastily and scooped up his bag. 'Anyway, I'd better get going.'

'Okay,' Becky said, avoiding eye contact with him. 'Bye.'

Dan nodded at Joe. 'See you, mate.'

'See you.' Joe watched Dan leave the corridor. 'What's goin' on?'

'Nowt,' Becky replied offhandedly.

'There must be coz normally you'd rip me a new one for getting detention when we're going to Bowen Hall.'

'It's okay,' Becky muttered. 'No big deal.'

'Were you being nice to me because of Dan Hardman?'

'What?'

'You don't fancy him, do you?' Joe asked. 'Because if you do, you haven't got a cat in hell's chance.'

'What do you mean?'

'All the girls fancy him,' Joe grinned. 'And some of those in his year are well fit. You're way out of your league.'

Becky looked furious. 'Out of my league?'

'God, yeah. He's like One Direction handsome. And you're – well – you're just you …'

Becky was about to explode when the strangest thing happened. A small cat-like animal with silky brown fur rushed past them, growling playfully, its open mouth revealing two long fangs much longer than those of any ordinary cat.

Horrified, Becky looked at Joe, whose face had frozen with shock. 'Sabian!'

'Bloody Hell!' Joe said. 'Get him!'

Becky set off like a rocket. Shoulder to shoulder, she and Joe sprinted down the corridor, the patter of Sabian's paws echoing against the hard wooden floor. Becky watched Sabian skid to a halt, before turning right and scampering up a flight of stairs.

Becky's heart threatened to burst from her mouth. She knew teachers always remained long after the school day had ended, and, if they were caught, how could she and Joe possibly explain away the existence of a twelve thousand year old Sabre-tooth tiger cub?

What on earth was Uncle Percy thinking? And where exactly was he?

Becky and Joe powered up the stairs, anxious not to lose sight of Sabian's tail.

Floor one.

Floor two.

Floor three.

Floor four.

By the time she had reached the fifth and final floor, Becky's limbs were on fire. Not stopping to draw breath, her eyes scanned the corridor ahead. Sabian was nowhere to be seen.

'Where is he?' Joe panted heavily, leaning against the bannister.

Suddenly, a faint yelp clipped the air.

Looking round, Becky spied Sabian's silhouette beside a door that was slightly ajar. Racing over, a stitch welling in her side, she watched him disappear through the doorway.

'That's the roof,' Joe panted, catching her up.

Tentatively, they followed Sabian outside. A golden sun filled the deep blue sky. Scanning the area, Becky could feel the baking corrugated iron roof through her shoes.

'If we're caught,' Joe said, 'we are in such deep –'

Before he could finish, a throaty cough sounded from their rear. Becky and Joe swivelled round. A tall, slender figure, elegantly dressed in a pristine suit, strolled into the light, his thin mouth curved in an ugly sneer. The man was sliding a lifeless Sabian into a leather satchel.

'Good afternoon, kiddies,' Emerson Drake said. 'Long time, no see…'

Chapter 3

Falling Down

Becky fought back the tears as she watched Drake close the satchel. She knew immediately what had happened. Sabian had been murdered and transformed into a Cyrobot just to get to her attention.

Drake seemed to read her thoughts. 'Don't upset yourself, Rebecca. It isn't your furry chum from Bowen Hall,' he said. 'Your uncle's security measures prevent my entering Bowen Hall's grounds, otherwise I would've happily got the real thing, but no …' he nodded at the satchel, 'I found this cub wandering the plains of Lagoa Santa in the Cenozoic Era … so nothing to worry your pretty head over.'

'But you still killed it!'

'Well, to employ a cliché - you can't make an omelette without breaking a few eggs.'

'You're sick in the head.'

'Sticks and stones, my dear...' Drake walked to the roof's edge and looked out. 'How nice to be back in Manchester. You know, it's always held great fascination for me – the world's first industrialised city, the site of the first splitting of the atom, and the birthplace of the modern computer. Of course, it's also home to some of the most notorious serial killers in history … ' He chuckled to himself. 'It must be all the rain.' His face brightened as he turned back to Becky and Joe. 'And, of course, I've always had a soft spot for Manchester United.'

'That explains so much,' Joe growled.

'Why are you here?' Becky asked. 'What do you want?'

'A question worthy of Aristotle himself,' Drake replied. 'What do I want? Well, in short, everything. And I believe I'm well on my way to achieving that goal. However, why do you assume I'm here for myself, that I'm always so self-serving? I really think you've misjudged me.'

'We haven't,' Becky replied coolly. 'You're an evil, psychotic, lying, devious scumbag. Simple as...'

Drake shot Becky a look of feigned indignation. 'Oh, Rebecca, I might be many things but I'm not a liar. And therein rests the irony ... ' He paused, leaning in slightly as if revealing a confidence. 'Lies surround you - surround both of you ... a web of glorious lies, and you have no idea. You just live quite happily, content in your ignorance, blissfully unaware of the truth, unwitting pawns in someone else's game, blindly trusting those you really shouldn't trust...'

Becky's disgust was fleetingly replaced by confusion.

'You see, I've been doing my research,' Drake continued. 'In fact, I've been so fascinated putting pieces of a quite elaborate jigsaw together, I've neglected hunting down the last two Eden Relics. But I've not been able to stop myself. It's been such fun. Still, I've nearly completed the jigsaw now and believe me it paints a most illuminating picture.'

'What are you talking about?' Becky snapped.

'Oh, it's not for me to say,' Drake replied. 'But let me say this – you live in your own Plato's cave, only seeing the world you're presented with and not the world as it is, spoon-fed a fictitious reality by the people you trust most like a mother feeds a baby.'

Joe fixed him with an angry glare. 'Are you gonna try

something or are you just gonna bore us to death with crap?'

'Try something?' Drake's face-hardened. 'I've merely come to deliver a message, boy. And as matter of fact, it's a message for you.'

'Go on,' Joe said.

'It's a private message,' Drake replied. 'For your ears only.'

Joe didn't move. 'Anything you want to say, you can say to both of us.'

'Then you don't get it,' Drake replied. 'Come here. I'll whisper it to you.'

'Don't, Joe!' Becky said.

Joe ignored her. In three steps, he was standing toe to toe with Drake. 'What's your message then?' he asked. 'I'm not afraid of you.'

Drake leaned in, his eyes wild. 'My message is this … you should be!' In a flash, he had flipped Joe round, clamped his arm around his neck and wrenched him close, choking him.

'LET GO OF HIM!' Becky screamed.

'It's your fault I'm doing this, Rebecca,' Drake hissed, tightening his grip. 'I'm concerned your telekinesis has developed to a point where you could prevent me going anywhere, while this boy alerts your uncle in the car park. And that wouldn't be good for me. However, I think I can make a safe retreat if your powers are otherwise … engaged.'

'Just let him go!'

'As you wish, Rebecca…' With surprising strength, Drake hoisted Joe in the air. Then he threw him off the roof.

Like a bullet, Becky sprinted to the edge. She looked down. Joe was falling fast, the hard ground rising to smash his body into pieces. Heart pounding, she extended her hand, at the same time focussing on him with all her might. Immediately, a peculiar feeling swept her skull, like warm water, every nerve in her body on fire.

Joe thrashed and flailed as he clawed at nothing. But then with a sudden jerk, he stopped mid-air, six feet or so from the ground.

Becky guided him down, until his feet met the path beneath. Then she collapsed to her knees, panting, every bit of strength deserting her. To her left, she heard a loud crack and knew Drake had gone, his portravella taking him to who knew where. With renewed energy, she leapt to her feet and charged across the rooftop, through the open door. Flying down the corridor, everything a blur, she hurtled down the stairs, and was soon charging down the exit corridor to the world outside. Crashing through the front door, she forked right along the north face of the school and saw Joe. Flooded with relief, she approached him. 'Are you all right?'

Joe didn't answer.

It was then she noticed he looked troubled, his eyes angled downward. Tracing his eye-line, her stomach churned. Dan Hardman was sitting crumpled on the grass, his face empty of colour. He was staring up at Joe as if he was from another planet.

'He saw everything,' Joe said flatly. 'He's feeling a bit queasy.'

Becky gulped.

Dan glanced up at her. 'I don't understand,' he said, looking back at Joe. 'H-how?'

Just then, they heard footsteps from behind.

Fearing they had attracted even more of an unwelcome audience, Becky turned to see Uncle Percy sprinting over, ashen-faced and distressed.

Reaching them, he glanced down at Dan and forced a smile. 'Good afternoon, everyone.'

'Drake was here,' Joe said.

'That would explain your recent attempt at flight.'

'You saw it?'

'From a distance,' Uncle Percy replied. 'Are you okay?'

'Fine. Drake was talking weird. He said that -'

'You can tell me about it later,' Uncle Percy interrupted. 'Let's deal with one thing at a time. Now, who's this?'

'This is Dan,' Joe said.

'Hello, Dan,' Uncle Percy said. 'I'm Percy Halifax. You've had quite an eventful start to your Easter holidays, haven't you?'

'I – I err –'

'He saw me,' Joe cut in.

'Of course he did.' Uncle Percy slipped his hand into his jacket pocket. 'Then I'm sure you're wondering what on earth is going on. Am I right?'

'Y-yes,' Dan replied.

'I wouldn't even know where to begin,' Uncle Percy replied. 'But I'll tell you what…' He pulled out what looked like a digital camera. Becky recognised it at once as a Temporaliser – a device to render someone immobile. 'May I take your picture?'

Before Dan could respond, a thin jet of blue light surged from the lens and encircled his head, before fading away, leaving him as still as a statue.

Joe beamed from ear to ear. 'I love it when you do that.'

'It's necessary,' Uncle Percy replied. 'Now, Dan doesn't really need to remember the last few minutes, does he?' He withdrew a small gadget that resembled a torch.

This time, Becky recognised it as a Memoraser – a device to eradicate someone's memory.

Uncle Percy pressed two digits on the Memoraser. 'I'll tell you what, why don't we memorase his last twenty minutes, just to be on the safe side.'

Becky made a strange squeak. Her first ever date, one with the hottest boy at Coppenhill High School, would cease to be along with his memory.

'Are you okay, Becky?' Uncle Percy asked, concerned.

Becky sighed miserably. 'Yep.'

Joe frowned at her. 'What is the matter with you?'

'Nothing.'

Uncle Percy clicked the Memoraser. A shaft of silvery light ignited Dan's eyes, which swirled like marbles in their sockets. 'Now let's Retemp him.' He reset the Temporaliser and clicked it again. At once, a shaft of green light spurted from the lens, shrouding Dan's head in a shimmering green mist. As it dissolved, Dan emerged from his daze, shaken and confused.

'Hello, Dan,' Uncle Percy said, flashing him a reassuring smile.

'H-hello,' Dan replied.

'You've had a little turn, but you're okay now.'

'Oh, err, right.'

'I'm Percy Halifax.'

'Hiya,' Dan said, shaking Uncle Percy's extended hand. 'I'm Dan Hardman.' He noticed Becky. 'I – I know you. You're Becky Mellor. I used to deliver newspapers to your mum's house. She gave me a tenner tip last Christmas.'

Becky's heart sank. They had had the very same conversation only minutes before. 'Did she?'

'Yeah,' Dan replied. 'She seems really nice.'

'She is very nice,' Uncle Percy agreed, helping Dan to his feet. 'But Dan, perhaps it would be best if you made your way home. We don't want you to have another turn, do we?'

'No,' Dan replied, nodding. 'I think you're right.' Unsteady on his feet, he picked up his school bag. 'Well, see you. Thanks for, err, helping me out.'

'Not a problem,' Uncle Percy said. 'Goodbye, Dan.'

'See ya, mate,' Joe said.

'Bye,' Becky muttered.

Dan's eyes met Becky's for a lingering moment, his mouth offering the hint of a smile, before he turned and sloped off.

As she watched him leave, Becky's stomach churned. And there and then, she knew her Easter holidays would be devoted to taking a bucket load of photographs of the Silver Ghost and uploading them on to Facebook.

Chapter 4

At the Hop

The moment Dan disappeared from sight Uncle Percy lost his self-control and seized Joe in a crushing hug. 'You nearly gave me a heart attack, Joe.'

'In all fairness,' Joe mumbled into Uncle Percy's shoulder. 'I think Drake should take some of the blame.'

'I know,' Uncle Percy replied. 'But are you sure you're okay? No breaks, no strains.'

'I'm fine, but you do know I'm at school … this is not cool.'

Uncle Percy released him. 'I wouldn't want to shatter your street cred.'

'Don't worry,' Becky mumbled, still peeved about Dan. 'He hasn't got any.'

Uncle Percy noted her glum expression. 'Are you all right, Becky?'

'She's fine,' Joe said. 'She's got the hots for the school stud and she's miffed your brain zap blew the only chat she'll ever have with him.'

'I am sorry, Becky,' Uncle Percy. 'I had no idea.'

'There's nowt to have any idea about,' Becky snapped back. 'I don't have the hots for anyone.'

'Course you don't,' Joe muttered sarcastically.

'Up yours.'

'Up yours, too.'

'Now, now,' Uncle Percy said firmly. 'Let's not go up anybody's, shall we? Your Easter holidays have already started somewhat eventfully. Why don't we let bygones be bygones, put this squabbling behind us, and try and have a nice time?'

'Okay,' Joe replied. Becky nodded.

'I've picked up your bags from your mother's house,' Uncle Percy said. 'So shall we make tracks?' He walked off in the direction of the car park. As Joe caught up with him, he said, 'Now, young man, what was this detention all about?'

'Scrapping,' Joe replied. 'But it was —'

Uncle Percy's mouth pressed into a stern line. 'There can be no excuses for mindless fisticuffs, Joe, regardless of what you consider a reasonable justification.'

'This Year 10 bully grabbed my mate, Zammo, dragged him into the girls' bogs and was about to flush his head down the toilet, when I stopped him.'

Uncle Percy looked conflicted. 'This could be a rare occasion when there may be some just cause. As Edmund Burke famously said, "All that is required for evil to flourish in the world is for good men to do nothing." So in the spirit of Mister Burke, I hope you gave the scoundrel a good thrashing.'

'I did okay.'

'Just don't go making a habit of it.'

'I won't.'

Uncle Percy, Joe and Becky entered the visitors' car park to see Beryl, Uncle Percy's Hackney cab and time machine, was the last car parked there. They climbed in.

Uncle Percy turned the ignition over and pulled onto the street.

'If you're planning on time travelling to Bowen Hall,' Joe said. 'You're not gonna find a free space around Manchester to make the trip.'

'Not a problem,' Uncle Percy replied. 'Percival Totteridge has kindly loaned us the use of his garage for said purpose. He lives in Whalley Range, so we're not far away.'

As they weaved through the busy streets, Becky gazed out of the window. She recalled the last time she had travelled in Beryl, her amazement at discovering the car was also a submarine, and the relentless attack by zombie sharks that left the car ravaged and devastated. Shivering at the memory, her thoughts drifted eagerly to Dan Hardman. Her heart skipped a beat. Okay, he couldn't remember asking her out now, but at least he had, and maybe he would do so again. A glorious vision entered her head – she and Dan were eating lunch together in the school canteen, opposite Debbie Crabtree, whose fat face had turned sprout-green with envy. Just as a smile curled on her mouth, another image surfaced, tarnishing all that had gone before: Emerson Drake. Her delight turned to revulsion. Before she could stop herself, she stared at Uncle Percy and said in an icy voice, 'Emerson Drake said you're lying to us. What does he mean?'

'What?'

'He didn't mention you by name, but he might as well have.'

'And what did he accuse me of lying about?'

'He didn't say,' Becky replied. 'But he did say we were surrounded by a web of lies and ignorant of the truth. So … are we?'

Uncle Percy fell silent. He looked uncomfortable. 'And is this why he paid you a visit?'

'Other than to throw Joe off a roof, he didn't seem to have come for any other reason,' Becky replied. 'So … is he right?

Are you lying to us about something?'

Uncle Percy sighed. 'Emerson Drake is a deceiver, a manipulator and he'll use any weapon at his disposal to inflict harm on others. In this instance, it's words.'

'He said he doesn't lie.'

Uncle Percy gave a hollow laugh. 'And isn't that the biggest lie of all? Drake will stop at nothing to destroy anyone and everything that opposes him. We oppose him. We stand for everything he isn't. And he's trying to destroy our faith in each other. He's trying to drive a wedge between us.'

Joe frowned at Becky. 'Drake's full of crap. Stop stressing about it.'

Becky ignored him, and looked warily at Uncle Percy. 'You would tell us if there was something we didn't know, wouldn't you?'

'There are many things you don't know, Becky,' Uncle Percy replied. 'And many things I don't know, either. And yes, perhaps there are some things I haven't told you, because I don't think it's in your best interest to know them.'

Becky was about to challenge when Uncle Percy continued.

'As I'm sure there are things in your life you would prefer to keep from me…'

The conversation with Dan Hardman popped straight into Becky's head.

'Now, I respect your decision on such matters,' Uncle Percy said simply. 'And you … you should respect mine. I don't know exactly what Emerson Drake is referring to, if anything at all, but I do know we're supposed to have a wonderful Easter holidays together, so let's concentrate on that, shall we? And not on some pestilential bile spouted by a maniac…'

Becky didn't feel satisfied at all. 'But –'

Joe had had enough. 'Cane it, will you, Becks?' he said. 'You keep stuff from me all the time. And if Uncle Percy doesn't want us to know something I'm sure there's a reason. Why're you always poking your big conk into other people's business.'

Becky huffed loudly, folded her arms and slouched into the chair. 'I don't,' she muttered. 'And I haven't got a big conk, fat head!'

A few minutes of stony silence later, Uncle Percy drove on to the long shingle drive of a large detached house. He curved left into an open garage, far away from the roadside. Cloaked in a sudden darkness, he brought Beryl to a halt, and looked back at Becky.

'Now, have we had enough of the silent treatment? We won't have a particularly memorable time if we don't talk to each other.'

Becky took one look at him, his face hopeful. 'Okay.'

'Good,' Uncle Percy said with a smile. 'I really enjoy Easter, and I've got plenty of Easter treats lined up for you.' He leaned over and typed six digits on to Beryl's time pad. At once, a thick mist of light poured from the dashboard, illuminating the interior of the car.

'Bowen Hall, here we come!' Joe shouted joyously.

For once, Becky couldn't share his enthusiasm. She couldn't shake the feeling Drake's accusations had left Uncle Percy peculiarly troubled, distressed even. And, as far as she was concerned, he could be as slippery as he wanted, play whatever word games he chose, but there was something significant he wasn't telling them, something that involved her and Joe. And she was determined to find out what that was. No matter how difficult it was to hear.

*

A moment later, Becky was staring up at Bowen Hall, its hundreds of windows glinting like polished diamonds in the high sun. At once, all thoughts of Drake dissolved, replaced by the burning excitement of the week to come. Her gaze shifted to the front door, fully expecting it to burst open, to reveal Maria, arms waggling, hurtling toward them at full pelt, Jacob limping close behind, as fast as his impaired leg would allow. But the door remained firmly shut. She was about to ask where they were when Uncle Percy seemed to anticipate the question.

'Now there's something I should tell you,' he said gravely. 'Maria and Jacob are away.'

Becky's eyes narrowed. 'Away?'

'They're travelling.'

'Time travelling?'

'Yes.'

Becky was shocked. It was the last thing she'd expected. 'When? Where've they gone?'

'Berlin,' Uncle Percy replied.

'When?'

'Nineteen Fifty Three.'

'Why?' Joe asked.

Uncle Percy took a solemn breath. 'Yesterday was the anniversary of the death of their son, daughter in law and grandaughter. They return to Berlin every year for a few days to visit their grave.'

Silence filled the car.

'Why Nineteen Fifty Three?' Joe asked.

'They choose a different year each time they return, so they don't bump into themselves.'

'When will they be back?' Joe asked.

'Late tonight, I believe,' Uncle Percy replied. 'Obviously it's a sensitive time for them, so please don't bring the subject up unless they do.'

'We won't,' Becky said.

'Course not,' Joe added.

'But Maria did leave strict instructions you weren't to feel sad for them,' Uncle Percy said, managing a smile. 'She's looking forward to seeing you both and she intends to spoil you rotten with all kinds of edible goodies. Infact, she's already baked an Easter Lamb cake the size of a Great Dane.'

'Easter lamb cake?' Becky said. 'A cake made out of lamb?'

'A sponge cake in the shape of a lamb,' Uncle Percy clarified. 'It's called Osterlamm Kuchen, and is a very old Eastern European tradition. Quite delicious.' He opened the driver's door and climbed out.

Exiting the car, Becky heard a shrill yelp and saw Sabian scamper from the nearby trees, his mother, Milly, striding majestically behind him. Sabian rushed toward her, weaving excitedly between her legs. After all that had happened at school, she couldn't begin to express how happy she felt to see him alive and well.

Will Shakelock followed the cats into the open. 'A fine evening to you all.'

'Hey, Will,' Becky waved.

Joe raced over to him. 'Drake chucked me off a roof,' he said as eagerly as if reporting a good football result.

Will was lost for words.

'He was at our school,' Joe continued. 'He used a dead Sabre tooth cub we thought was Sabian to lure us onto the roof, and then he threw me off it. I thought I was mush, but Super Becks saved the day with her *googly* powers.'

Bewildered, Will glanced at Uncle Percy.

'I'm afraid it's true, William,' Uncle Percy confirmed.

'And where's Drake now?' Will asked.

'He's long gone,' Joe replied. His eyes ignited as he remembered something. 'I joined a sword fighting class in Hulme. The teacher says he hasn't seen anything like me before. He reckons I'm a natural. Wanna test me?'

'Why not?' Will replied, smiling. 'But first you should settle in your quarters.'

Joe beamed. 'Okay.' He raced to the taxi's boot, opened it and grabbed his suitcase. Then he and Will approached the front door, talking animatedly, neither of them pausing for breath.

Becky grinned as she watched them disappear into the house. 'He has, you know,' she said to Uncle Percy. 'Every night after school, when he's not doing his archery, he's been going to that sword club. And I hate to admit it, but he's well good. No, he's better than that, he's brilliant. What with that and the archery, he's become Will-lite … a spotty, smelly, irritating Will-lite.'

'I'm glad he's found a hobby,' Uncle Percy replied, taking Becky's suitcase out of the boot.

'Yeah, but everything he's good at is to do with violence,' Becky replied. 'And that's not so good for me.'

Uncle Percy hooked his arm into Becky's. 'As far as I can see, young lady, your *googly powers* make you just about the most powerful human being on the face of the planet. I don't think you have any worries in that department.'

Becky had never thought about it like that. As they walked up the high stone steps, she said, 'Any news on the next Eden Relic?'

'I've been doing some research,' Uncle Percy replied. 'But

nothing concrete as yet. It seems there are more stories of powerful relics in history that just about anything else. Most are just bibble babble.'

'And what about Dad?'

Uncle Percy sighed. 'Nothing at all, I'm afraid. However, despite Drake's intimidatory tactics, the community is still searching as hard as ever. No one's giving up. I promise you that.'

With a shiver, Becky recalled Drake's threats at the Enchantment Beneath the Sea Dance the previous Christmas. 'That's really kind of them.'

'Not at all. They want to do it.'

'And Drake's made no attempt to hurt anyone?'

'Not as yet,' Uncle Percy replied. 'But we have taken some measures to protect the travelling community. Rather significant measures, as it so happens.'

'What kind of measures?'

'I'm hoping to show you tomorrow afternoon,' Uncle Percy replied. 'I'll keep it as my little secret for now, but I think you'll enjoy it.'

Becky recalled his enthusiasm on the phone. 'So is that what's "totally awesome"?'

'Oh, no,' Uncle Percy chuckled. 'The total awesomeness shall be revealed tomorrow morning.'

'And do I get a clue?'

'Nope,' Uncle Percy grinned. 'But just one more sleep and you're in for an absolute treat. Trust me…'

From nowhere, Drake's words seared her thoughts. 'You just live quite happily … trusting those you really shouldn't trust.'

And for all her confusion, for all her uncle's strange,

evasive response when questioned, she knew she trusted him with all her heart. She really did.

*

Becky went to her room and unpacked her suitcase. She changed out of her school uniform, and into a t-shirt and jeans. Then she sent a text her mother to say they had arrived safely, before staring out of the window and surveying the grounds. It was then she heard a firm rap at the door. 'Come in.'

The door didn't open.

'Come in,' she repeated.

Still, the door remained shut.

Surprised and somewhat puzzled, she opened it. At once, her eyes nearly popped from her skull.

A gigantic rabbit, the size of a small cow, was standing there, its salmon pink nose twitching, its chopstick-sized whiskers quivering madly. It had a coat of silken grey fur, tiny chestnut-brown eyes, and a pair of small but floppy ears. The rabbit shuffled into the bedroom, causing her to step back with shock. Then she heard suppressed giggles from the next room.

'Get out here … NOW!' she shouted in a half laugh, half shriek.

Uncle Percy and Joe appeared at the door, clutching their sides with laughter.

'What the hell is that thing?' Becky fired at Uncle Percy.

'That, Becky, is Nuralagus Rex,' Uncle Percy replied. 'The largest rabbit in history. I found him on Minorca in the Messinian age, four million years ago. Isn't he smashing?'

Becky's disbelief became amusement. 'You are such a big kid!'

'He's so cool,' Joe said. 'Can we keep him?'

'I don't think so,' Uncle Percy replied. 'Barbie's already

furious at me for bringing him out of his time.'

Becky watched as the rabbit loped over to the four-poster bed and began to nibble at her duvet. 'And what's his name?'

'Bernie.'

Becky laughed. 'Bernie the Rabbit!'

Uncle Percy grinned back at her. 'I told you I had some Easter treats for you … this is Bernie the Easter Bunny…'

Chapter 5

Broken Glass, Broken Lives

The next hour passed by in a blur. Becky, Joe, and Uncle Percy stopped off at the kitchen to collect a bucket of freshly picked carrots, before taking Bernie outside to explore the grounds. He was inquisitive about everything, lumbering round happily, from tree to flower patch, munching relentlessly on an endless stream of carrots. Soon after, Will joined them, wielding two wooden swords, and an eager Joe showed him his abilities as a swordsman. Will was impressed, and to Joe's delight, stated that Joe was as capable with a sword as any trained medieval knight.

Becky was eager to visit the stables to see Pegasus, the winged foal, but, to her frustration, a strangely insistent Uncle Percy suggested she do that the following day.

As the sun sank on the horizon, leaving the grounds blanketed in shade, they returned to the Hall. An enthusiastic Uncle Percy had promised to cook evening dinner, and Becky was delighted to discover that, although he was an unparalleled genius at everything else, he couldn't cook to save his life. He spent two hours ruining everything he touched, incinerating a roast beef joint, over-boiling broccoli and cauliflower until they liquefied into goo, and splashing gravy everywhere, until more spattered the kitchen walls than was in the pan. In the end, he admitted defeat, threw all of his culinary efforts in the bin, and

41

slumped with a huff on to his chair, whilst Becky made everyone beans on toast.

It was approaching eleven when Becky collapsed into bed. Exhausted, she buried her head in her pillow and curled up beneath the sheets. She fell asleep almost immediately.

In the blink of an eye, she was awake again. The room was tar-black and the air as thick as treacle. She picked up her phone. 1.46am. She lay there for what seemed like an age, tossing and turning. Her mind began to work overtime, reflecting on all that had happened the previous day – the good and the bad: Drake's appearance, Joe freefalling to certain death, Uncle Percy's curious response to Drake's accusations. She knew at once sleep was out of the question.

Lifting herself out of bed, she went to open the window, hoping some fresh air might help. Opening the curtains, she unfastened the latch, and pushed open the window. A frail breeze stroked her face. As she stared into the blackness, a blast of light, lasting no more than a second, exploded at the edge of the forest. Simultaneously, she heard a faint cracking sound. Dumbfounded, she rubbed her eyes and looked again.

The light had gone.

Becky's heart pounded over the breeze. She was in no doubt a time machine had materialised in the grounds. But who was the traveller? Uncle Percy? Barbie? Maria and Jacob returning from their trip to Berlin? But why would any of them choose to arrive in Bowen Forest? She stared at the same spot for a further few moments hoping for an answer, but all was veiled in darkness once more.

Her mind awhirl, she stood there eager for an explanation. For an instant, she thought she'd visit Uncle Percy's room to see if he was there or knew what was going on, but it was so late. She didn't want to wake him if she was mistaken.

Deep down, however, she knew she wasn't.

Pacing up and down the room, her curiosity ablaze, she threw on her dressing gown and slippers, before marching to the door. She had to know what was going on. She rushed down the corridor, onto the landing, before racing down the left flight of stairs into the Entrance Hall. It was then she came to an abrupt halt. The Morning Room door stood ajar, masking a soft butter yellow light that beckoned from within. It had to be Uncle Percy, but what was he doing up at this time of night?

Tentatively, she pushed at the door and said in a quiet voice, 'Uncle Per –' But as the door swung open, she saw Jacob, illuminated by candlelight, sitting at a walnut trestle table, placed on which was a pot of tea, steam rising in spirals from its curved spout. His hand trembled as he sipped from a china cup. She knew at once she'd interrupted a very private moment.

Jacob looked over, startled. 'Fräulein Becky?'

Becky didn't know where to look. 'I'm sorry, Jacob,' she said. 'I … I thought you were Uncle Percy.'

'Why are you up, child?'

'I thought I saw something … in the grounds. I was going to investigate. Then I saw the light on, and –' Becky faltered. 'I'm sorry to intrude.'

'Not at all,' Jacob replied. 'But you should not be leaving the Hall, not under any circumstance. These are perilous times.'

'I s'pose.' Becky saw that Jacob's eyes, usually so kind and engaging, were inflamed and bloodshot.

'Would you like to join me in cup of tea?' Jacob asked.

'Are you sure?'

Finally, Jacob found a smile. 'An old man appreciates youthful company. I would like it very much.'

Becky walked over and sat down beside him. Jacob pushed himself to his feet, took a cup and saucer from an adjacent cabinet, and returned to his chair.

He poured her a drink.

'I never drank tea before I arrived in your time, now I'm not sure how I'd breathe without it.' Jacob passed over the cup.

'Thank you,' Becky said. 'Is Maria in bed?'

'Yes,' Jacob replied. 'She has been through a great deal, and is very tired. Did your uncle explain where we were?'

'Yes.'

'And why we were there?'

Becky nodded. 'He did,' she said faintly. 'I dunno what to say except I hope it - well, you know, gave you some comfort.'

'It does…every time.' Jacob exhaled heavily. 'It is always a demanding trip, on our bodies, our minds and our souls, but one that is always necessary. Maria and I are old now, it is right we spend time with our memories. The good ones … and the bad. And we are blessed to have a thousand more happy ones than sad.'

'I'm glad.'

Jacob's eyes regained their usual glow. 'You are a very special child, Fräulein Becky. And although in many ways you resemble my late granddaughter, it is my son, Karl, you remind me of most. He was like you – strong, kind, decent, free, with a heart as big as the Rhine.'

'I'm sorry he was … err, taken away from you.'

'Thank you.' Jacob took a sip of tea. 'Would you like to

hear about it? I would not wish to give you nightmares.'

Becky hadn't expected this. 'Only if - if you want to tell me.'

Jacob smiled. 'It is not always a matter of want. Some stories should be voiced, not for the pleasure of telling them, but as a lesson, a lesson for those to come in the future...'

'My son, Karl, was an architect and a builder.' The hint of a smile skirted his lips. 'Even as a boy, he showed such remarkable talent. As a man, he was very successful.' Pride welled in his voice. 'And in Berlin, in the nineteen twenties there was much building to be done. Anyway, Karl bought a derelict farmhouse in Falkensee on the outskirts of the city. He and his wife, Liesel, spent two years mending it, and when they finished, they invited Maria and me to live with them and their daughter, my granddaughter, Celia. We were delighted to do so. We were the happiest of families. But as our joy grew, so Berlin was changing, the country was changing. A cancer was spreading ... spreading fast ... and soon it spread throughout Germany - that cancer was the *Nationalsozialistische Deutsche Arbeiterpartei:* The Nazi Party. It spread its ugly message of hatred, intolerance, and extremism throughout the land. And those that would not listen – well, they became victims of such terrible violence by the Sturmabteilung, the brownshirts, and all of it advocated by that vile little man with the devil in his eyes...'

'You mean Adolf Hitler?'

'I do.'

'But you know what I've never understood - how could such evil come to dominate a country? Why wasn't he stopped before it got out of control?'

'I am not sure I can answer that,' Jacob replied. 'All I can say is that after the Great War, Germany was lost, the people weary, disenchanted, without money or pride or hope. The compensations required as part of the Treaty of Versailles made it impossible for the country to rebuild. And that's exactly what Hitler promised – resurrection, renewal, rebirth … he promised to give my people a Germany they could be proud of again, to fix the economy, to give employment, to restore pride in a once great nation. And a desperate, despondent people were prepared to listen. What they didn't know was his true agenda…' He paused. 'But I knew. I read his despicable book, *Mein Kampf,* and Karl and I saw him speak in Berlin. And it terrified me to the depths of my soul. Karl, too.'

His expression changed from sorrow into anger.

'But it was when the Nazi Party began to actively target the Jews that Karl and I knew we had to do something. Many of my best friends were Jewish and we couldn't just stand by and do nothing. We discussed many ideas, but it was after *Kristallnacht,* The Night of Broken Glass, when the stormtroopers started destroying synagogues, Jewish businesses and homes, all across the country, killing too many to mention, that we knew we had to act.'

'What did you do?'

'We transformed Karl's house into a refuge, a safe house. And we used his business transportation to smuggle Jews from Berlin and out of the country. Over the next six months we aided over a thousand Jews to flee Germany. But then we were betrayed. Someone informed the authorities…' His head tilted down. 'Before we knew anything, stormtroopers were at our house…. Otto Kruger was with them.' He spat the name out. 'At that time, there were three Jewish families lodging with us in the cellars. The stormtroopers slaughtered them all.' His entire body was shaking now. 'Then Otto Kruger took out his Luger and, one by one –' He struggled to find the words. ' – He shot my son ... his wife ... my beautiful granddaughter... And he would've shot Maria and me, when an angel appeared. Your uncle created a diversion and saved us. In the chaos, I was shot in the thigh. I still have the limp to this very day. But we escaped...'

Fighting back the tears, Becky reached over and held his quivering hand.

'Then your uncle brought us to your time, to safety. He tried to return to Falkensee, to the house, to change events but this Omega ... what does he call it?'

'The Omega Effect.'

'This Omega Effect prevented it. We had to accept our family died that day, and that such events could not be altered. Of course, at first we wanted to die with them, to join them in the afterlife. But, in time, your uncle convinced us to live... to share his life. He is the finest of all men. And I shall never thank him enough for what he did, and what he tried to do. Slowly, he helped us to live again. But ...' he paused, 'my son, my granddaughter will never live again, except in my memories. And for this, I pray God can forgive Kruger and the other beasts for their involvement ... for I cannot. Of course, it was only after I came to your time, that I read books about the second Great War, and about the millions murdered by that little man and his puppets - a symphony of death orchestrated by the few, to the everlasting shame of the many. For years, I could not comprehend it all. But if there can be one lesson learnt, one flicker of good to come out of all that happened, it is that we must always stand up to such tyranny.

47

The tale of my country is a tale that should never be retold. And it saddens me that stories such as this still occur to this very day. This Emerson Drake is proof of that ...'

Jacob collapsed into his chair, all energy deserting him.

Becky didn't know what to say. 'I'm so sorry for everything you've been through.' She squeezed his hand tightly.

'My child, there are many that have been through much worse than even I. But there it is ... that is my story.'

Becky's eyes met Jacob's. 'Jacob ... may I kiss you?'

Jacob looked taken aback. Then he nodded.

Becky leaned in and kissed his cheek. 'Thank you for telling me.'

'No, thank you, Fräulein Becky,' Jacob replied. 'You have the best of hearts. And I want nothing more for you than to have the best of lives...'

Then together they cried deep into the night.

Chapter 6

Hold your Horses

It was gone three when Becky and Jacob parted ways. Becky stumbled into bed, physically and emotionally exhausted. It had been such a long and draining conversation with Jacob she had forgotten why she went downstairs in the first place. She was woken by her door crashing open.

'Are you getting up or what?' Joe hollered, marching in. 'It's nearly ten. Everyone's had breakfast and Uncle Percy's waiting to show us this big surprise.'

Becky launched herself out of bed. 'I'll be in the kitchen in ten minutes.' She showered quickly, cleaned her teeth and flung on some clothes. Shortly after, she was charging down the stairs, across the Entrance Hall, to the kitchens, where she saw Maria standing at the sink.

Maria's weary face cracked with joy. 'Ah, here is my beautiful angel.' She scuttled over and grabbed Becky in a spine-snapping embrace. 'Why are you sleeping so late? Maria has been longing to see you.'

Becky knew from Maria's tone Jacob hadn't discussed their conversation. 'I had a late night. But it's great to see you. I'm glad you're back.'

'And I am back.' Maria gulped hard. 'I would be no where else.'

As they released each other, Uncle Percy breezed into the room, fresh-faced and smiling. 'Ah, Becky, I see you've finally entered the land of the living.'

'Yeah.' Then Becky remembered the curious incident the previous night. 'Were you in the woods last night?'

'No. Why do you ask?'

'I thought I saw a light blast from a time machine near the woods. I was wondering if it was you.'

'No,' Uncle Percy replied. 'And you know no one can enter the grounds without my sanctioned codes. So you must be mistaken.'

'Perhaps,' Becky said. She thought hard for a moment. 'But couldn't someone steal the code and enter the grounds without your knowledge?'

'Ah, but as a precaution against that I've installed a Pretonicator which scans the grounds constantly for unfamiliar travelling devices. I'd be immediately informed if a time machine not of my creation had entered the grounds. Infact, the Pretonicator is programmed to repel such a time machine to a different time zone and a somewhat remote location.' His grin widened. 'Presently, it's set to send any unwelcome time machine to the Wingecarribee swamp in Australia, in 83BC. However, as I haven't had any notification from the Pretonicator I can assume we've had no visitors.'

'Could it have been Barbie then?'

'Barbie's away at the moment.'

'Away?' Becky asked, surprised. 'Where is she?'

'She's on loan.'

'Who to?' Becky replied. 'And what for?'

'She's doing some work for the travelling community,' Uncle Percy replied. 'But don't worry, you'll see her this afternoon.'

Becky's ears pricked up. 'We're going on a trip?'

Uncle Percy nodded. 'We are, indeed.'

'Where to and when?'

'Balestrino, Italy. 1954.'

Becky's heart fluttered. She had always longed to visit Italy. 'And what work's she doing there?'

'You'll see.'

'And is that the big surprise you've been harping on about?'

Uncle Percy chuckled. 'Oh, no,' he replied, a twinkle in his eye. 'The surprise is something much more *uplifting*. And we certainly don't have to go to Italy to experience it.' He looked at Becky who looked more puzzled than ever, and said, 'So hurry up, enjoy your breakfast and I'll show you...'

Becky couldn't eat quickly enough.

*

'So what is this surprise?' Joe asked eagerly, walking alongside Becky and Uncle Percy as they crossed the lawns. 'Do you have a new time machine?'

'It's considerably more thrilling than that...'

Within minutes, Bowen Lake loomed on the horizon, its powder blue water glistening like frosted glass. Following the winding path, they turned at the boathouse and approached the stables. It was then they spied the outline of a three-horned dinosaur stretched out lazily on the ground, thick strands of grass dangling from its powerful jaws.

'Gumpy!' Joe shouted excitedly.

Gump's plated head jerked up. He pushed himself onto his sturdy legs and mooed loudly.

Joe stopped dead in his tracks. 'Flippin' heck, he's as big as a tank!'

Uncle Percy chuckled. 'You're quite right. And he's not the only one who's had a growth spurt of late.'

Becky was about to ask about Pegasus when, from behind

Gump's colossal frame, a sleek, elegant animal paced into view, its long silky white tail whipping the air. 'Peggy!'

Pegasus clearly recognised Becky's voice. With a joyful whinny, she galloped over, her silken mane bouncing like smoke on the wind.

Becky couldn't speak. Like Gump, Pegasus was almost unrecognisable. No longer a foal, Pegasus was a fully-grown mare. Pegasus came to a halt at her feet, her enormous feathered wings clamped tightly to her sides. Then she leaned down and pressed her nose fondly against Becky's face.

Becky cupped Pegasus' snout in her hands and kissed her softly. 'Hello, you.' At that moment, she noticed four thin metal bands attached to each of Pegasus' ankles. 'What are those?' she asked Uncle Percy.

'You'll see.'

In a low, graceful bow, Pegasus sank to her knees.

'I knew this would happen the moment she saw you. She's been waiting for this for weeks … She wants you to ride her, and only you...'

Becky froze.

'Go on, you big chicken,' Joe said, nodding feverishly. 'Get on.'

Wordlessly, Becky climbed on Pegasus' back; her legs fitted neatly below the wing joints. Then Pegasus stood up and neighed happily.

Looking down at Uncle Percy and Joe, Becky's insides tumbled.

'I said last summer it was important to learn horse-riding,' Uncle Percy said, stroking Pegasus' nose. 'Of course, back then I had no idea just how important it would be.'

Immediately, Becky recalled Charger, the elderly horse on

which she had first learned to ride. 'This is a bit different.'

'I should say,' Uncle Percy replied with a wink. 'Peggy can fly now…'

Before Becky had time to respond, Pegasus set off with a start.

Fear and adrenaline surged through Becky. She clung to Pegasus' neck for dear life. As they gathered pace, she could hear Joe's yelps of joy. Then her heart jolted further. Pegasus' wings had extended. She braced herself, when suddenly she felt the oddest sensation. The thunder of galloping hooves had gone. The only sound she could hear was the wind thrashing her ears and the soft swish of wings carving the air, powering up and down in consistent rhythm.

Pegasus climbed higher, as if scaling invisible steps.

Just then, Becky spied a flash of green light above Pegasus' hooves. She knew at once the anklets were Invisiblators.

To the world below, they had vanished without a trace.

Glancing down, Becky's fear turned into awe. She saw the countryside unfold like a picnic blanket, green and yellow and ochre. Cars, houses, rivers, roads appeared before her like miniature pieces on a giant chessboard. Feeling safer with each passing second, Becky sat back and took it all in.

She never wanted it to end.

After the most wonderful ten minutes, Becky felt Pegasus turn about and head back. Soon, Bowen Hall, the lake, the stables came into view. Pegasus dipped lower, angling her descent.

Becky could see Joe and Uncle Percy now. About thirty feet from the ground, she saw their expressions change. She knew she and Pegasus had materialised. Joe yelled something she couldn't hear, a beaming Uncle Percy clapped vigorously. She watched Pegasus' legs move in a galloping motion, anticipating the hard ground ahead. Bracing herself, she closed her eyes, her grip tightening around Pegasus' neck. And then hooves met hard earth, causing Becky to jolt on impact. But she held on.

Becky's head spun as they decelerated to a halt. Flinging her arms around Pegasus' neck, she breathed, 'Thanks for not letting me die, Peggy.'

Joe sprinted over. 'My turn ...'

Pegasus shook her head and whinnied loudly.

Becky laughed. 'I think that's a 'no', bro.'

'And how was it?' Uncle Percy said.

'Awesome,' Becky said, leaping to the ground.

'I can only imagine,' Uncle Percy replied.

A raised voice drifted on the air. 'That is something I'd never have believed, but for seeing with mine own eyes.'

Becky turned and saw Will approach. She was about to reply when her eyes widened with horror. His face was a patchwork of cuts and bruises, his mouth swollen.

He looked like he'd been in a war.

Chapter 7

Pig Out

'What the hell happened to you?' Joe gasped.

Will's face was difficult to read. 'I suffered a misfortune.'

'A misfortune?' Joe replied. 'Have you been scrapping with Godzilla?'

'I fell.'

'From what ... a plane?'

'From the tree-house.'

'The tree house?' Joe puffed with amazement. 'That's like thirty feet high. It's a good job you're not dead.'

'I'm not dead yet,' he smiled.

'And exactly how did you fall out of the tree?' Uncle Percy asked, puzzled.

'It was my error,' Will replied. 'And of no matter.'

Becky remembered the strange light in the forest the previous night. 'When did you fall?'

'In the deep of night.'

'I thought I saw a light blast from a time machine around two. Was that you?'

'There was no time machine, miss. Perhaps you saw my torch?'

Becky was considering this, when Uncle Percy spoke up. 'Any broken bones?'

'Nothing a bathe in the lake won't remedy.'

Uncle Percy smiled. 'I think a more thorough examination may be in order, William. Let's go to the Medi-room.'

'There is no need.'

'Nonsense,' Uncle Percy replied. 'And you can have a proper bath while you're there.' He turned to Becky and Joe. 'Now this may take some time, but I've got plans for later, so meet me at the marble fountain at one o' clock.'

'The marble fountain?' Becky asked, surprised.

'In the courtyard.'

'What kind of plans?' Joe asked.

'A trip.'

'Where to?'

'As I mentioned to Becky earlier, we're going to Italy.'

'Ace,' Joe said. "Are we going to Ancient Rome? I'd love to see a gladiator fight in the Colosseum.'

'Really?' Uncle Percy replied. 'I wouldn't. Very nasty affairs. Anyway, no we're not going to Rome.'

'Why Italy then? Is it to do with Drake? The next Eden Relic?'

'No. I just want to show you what I've arranged for the travelling community.'

'What d'you mean arranged?'

'Following the Megalodon attack at Christmas, I said it was Drake's intention to "spawn a climate of fear" within the community. Anyhow, I decided to do the opposite … to make provisions to spawn a climate of peace and safety.'

Becky looked confused. 'And?'

'And I did … in 1950s Italy.'

'What kind of provisions?'

'You'll have to wait and see.'

'Okay,' Joe said. 'So if we're going on a trip then why are we meeting at the fountain and not the Time Room?'

'Because it's time to meet Beatrix,' Uncle Percy replied, eyes twinkling. He gestured at Will. 'Now come, William, let's go and take a look at your injuries.' He turned to Becky and Joe. 'See you at one…'

Becky and Joe watched them walk away.

'Beatrix, eh?' Joe said. 'That must be the last of his time machines… he said he had five.'

'I guess so. What do you reckon it'll be?'

'I hope it's a Ferrari.'

'But it's more likely to be a fire engine.'

Joe took a few seconds to ask his next question. 'D'you really think Will fell out of a tree?'

'Why would he lie?'

'I dunno,' Joe replied. 'It all seems a bit suss to me.'

Becky didn't answer. She didn't want to voice the fact she agreed with him – that there was something about Will's explanation that did seem suspicious. And there was something different about him, too - something in his eyes, in his mannerisms, in the tone of his voice, something she couldn't quite put her finger on. And she couldn't tell if it was something very good or extremely bad.

*

The next few hours passed in a heartbeat. Becky and Joe remained with Pegasus and Gump, playing in the fields, traversing the lakeside, skimming stones on the serene water. After returning to the Hall for lunch, they made their way to the marble fountain, still curious as to why they should meet there if they were embarking on a time trip. The sun had buried itself behind heavy cloud, tinting the air with a slight chill.

At one o' clock, Becky and Joe stood at the fountain's base. Crafted from Apuan marble, it depicted Neptune rising from a tempestuous ocean, wielding a trident in one hand and a seashell in the other; a giant eel enwrapped his body like a vine, spouting water from its open mouth, which crashed into a wide basin below.

Becky, however, barely noticed. She was disappointed to find no sign of Uncle Percy or his latest time machine. After a few minutes of waiting, she was about to suggest they go and find him when Neptune's eyes flashed scarlet and a thunderous grinding echoed beneath their feet, making Becky and Joe take two steps back with astonishment.

'What the –?' Joe said.

All at once, the entire fountain moved steadily right as if on invisible wheels, revealing a large crater in the ground, fifty feet wide. Then, from below, a mass of shocking pink nylon swelled into view, filling the hole. Climbing higher, recognisable shapes appeared before them: a pair of jet-black eyes, a short, stubby snout, a set of tiny wings, and a broad toothy smile.

Becky's heart was in her mouth. Beatrix was a hot air balloon in the shape of a winged pig.

Rising like a bubble-gum cloud, Beatrix soon filled Becky's gaze. Then, just below her inflated trotters, suspended on six metal cables, a wicker basket emerged from below. Inside, Uncle Percy grinned at them. 'Good afternoon … this is Beatrix,' he announced, enjoying the shock on their faces. 'What're you waiting for? Climb aboard.'

Becky found herself rooted to the spot. 'I-is it safe?'

Uncle Percy chuckled. 'Of course, it's safe.'

Stunned, Becky stepped forward as Uncle Percy opened the basket's door. She walked in, quickly trailed by Joe. Clinging tightly to the basket's handrail, she said, 'Why did you make a balloon in the shape of a pig?'

'I wanted to prove pigs really can fly,' Uncle Percy replied. 'Seriously, I've always been inspired by the novels of Jules Verne.' He locked the door. 'And his novel 'Five weeks in a balloon' was one of my childhood favourites, and triggered my interest in hot air balloons. Infact, I'd say I was something of a balloonatic.' He laughed.

Becky and Joe didn't join in.

'So are you ready?' Uncle Percy turned the blast valve. 'Ballooning is such a wonderful way to travel.' With a deafening roar, flames, six meters high, shot from a propane burner, filling the fabric above. They ascended quickly.

Becky looked down again. She couldn't quite believe it. For the second time that day she was flying. But this time, she felt secure, relaxed even, as the world opened up leisurely below her.

They had only risen thirty feet or so when Uncle Percy said, 'Much as I'm an admirer of the English countryside, we don't want the residents of Addlebury distressed by a vanishing pig balloon. Let's go to Italy.' He typed in six digits on a chronalometer set beneath the burner. Just then, hazy light poured out of the control panel, igniting the cables above. Within moments, an echoing boom rent the air.

Becky's stomach gave a jolt. They were suddenly thousands of feet in the air, drifting gracefully through a cloudless sky. Finding the courage to look down, she saw rolling hills, chestnut trees, winding streams and lengthy meadows of yellow and orange. She glanced over at Uncle Percy, who wore the most serene smile on his lips.

'Ah, Italia ...' he whispered to no one in particular.

For some time, Becky and Joe watched the world pass them

by in a captivated silence, exchanging smiles and pointing down from time to time. Then, on the horizon, they saw a large hill, carpeted deep green from countless olive trees, atop of which stood a medieval castle, which overlooked a partially walled city enclosing dozens of buildings.

'The town of Balestrino,' Uncle Percy said. 'It dates back to the 11th century. It was abandoned in 1953 due to geological instability. And that's precisely why we've arrived in 1954.'

'But I still don't get it,' Becky said. 'It's pretty and all that, but why are we here?'

'Well, as you know, Emerson Drake made some quite serious threats against the community. I told you I would take them seriously. To cut a long story short, after Christmas I started to work on an idea to keep everyone in the travelling community as safe as I could. As time travellers are scattered all across the world, I thought I'd establish a safe haven where travellers could relocate, at least until Drake has been apprehended. Of course, I needed somewhere large enough to house upwards of two hundred travellers and their families. Anyway, I did my research and Balestrino fitted the bill.'

'You put all the travellers all in one town?' Becky said, surprised.

'Those that wanted to come. As I said before, in 1953, the entire town was abandoned so there's plenty of room. Now, obviously, because of my knowledge of the future, I know the area will suffer no significant seismic activity for nine months, so it's safe enough for the time being, and that gives us enough time to perhaps find the remaining Eden relics and stop Emerson Drake. Anyway, after approval from the GITT committee, Barbie and I began to make the town fit for our needs. I've installed state of the art security and believe the community is as safe here as I can possibly make them. It also means there are plenty of experienced people working on finding your father. In fact, they're more focussed on that than ever.'

Becky smiled gratefully. 'That's very kind of them.'

'Nonsense, they want to do it, ' Uncle Percy replied.

As Uncle Percy began their descent, Becky inhaled deeply and looked down at Balestrino, its churches, terracotta roofed houses, narrow rickety streets appearing like tiny pieces in a board game. Even from this distance, she could see the light blasts of time machines, coming and going. And then it occurred to her just how different her life was from others her age. She was about to land in an abandoned town in 1950s Italy, a town inhabited entirely by time travellers.

And she was arriving in a flying pig.

Chapter 8

The Celestial Stowaway

The closer they descended toward Balestrino, the more Becky saw people rush from the tiny houses and wave excitedly at them, the treacly air soon filling with faint but enthusiastic shouts of welcome.

'Beatrix certainly knows how to make an entrance,' Uncle Percy beamed, waving back. Minutes later, he guided the balloon onto the town square. Upon touch down, applause echoed all around.

Overwhelmed, Becky scanned the hundreds of beaming faces, some of which she recognised - Keith Pickleton, Mary Cassidy, Malcolm Everidge, Terence Brown, and many more she didn't.

As Uncle Percy opened the basket door, a mass of bodies rushed forward like a tidal wave, surrounding them.

'Buon Giorno, everyone,' Uncle Percy yelled over the din. He stepped out of the basket and began to shake as many hands as he could. 'Hello, Keith, Saleem, Shirley, Katya … Deary me, what a wonderful welcome.' He waited for the clamour to die down. 'Everyone, may I introduce my niece and nephew, Becky and Joe Mellor. Some of you met them at Christmas, others may have been too concerned with being eaten by a prehistoric shark.'

As if some kind of celebrity, Becky was besieged with hand shakes, smiles and hearty slaps on the back. Then, amidst the horde of well-wishers, she heard a voice she recognised.

'Well, well … if it ain't me little pirate pals.'

A hulking man, his face hidden beneath a thicket of grey and brown whiskers, pushed his way to the front. He wore a wide-brimmed Stetson hat and walked stiffly as though wearing ill-fitting shoes.

'Bruce!' Joe bellowed.

'Howdy, kid.' Bruce Westbrook shook Joe's hand, his grin wide and infectious.

Becky ran over and hugged him. 'How are you, Bruce?'

'As happy as a hyena seein' you again, purdy lady.'

'How's the bullet wound?' Joe asked.

Bruce gave an unconcerned shrug. 'Gives me somethin' to yak 'bout in Famous Sam's Bar, don't it?' he replied cheerily. 'If anyone asks, I always say I got it brawlin' an armed bank robber in Toledo.' He laughed. 'Best of all, the ladies just 'bout love cooing over the battle scar. I'll tell ya … I spend more time with my shirt off in Famous Sam's than with it on. Shame the ladies don't do the same. Anyhows, what's been happenin' with you, kid?'

'Emerson Drake threw me off my school roof,' Joe replied happily.

Bruce looked shocked for a moment. 'Then you look pretty darn good all things considered. And what's this 'bout you findin' this Spear of Fate without me?'

'Yeah,' Joe replied. 'And we fed a Nazi to a load of mythical creatures.'

'Good.' Bruce nodded his approval. 'I hate those damn Nazis.'

Uncle Percy walked over and shook Bruce's hand. 'Good day to you, Bruce.'

'Howdy, Halifax,' Bruce grinned. 'Mighty fine town you found for us here.'

'I'm glad you approve.'

'What's not to love? Italian food, first-rate Vermentino, and there's a village nearby where there's a signorina as sweet as a sunset and as obliging as a judge on the take, if ya catch my drift.' He winked at Uncle Percy.

Uncle Percy frowned. 'I don't wish to catch anything from you, thank you very much.'

Becky scanned the town. Beyond the wall of cheery faces, time machines were parked chaotically in every available space – dozens of cars, old and new, motorbikes, a hang glider, a kayak, a Jet Ski, and, to her great surprise, what looked like a Western Stagecoach, pulled by two giant horses.

Becky watched as a tall, middle-aged woman with custard blonde hair approached Uncle Percy. She had brilliant blue eyes and an attractive yet purposeful face that radiated an aura of quiet authority.

'Hello, Percy,' the woman said with a pronounced accent. 'Good to see you.'

'Olivia,' Uncle Percy replied warmly. 'Lovely to see you.' He kissed her on each cheek. 'Becky, Joe, this is Olivia Larsen, the new chairwoman of the GITT committee.'

'Hello,' Becky and Joe said.

'Velkomen.' A warm smile curved Larsen's mouth. 'And, as we say in Norway, God påske … Happy Easter.'

'Happy Easter to you,' Becky replied.

'We hope you'll stay with us a few days,' Larsen said. 'We've prepared a charming house for you both.' Her eyes found Joe. 'Joe, we've even decorated your bedroom wall in pictures of, I believe, Manchester City Football Club. I've been informed they're your favourite. Is this the case?'

'Yeah,' Joe replied with surprise. 'That's ace. Cheers.'

'Our pleasure.' Larsen's smile morphed into a line. 'Now, before we show you around, I want to update you on where we are in locating your father. We've created an incident room in the church of Saint Andrea. So far, we've investigated six hundred and seventy timelines and over nine hundred sectors. There's still some way to go, but we think we're making progress. As a matter of fact, we have two very strong leads as to his location. And the second we have a confirmed sighting, Tracker division are on the alert to retrieve him immediately. And, believe me, they're very, very capable.' A smile returned to her face. 'So, please, be assured we are doing everything we can and are confident of finding him shortly.'

There was something in Larsen's face that made Becky trust every word she said. She was about to express her thanks when an ear-splitting pop shattered the silence. She didn't even blink. Convinced it was just an arriving time machine, it was only when a scream rang out that her spine froze. Glancing over, she saw an old fashioned motorcycle had materialised at the edge of the square. A Chinese man, his face pale and drawn, was hunched over the handlebars, clutching his arm, which was drenched in blood.

Uncle Percy rushed over to him. 'Liang?'

The Chinese man looked up. 'Thank God you're here, Percy,' he rasped.

Uncle Percy turned to the stunned crowd, and shouted, 'Is Doctor Aziz here?'

'Not necessary, Percy,' the Chinese man said, wincing in pain. 'It's a flesh wound. Nothing more. I was lucky.'

'Nevertheless,' Uncle Percy replied, 'I think we should let a professional take a look at it.'

A short, rotund woman with a stern but kindly face, her hair scraped back in a severe bun, hurried to Uncle Percy's side.

Becky recognised her as Emily Appleby, the nurse who had cared for Edgar at Christmas. 'Let me take a look,' she insisted.

The Chinese man shook his head. 'Emily, it can wait,' he replied, his words urgent and resolute. 'Percy, I need you to meet someone.'

It was only then Becky noticed the motorbike had a sidecar. Sitting inside was a scrawny young man, wearing a tar-stained jacket and ragged trousers, his face matted with grime and sweat. Looking round, his eyes ballooned with a mixture of fear, bewilderment and something that resembled relief.

'This is Shamus,' the Chinese man said, climbing off the bike. 'Shamus Cusack.'

From Uncle Percy's surprised expression, Becky knew Shamus had been brought here from the past.

'Nice to meet you, Shamus. I'm Percy Halifax.'

'H-hullo,' Shamus replied in a thick Irish burr.

Uncle Percy smiled back at him. 'Now, I don't know what's happened, but I can assure you that you're completely safe now and amongst friends.'

Shamus nodded hesitantly. 'Aye ... Okey.'

'I'll tell you what happened, Percy,' the Chinese man offered. 'Three Associates happened.'

Uncle Percy's face grew solemn. 'When and where?'

'1872. The Azores. In the town of Santa Barbara, São Jorge Island.'

'What were they doing there?'

The Chinese man motioned at Shamus. 'Looking for him.'

'Is that so?' Uncle Percy's eyes returned to Shamus. 'And, Shamus, do you know why these three men were looking for you?'

Shamus didn't reply.

'Show him, Shamus,' the Chinese man insisted. 'If anyone can shed light on all of this, Percy can.'

Tentatively, Shamus drew a package from beneath his jacket. 'They were afta this, sir.'

Becky watched as Shamus raised a long thin object into the light. It was wrapped in a tattered cloth and secured with a thin coil of twine. Shamus was about to unravel it when Uncle Percy interrupted him.

'I think that can wait a few minutes, Shamus.' Uncle Percy turned to Olivia Larsen. 'Olivia, I think Shamus would appreciate a less sizeable audience … perhaps we could relocate to somewhere more private?'

'Of course,' Larsen replied. 'We've set up a temporary committee room in the Municipio, the town hall, you're welcome to use it.'

'That's very kind of you,' Uncle Percy replied, offering Shamus his hand. 'Please, young man, allow me.' He aided Shamus out of the sidecar, before glancing at Becky and Joe. 'Becky, Joe, can I assume you wish to come, too?'

'Too right,' Joe said with hesitation. Becky nodded.

Uncle Percy turned to the Chinese man. 'Liang, I really think you should let Emily examine your injuries? I'm sure Shamus can recount all that's happened.'

For the first time, the Chinese man appeared unsteady on his feet. 'Perhaps you're right, Percy. It has been an eventful half hour.'

Bruce Westbrook rushed forward. 'Lean on me, buddy.' He

curled the Chinese man's uninjured arm around his shoulder.

'Thank you, Bruce,' the Chinese Man replied.

'Come on, Liang,' Emily Appleby said. 'Let's get you a cup of tea, maybe a slice of Madeira cake, and take a good look at that arm.'

Becky watched as Bruce and Emily aided Liang to a nearby building she assumed had been set up as a medical facility.

'I pray to Saint Michael he'll be okey,' Shamus said, watching them disappear inside. 'He saved ma darn life.'

'He'll be right as rain in no time at all,' Uncle Percy replied. 'But for now, let's concentrate on you, shall we?'

Within moments, Becky, Joe, Uncle Percy and Shamus were trailing Olivia Larsen northward across the piazza, in the shade of a crumbling ancient church with a bell tower that resembled a macaroon.

Becky couldn't take her eyes off Shamus, whose nervy gaze flicked between the mass of stunned faces and the wide array of strange and unusual time machines. Who was he? Why were Associates after him? What was inside the package? She couldn't help but feel sorry for him.

It was clear Uncle Percy felt the same way and did his best to put him at ease. 'So, Shamus, can I assume Mister Chow has told you about the time travelling community?'

'Aye, sir.'

'I bet that came as something of a shock.'

'It wudda, sir. But not after all I've seen...'

They entered a cobbled side street and approached a tall building, its cracked sandstone walls obscured by thick knots of rust coloured ivy.

Moving inside, Becky felt like she'd entered a different world. A modern ceiling fan spun silently above their heads, driving cool air onto the freshly plastered high walls, hanging upon which were some of the most spectacular paintings she had ever seen. A giant table in the form of an egg timer was set in the middle of the room, peppered around which were eight chairs.

'Now I do like what you've done with the place, Olivia,' Uncle Percy said admiringly.

Larsen smiled. 'I thought you'd approve, Percy. As an art aficionado yourself, I'm sure you appreciate the brushstrokes of the old masters – Giotto, Rubens, Masaccio, Botticelli, Rembrandt, Goya and, of course, Da Vinci. All originals, of course.'

'Of course.'

Olivia Larsen extended her hand. 'Please, everyone, take a seat. Now, Shamus, can I offer you a drink?'

'No, Ma'am.'

Uncle Percy pulled out a chair and gestured for Shamus to sit, before taking one for himself. 'Now, Shamus, I understand all of this must be quite overwhelming.'

'Aye. A tad.' Shamus nodded at the package. 'Do ya wish ter see this now, sir?'

'In time,' Uncle Percy replied. 'But first I want you to put everything into context, to start at the very beginning. Tell us about your involvement in all of this - about the package, the Associates … try to leave nothing out. We have plenty of time.'

Shamus sucked in a deep breath. 'I left Ireland three years ago, in 1869. I left for the new world, sir … America. Ne'er had much luck at home, figured I'd try my hand out there. I works my way 'cross the Eastern Seaboard - Boston, Providence, New Haven, before findin' meself in New York

City. Anyhow, one night, as I'm workin' the docks, I bumps into an old chum of mine from Kilkenny, fresh off da boat. He tells me my Ma was sick. Very sick. I knew there and then I had to get back ter Ireland ter be with her. But I had no money fer passage. Anyway, I learn there's a ship, a brigantine carrying 1700 barrels of raw alcohol, bound for Genoa, Italy. I figures if I can get to Italy, I can get home. So I stowed away. Anyway, a few days a' sea, I was discovered. All fairness, Captain Briggs wus a good man. He listened to me situation, and agreed ter take me ter Italy. From there, he said he'd help me find a sailin' back ter England. From there I'd have no problem getting home.'

Something stirred in Uncle Percy's memory. 'Captain Briggs? The ship... it was the Mary Celeste?'

Shamus nodded. 'Aye, sir. That be her name.'

Uncle Percy sank deep into his chair.

'The Mary Celeste!' Joe said. 'I've heard of that.'

'I'm not surprised, Joe,' Uncle Percy said flatly. 'The story of the Mary Celeste is perhaps the most famous maritime mystery of them all. If memory serves, she was found abandoned off the coast of Portugal on the 5th December 1872 - no crew, no captain, and no passengers. Yet all the cargo was intact, all the crew's personal belongings were in their quarters, and there was a six-month supply of food and water on board.'

'What happened to the crew?' Becky asked, shocked.

'No one knows what happened to them,' Uncle Percy replied darkly. 'And they were never heard of again.'

'Well I do, sir.' Tears dampened Shamus' eyes. 'I know what happened ter them coz I wus there. And I saw da whole abominable thing.' He hesitated. 'They were butchered, sir ...

butchered like rabid dogs … every last one of them. The sharks ate well that day…'

Chapter 9

The Ship of Ghosts

Heartbroken, Becky watched Shamus wipe his eyes.

'We musta been at sea fer 'bout a month,' he said. 'Be da jaysus, we battled some heavy weather, storms that woulda blown the horns off Satan himself, but we came through to fine waters. Fair play, it were a good crew. Alongside Cap'n Briggs there were seven others – first mate, Albert Richardson – a tough man, but fair. Second mate Gilling, a Dane, and a moocher if there ever were one – and five others, mainly Germans. Tough loyal men. Good sailors. We were headin' toward the straights of Gibralter, when one afternoon as I were cleanin' the Captain's quarters, I hear this mighty explosion outside. I look outta da cabin door and see five men standin' on deck … just 'bout came outta thin air, they did… Massive men, with guns unlike any shooters I'd ever seen. One man, biggest o' da lot, with cold blue eyes that cud freeze whiskey, were bellowin' orders.'

'Did you hear this man's name?' Uncle Percy asked.

'Aye. He called himself Kruger.'

Becky's stomach turned. 'Otto Kruger?'

'I heard no Christian name, Miss,' Shamus said. 'But then there were no Christian in him. He were pure devil, he were.' He detected something in Becky's eyes. 'D'ya know of him?'

Becky nodded. 'Yeah. He's a psycho.'

'Last time we met him we cut off his arm,' Joe said. 'It

seems like that wasn't enough to stop him.'

'No,' Shamus said. 'But then that wud explain his false one …'

'A false one?' Joe gasped.

'A metal one. I've seen many a fake limb in ma time, but none that looked like tha'. It moved every bit like a normal one.'

Uncle Percy remained impassive. 'What did Kruger want?'

Shamus nodded at the parcel. 'This...' He unravelled the cloth to reveal a black leather scabbard, about ten inches in length, decorated with glittering rubies and opals, inside which was a snow white ivory dagger. He pulled free the knife. A verse of Latin words was clearly inscribed on the double-edged blade, which tapered to a point. The ebony grip fed a pommel, engraved on which was a black eight pointed cross on a white background.

'May I, Shamus?' Uncle Percy offered his hand to take the knife.

Shamus passed it over.

'Is it an Eden Relic?' Joe asked.

Uncle Percy rolled the dagger between his fingers, half expecting something unusual to happen. 'Judging by the last time I touched one, I would say no.'

'Wut's an Eden Relic?' Shamus asked.

'Otto Kruger is working for an evil time traveller, Emerson Drake,' Uncle Percy replied. 'Some years ago, Emerson discovered a legend that claimed five ancient relics, supposedly crafted by God, were planted in the Garden of Eden at the dawn of time. These relics would imbue their possessor with untold power. Subsequently, a megalomaniac like Drake has devoted his life to getting them. Now, it turns out the legend, to a great extent, is true. We know, because we've found three of the Eden Relics. We are now searching for the fourth. However, we don't know where or indeed what type of relic it is.'

'An' wut's it gotta do with da knife?'

'I've no idea,' Uncle Percy replied honestly. 'But if it's important to Drake, then it's important, full stop. We just have to find out why.'

'Do you know what the words on the blade mean?' Becky asked. 'Are they in Latin?'

'Indeed.' Uncle Percy studied them closely. 'My early Latin's somewhat rusty, but I believe it says something along the lines of:

> **I leave, for thy finding**
> **O, future prince**
> **The fiery blade forged**
> **With divine providence**
> **Tramp the land of my fathers**
> **To the shrine that I raised**
> **In the steps of Columba**
> **See my guide, held in glaze**

'So it's a riddle?' Becky suggested.

'It certainly seems that way. But a rather vague one.'

'But it says we're looking for a 'fiery blade," Joe said. 'So the next Eden Relic's a sword or a dagger?'

'That would be a logical assumption,' Uncle Percy replied. 'And the fact that it's forged with "divine providence" certainly suggests it's a clue leading to an Eden Relic.'

'Who's Columba?' Becky asked. 'Is that another name for

Christopher Columbus?'

'Columba's an Irish Saint, missy,' Shamus interrupted. 'A very righteous man, he were. Me Ma used ter tell me stories 'bout 'im.'

'That's quite right, Shamus,' Uncle Percy said, turning back to Becky. 'Columba was an Irish Missionary from the 6th Century, and primarily recognised for spreading Christianity throughout Scotland. He founded many churches and abbeys across the country… most notably the renowned monastery on the Island of Iona. Many years after his death, the Catholic Church canonised him for his work.'

'What does that mean?' Joe asked.

'They made him a Saint.'

'And rightly so,' Shamus said.

Joe's eyes fell once more on the dagger. 'And what does "see my guide" mean?'

'I've no idea.'

'And that symbol?' Becky asked, pointing at the dagger's pommel.

'Ahh, now that I can answer. It's the emblem of the Knight's Hospitaller.'

Joe leaned forward. 'Who are they?'

'They're an order of Medieval Knights, Joe,' Uncle Percy replied. 'In the mid-11th century, a Benedictine abbey was established in Jerusalem. A number of years later, a hospital was created beside the abbey to care for sick or injured pilgrims that visited the Holy Land. Of course, these were dangerous times and the abbey and hospital needed protection. A number of trained Knights, highly religious men, came forward and undertook monastic vows of chastity, poverty and obedience, devoting their lives to the order. After the First

Crusade in 1099, the Knights Hospitaller expanded and soon became a powerful and feared military power, eventually being charged with the guardianship of the Holy Land. Subsequently, in time, their wealth and influence grew, and they existed for many hundreds of years as one of the most respected armed forces in the world.'

'So they're like the Knights Templar?' Joe said.

Uncle Percy looked impressed. 'You know of the Knight's Templar?'

'He's played Assassin's Creed,' Becky said. 'Whatever historical knowledge exists in his pea-sized brain comes from computer games.'

Joe threw her an offensive hand gesture. 'Bite me.'

'Now, now,' Uncle Percy said firmly. 'Anyway, Joe, in reality the Knights Hospitaller were slightly different from the Templars.'

'How?'

'The Templar Knights have been in existence for thousands of years, much longer than the popular belief, and much of what has been documented about them was a cleverly fabricated deception to disguise their real purpose. No, the actual Knights Templar had a somewhat different agenda to the one recounted in history books, or computer games for that matter.' Uncle Percy bent forward, his eyes alive. 'And, furthermore, they still exist in the twenty first century and are still fighting their age-old cause to this very day.'

'Really?' Joe said. 'There are still Templar Knights knocking about?'

'Yes. And as a matter of fact, you've met one.'

'I have?'

'You have, indeed,' Uncle Percy replied. 'Do you remember

visiting The Magpie Inn in Addlebury and I introduced you to an elderly chap, Sidney Shufflebottom?'

'Yes.'

'Sid's a modern Templar Knight.'

Joe looked unimpressed. 'Really? He was a bit old, wasn't he?'

'Yes – well, he's retired now, but he certainly was one. And believe it or not, there are thousands of Templars across the world, even now engaged in a never-ending battle with an ancient foe.'

Joe was interested now. 'What foe?' he asked. 'What's their real cause?'

'Ah, that would take far too long to explain,' Uncle Percy replied. 'It's another story for another day.'

Although Becky found this enthralling, she was keen to return to the task at hand. 'So back to this knife ...' She looked at Shamus. 'Did Kruger say anything else about this dagger? Why he wanted it or what he was going to do with it?'

'No, missy. He jus' demanded that Cap'n Briggs get it for him or there'd be consequences. Course, most of da crew didn't know what Kruger were talkin' about. But I did. The Cap'n had shown me da knife da night before, ya see.'

'Do you know how Captain Briggs acquired it?' Uncle Percy asked. 'Or where he got it from?'

'Nope, sir, he neva said,' Shamus replied. 'And I'm sure if he'd known what kinda carnage Kruger was capable of, he wudda given it ova in a heartbeat. But Kruger never gave him a chance. Before anyone knew owt, Kruger was killing everyone on deck. No one stood a chance.' Shamus was shaking now. 'Kruger snapped Volkert Lorenson's neck like it was a twig ... an' Lorenson was one of the hardest beggars I've ever met.

The rest of the crew fought back, but, one by one, he put them down like he were steppin' on ants. Never seen such a massacre.' His voice lowered to a whisper. 'Kruger were sent straight from da bowels of Hell, I reckon, and no mistake.'

'How did you escape with the dagger?' Joe asked.

'Well, the blade were right there in da cabin I wus cleanin'. I saw the carnage from da window, grabbed da knife, snuck round da stern and leapt overboard.' Guilt laced his every word. 'Maybe if I'd given him da knife he wudda spared some of them.'

Uncle Percy gave Shamus a sympathetic look. 'Shamus, we know these men, and we know Otto Kruger. It's highly likely everyone's death warrant was signed the moment he appeared on the ship. That's the kind of monster you were dealing with. You mustn't blame yourself.'

Shamus sighed heavily. 'Guess we'll never know.'

'So what happened next?' Joe asked.

'I swam ter shore,' Shamus replied. 'It were maybe four miles, maybe five. I found meself in Santa Barbara, at a tavern. The landlady, a lovely old gal, Catarina Rosario, were good ter me, God bless her. She took me in, fed me, gave me a bed, not that I cud sleep with those god-awful images in me head. Anyway, I kept da whole revoltin' story ter meself, but did mention I'd been a stowaway on da Mary Celeste. A couple of days later, Mister Chow wanders in da bar and buys me a drink – very interested in da ship, he were. Anyways, I liked him, trusted him, so I tells him da whole crazy tale … expecting him not ter believe a word. But he did. He believed everything. It were then he told me told me about time travellers, about you and yer ventures. Then three of them Associates enter da bar, and start shootin' up the gaff. We managed ter escape, and he brings me here. And that's all I got ter tell ya…' He exhaled a weary breath. 'I've witnessed da opening of the gates o' Hell, and all I ever wanted ter do were get back ter Ireland ter see me sick Ma.'

Uncle Percy patted his shoulder. 'Shamus, you shall see your mother again. We'll take you back to Ireland at once. And we'll send Doctor Aziz, a very capable physician, and he can examine your mother to see if he can help.'

'You will?'

'Of course we will. You've helped us a great deal. And we're very grateful.'

Shamus' eyes shimmered with gratitude. 'Thank yer, sir. Thank yer from da bottom of me heart.'

'No, thank you.' Uncle Percy raised the dagger. 'Now I'll have to take this.'

Shamus nodded.

'Come with me, Shamus,' Olivia Larsen said with a friendly smile. 'I think we should find you some stylish new clothes if you're to see your mother.'

'Thank you, ma'am,' Shamus said, pulling at the hem of his jacket. 'I don't do stylish, but these rags are reekin' a bit.'

'Thank you, Olivia,' Uncle Percy said.

Olivia Larsen helped Shamus to his feet

Becky watched Olivia Larsen leave with Shamus before she said anything. 'Will he be memorased?'

'Yes,' Uncle Percy replied. 'And after all he's seen I think it's a blessing in disguise, don't you?'

Becky nodded. 'Yeah.'

Joe nodded at the dagger. 'And what're you going to do with that?'

'I'm not sure yet,' Uncle Percy replied.

'You said the Knights Hospitaller had summat to do with the crusades … Wasn't Will in the crusades?'

'Yes. He was in the third crusade.'

'Then he may know something.'

'He may do, but it's a long shot. The Hospitallers existed over a century before Will was even born. However, I suppose it's as good a place to start as any.'

At that moment, the door opened, followed by the clump of heavy footsteps as Barbie, Uncle Percy's robot, marched over to them. 'Good afternoon, sir. Good afternoon, Miss Rebecca, Master Joseph.'

'Hiya, Barbie,' Becky and Joe said simultaneously.

'You're timing is impeccable, Barbie,' Uncle Percy said. 'Would you be a dear and transport us back to the tree house at Bowen Hall? We need to have a little chat with Will.'

'Of course, sir.'

'What are you going to do with Beatrix?' Joe asked Uncle Percy.

'I'll worry about her later,' Uncle Percy replied. 'Barbie, have you got enough Gerathnium to make the round trip?'

'Yes, sir.'

'Excellent,' Uncle Percy replied, returning the dagger to its scabbard and slipping it into his pocket. 'Then, Becky, Joe, hold on tight, please.' He gripped Barbie's shoulder. 'When you're ready, Barbie.' Becky and Joe held Barbie's hand. Immediately, the robot's eyes gleamed emerald; thin tendrils of light illuminated her open mouth.

Before Becky had time to process all that had happened in Balestrino - Shamus, the sickening truth about the Mary Celeste, Otto Kruger's return - they had gone.

*

The ground hardened beneath Becky's feet, as carpet became firm earth. A sudden chill clawed at her. Glancing up, she saw sunlight struggle to penetrate the branches of the ancient trees of Bowen Forest. To her left, the wooden platform to Will's tree house had been lowered to the ground. Then she heard Barbie make a faint humming sound.

'The Alto-Radar confirms Master Will is on the north bank of Bowen Lake.'

'Thank you, Barbie,' Uncle Percy said. 'If you could return to Balestrino and complete whatever work there is still to do, and then bring Beatrix back to Bowen Hall, I would be most grateful.'

Barbie bowed. 'Of course, sir.' A second later, she had gone.

Becky, Joe and Uncle Percy didn't waste any time. Soon, they were navigating their way along the path that bounded the lake, where they saw Will staring out across the velvety water. The plump figure of Deidre the dodo, her plume of snowy-white feathers fluttering in the breeze, was sitting at his feet, her giant beak nipping gently at his toes. Hearing their approach, Will turned toward them.

'Hi, Will,' Joe shouted over.

'Good afternoon to ye,' Will said, getting to his feet. 'And why have you returned from Italy so soon?'

Becky was delighted to see Uncle Percy had made an excellent job of patching up most of his injuries.

'Yeah,' Joe replied. 'We think we've had a breakthrough on the next Eden Relic.'

Will looked surprised. 'Is this true?'

'Yes,' Joe replied. 'And Kruger's back. He's been killing again.'

A strange expression flickered across Will's face, which he seemed to conceal immediately. 'I should have ended him when I had the chance,' he growled. 'Where is he?'

'In the nineteenth century,' Joe replied. 'He slaughtered an entire ship's crew himself. The Mary Celeste. It's like this dead famous ship that was found without its crew. Have you heard of it?'

'I haven't.' Will exhaled heavily. 'That crew is dead because I permitted him to live.'

'You mustn't blame yourself, Will,' Uncle Percy said quickly.

Will ignored him. 'Why did he slay them?'

'He was searching for something,' Joe replied. 'Show him Uncle Percy.'

Uncle Percy withdrew the scabbard from his jacket, before pulling free the blade. As he did, the colour bled from Will's face. 'God's blood!'

'What is it, Will?' Uncle Percy asked.

'Mine eyes hath seen it before.' Will could barely speak. 'At least, if not this one, then its brother.'

'Where?' Joe asked urgently.

''Twas the property of my companion and friend, my comrade in arms, my cleric ... Angus Tuck.'

Joe's jaw tumbled open. 'You mean Friar Tuck?'

'I do...'

Chapter 10

Morogh MacDougal

'Are you sure, Will?' Uncle Percy asked.

Becky thought Uncle Percy's voice contained a strangely dark inflection.

'I have no doubt of it,' Will replied.

'So what's so special about it?' Joe asked excitedly. 'I mean, Kruger offed a load of blokes to get his dirty mitts on it.'

'I know not,' Will replied, frowning at the flippancy in Joe's tone. 'What I do know is Tuck held it to be his most prized possession. He bore it at his side at all times, even in slumber.'

'So could this be the same one?' Becky asked.

Will reached out and took the knife, studying it front and back. 'I think not,' he said. 'I believe the script on the blade to be different.'

'What was written on the other one?' Joe asked.

'I do not know,' Will said. 'I know it was a riddle, but that is all. Tuck translated it for me once, but I did not listen. In truth, I rarely heeded the Friar's words in matters of the dagger, for they were often provoked by large amounts of mead. Still, I am firm these are not the words on Tuck's dagger. Furthermore, I believe this dagger completes a pairing Tuck often described with reverence.'

'What d'you mean?' Joe asked.

'Tuck claimed his blade to be one of a pair created by Morogh MacDougal, a Scottish noble and respected Knight of the First Crusade. He said that MacDougal had found an artefact on an expedition to the Holy Land – something of enormous power … something that filled him with both wonder and fear. For this reason, he concealed it from the eyes of men, but crafted the daggers as a guide, a pointer if you will to its location, for reasons known only to himself.'

'An Eden Relic?' Joe asked.

'In that time I knew nothing of such objects. I just believed the whole matter a fanciful tale with no foundation in truth. Many people, from peasant to patrician, would talk of finding such divine relics, and I believed this to be just another one of those untrue tales.'

'Was the object a sword or a dagger?' Joe asked, eyes bright.

Will looked shocked. 'Aye, boy. It was.'

'Uncle Percy,' Joe said. 'Read him the riddle.'

Uncle Percy took back the dagger and translated the Latin text.

'A fiery blade, eh?' Will said.

'Yeah … did Tuck ever mention something like that? Joe asked.

Will nodded. 'He referred to it as The Sword of Ages.'

Joe's face lit up. 'The Sword of Ages!'

'But more than that, I do not know. In truth, I rarely listened to the story. I had enough problems to ponder upon at the time, I felt no need to entertain myself with stories of fable and legend.'

'It is all very interesting,' Uncle Percy said thoughtfully, tenting his fingers.

'Why?' Becky asked.

'As I mentioned before, I've been doing research into possible Eden Relics, but found nothing concrete. However, there is a passage in the bible, in Genesis: 3: 22 -24 to be precise, that says, "So the Lord God banished Adam from the Garden of Eden to work the ground. After he drove him out, he placed Cherubims and a flaming sword to guard the way to the tree of life."

'A flaming sword?' Joe said.

'Yes.'

'So the Sword of Ages is mentioned in the bible?' Becky asked.

'Well, a flaming sword certainly is. But the bible is a complex book, with many authors and penned over a great deal of time. How much truth is contained within it is a matter of faith.'

'But it can't be coincidence,' Joe insisted. 'We know Eden Relics are real. We've got Tuck's story about that MacDougal bloke, and the fact that Kruger was trying to get this dagger means he must know about Tuck's story, too.'

Uncle Percy nodded his agreement. 'It certainly warrants further investigation.'

'Further investigation?' Joe snorted. 'We need to get to Medieval England pretty damn quickly, find Friar Tuck and …'

'No!' Will cut him off like a bullet.

'Why not?' Joe said, surprised by the bluntness in Will's voice.

'Do not question me on this, boy … You shall not be going!'

'But we need to –'

'ENOUGH!' Will roared, stunning them all to silence. 'My

judgement is final. And there shall be no more talk of it.' He marched off, his angry footsteps crunching the parched grass.

Becky's head swirled as she watched him disappear into the trees. She had never heard Will raise his voice before, never mind shout.

Joe took a few seconds to digest what had just happened, before spinning sharply toward Uncle Percy. 'What the hell was that all about?'

'I'm not sure,' Uncle Percy replied, clearly as shaken as Becky and Joe. 'What I do know is they were perilous times, and no one knows those perils better than Will. He cares for you deeply, for both of you, and I'm sure he just wants to keep you out of harm's way.'

Joe puffed loudly. 'They're all perilous!' he snapped back. 'Well, we don't need him. We'll go back to Medieval England, anyway. One way or another, we'll find Tuck, get that other dagger and find out more about the Sword of Ages. Who knows, maybe it's even there somewhere, locked away in a castle dungeon or summat.'

'I need to think about this.'

'What's there to think about?'

'Plenty,' Uncle Percy replied. 'But first I think I'd better have a private chat with William. I'll see you at dinner…'

As Uncle Percy left, Joe flopped on to the ground, confused and deflated. He cradled his head in his hands and sighed, 'What is going on?'

'I don't know,' Becky replied truthfully.

Joe shook his head. 'They're doin' my nut in. Now I'm convinced they're not telling us everything. Remember what Drake said about us being unwitting pawns in someone else's game. I'm positive now he was flippin' right.'

A knot grew in Becky's stomach. Once again, she couldn't bring herself to disagree with him.

∗

For the next few hours, Becky walked around in something of a trance, like a ghost drifting through the hallways of a haunted house, never quite being able to focus on anything. So much had happened that day, but for all the incredible things she'd seen, one single image revisited her again and again: Will's expression when Joe suggested they travel to Medieval England. What was going through his head? Fear? Panic? Worry? She couldn't quite tell.

Will didn't make an appearance at dinner. Instead, Uncle Percy passed on his apologies for the outburst to Joe, furthering this with his own explanation that Will was out of sorts following his recent accident and not feeling himself at all.

Becky still couldn't accept it. Devoid of any appetite, she prodded her Shepherd's Pie absently, until Maria stated her concern that she was becoming "Disblexic", and that she would never get a boyfriend if she were as thin as feathergrass. At this point Joe coughed the name 'Dan Hardman' and Becky tipped a glass of orange juice down his trousers.

The rest of the meal was cloaked in an uncomfortable silence. And it was only when Maria and Jacob left to wash up the dishes that Joe spoke up.

'So when are we going to Medieval England?' he whispered to Uncle Percy.

'Leave it with me, Joe,' Uncle Percy replied. 'We're not doing anything until I've done more research.'

'What's there to research? We need to find Tuck and see what he knows about the Sword of Ages. Simple as …'

Uncle Percy frowned. 'I don't think it is quite as simple as that, young man. And these things take some time to prepare. Now, once again, I'll ask you to leave it with me…'

Hours later, Becky returned to her bedroom feeling exhausted and drained. The day's events had finally caught up with her. She washed, cleaned her teeth, and was about to climb into bed when there was a low knock on her door. 'Come in,' she said.

The door opened slowly. Joe was standing there in his pyjamas, his face as white as chalk. She knew at once something was very wrong.

'What's the matter?' Becky asked quickly.

Joe didn't reply. Instead, he held up his hand and waved a strip of salmon pink paper. 'This…'

'What is it?'

'A lottery ticket.'

'What are you doing with a lottery ticket?'

'It's not my lottery ticket.'

'Then whose is it?'

Joe shuffled over and sat on the edge of the bed. 'Do you remember on the school roof when Drake grabbed me and said he wanted to give me a message. Well I think he did.' He stared at the ticket. 'I think he gave me this…'

'What do you mean?'

'I was starving and remembered I'd got some grots in my school blazer pocket. I went to look and found this.' He passed the over the ticket.

Hesitantly, Becky took it and scanned the six numbers: 13 – 19 – 39 - 41 - 43 - 48. The first three numbers were encircled in green ink, the others in red.

'Now look at the other side.'

Fingers trembling, Becky turned it over. Five words were written on the back of the ticket in an elegant script.

'For Harry, England and Saint George …'

Fear scaled Becky's spine. She recognised the handwriting instantly – she'd seen it before on a Valentines Day card she'd been given on a recent trip to 1920s Chicago.

A Valentines Day card from Emerson Drake.

Chapter 11

Going ... Going ... Gone

'We need to see Uncle Percy,' Becky insisted. 'And now.'

They wasted no time at all. Tearing out of the bedroom, they hurtled down the corridors and were soon racing into the Entrance Hall.

All the while, Becky felt revulsion grow within. She had no doubt Drake had slipped the ticket into Joe's pocket ... but why? What on earth did it mean? *'For Harry, England and Saint George?'* She'd heard the phrase before, but had no idea where or why Drake had written it. And what was the significance of the numbers, half circled in green pen, half in red?

They checked room after room, but there was no sign of Uncle Percy.

'Maybe he's gone to bed?' Joe said, after they'd checked the kitchen and parlor. 'Or maybe he's in the Time Room?' He sighed. 'I s'pose, we'd better wait until morning.'

'We haven't tried the library,' Becky replied.

Together, they sped up the stairs until they reached the topmost floor. Reaching the landing, they spied a soft orange light oozing from beneath the library door. Becky knocked twice. They heard movement and a second later the door opened, to reveal Uncle Percy, wearing a silk dressing gown, a pair of half moon reading glasses bridging the tip of his nose.

'Becky, Joe, can I help you?'

'We need to see you,' Becky said. 'It's urgent.'

'Very well,' Uncle Percy replied. 'Please, come in.'

Becky could see at once Uncle Percy had been busy. The circular table in the centre of the room was buried beneath dozens of open volumes, leather bound and brown with age. Nestled between the gigantic bookshelves that filled the room was a writing desk, set upon which were four wrist Portavellas.

'How's the research going?' Joe asked Uncle Percy.

'Slowly,' Uncle Percy replied. 'I've been learning what I can about Morogh MacDougal, but it's not been easy.'

'Why?'

'There's just very little out there,' Uncle Percy replied, approaching the table and sitting down. 'I've studied the work of Fulcher of Chartres, Ekkehard of Aura, Robert the Monk, Albert of Aix, Guibert of Nogent – all of them historians and chroniclers of this period, but there is little or no mention of Morogh MacDougal. The most useful thing I've found was Balderic, Bishop of Dol's work Historiae Hierosolymitanae libri IV, a detailed account of the First Crusade, including many of the individuals involved, but even then MacDougal is only mentioned in passing.'

'What about The Sword of Ages?'

'Not a sausage,' Uncle Percy replied. 'No mention, whatsoever. And believe me, I've looked. Anyway, to what do I owe the pleasure of this visit?'

Joe's face darkened.

'Go on, Joe,' Becky urged. 'Show him.'

Hesitantly, Joe held up the ticket. 'Drake slipped this into my pocket when we were on the school roof. There's a message on the back.'

Uncle Percy looked like he'd been punched in the gut. He snatched the ticket and studied the back of the ticket.

'We know it's from Drake, I know his handwriting,' Becky said in such a way it was pointless Uncle Percy trying to deny it. 'What does the message mean? And where have I heard it before?'

'It's part of a speech from Shakespeare's Henry V, Act III,' Uncle Percy said. 'It's one of the most quoted speeches in the English language.'

'And what's the point of it?'

'I … err … I don't know,' Uncle Percy replied.

Becky wasn't convinced. 'Are you sure?'

'Yes … I'm sure. I have no idea what he's up to.'

'Okay, then,' Becky said. 'Why has he circled some numbers in green and the rest in red?'

Turning the ticket over, Uncle Percy took forever to reply. 'Who knows what's going through that maniac's head? But what I will say is that anything he's touched deserves this fate...' Without warning, he tore the ticket into tiny bits. Then he marched over to a wicker bin and threw the bits inside. 'And that's the end of it.'

'But that's not end of it,' Becky said. 'He put the ticket there for a reason, and I want to know what –'

Fury flashed across Uncle Percy's face. 'Drake is playing mind games!' he shouted. 'And I'll hear no more about the matter!'

With his words still ringing through the room, Becky stared at him, dismayed.

'I – I'm very sorry,' Uncle Percy said, his anger subsiding. 'It's just … I loathe that man. And I loathe what he's trying to do to us.'

Becky didn't respond immediately. 'That's okay,' she said finally. 'But he must've meant something by it.'

'I think he's just messing with our heads. Perhaps to stop us focussing on what is really important.'

'The date on the ticket is for next week's lottery,' Becky pointed out. 'He could've come back from next week, from the future to deliver it.'

'The future could have been a second from when he travelled back. Or yes, he could have travelled from a temporal point some time away. However, as far as I know you can purchase lottery tickets in advance so we can't pinpoint precisely when he's travelled from. The date doesn't help us at all in this case.' He returned to the table and collapsed into his chair.

'So what do we do now?' Joe asked.

'This doesn't change anything,' Uncle Percy said. 'We get a good night's sleep, continue with our research and perhaps make a trip in the near future.'

'What about Will?' Joe asked. 'Will he mind if we go?'

'He'll know the right thing to do,' Uncle Percy replied. 'But I do think you should go to bed now and try and get a good night's sleep. I have a feeling tomorrow is going to be a very emotional day.'

Becky stared into Uncle Percy's eyes to see they were lifeless, blank, bereft of any of his usual vigour. 'I think it's you that needs a good night's sleep,' she said softly.

Uncle Percy sighed heavily. 'I agree. I'm going to finish up here and hit the hay.' He managed a smile. 'Goodnight.'

Becky climbed into bed at midnight. She felt nauseous, bewildered, and wondered if she would ever sleep. But, in time, she did. She awoke to the sound of a bird calling from deep in Bowen forest. Thin strips of hazy sunlight filtered in from a gap in her curtains. She opened her eyes and turned to her bedside clock. 6.30 am. She pulled herself up and yawned. Straight away, her blurry eyes were drawn to a scarlet envelope that had been slid beneath the door. Her heart stopped. She jumped out of bed and raced over to the letter, snatching it up and seeing it was addressed to her. Tearing it open, her blood pumping, she pulled out a sheet of cream paper and began to read.

Dearest Becky,

I know this will upset you to the very core, but Will and I have gone to Medieval England. I understand you'll be furious with me, and confused that I have come to this decision, but after long consideration I think it's best we embark on this trip alone. I am aware that you (and Joe) are as much a part of the Eden Relic quest as anyone, but you must trust me that this is for the best for everyone concerned. I shall see you upon our return and am aware, quite rightly, that you will vent your anger in the most vocal of ways. I am deeply sorry, but on this occasion this is the way it has to be.

All my love,
UP

Becky couldn't tear her eyes from the page. She felt like she'd been jabbed with a cattle prod. Rage grew within her, misting the words. Uncle Percy and Will had left for Medieval England without her and Joe.

They had been left behind.

Chapter 12

Numbing Numbers

Enraged, Becky threw on her dressing gown, hurled open her bedroom door, and marched to Joe's bedroom, the letter gripped tightly in her balled fist. She pounded at Joe's door with such force it rattled its hinges. A second later, she heard a groggy voice shout 'Come in'. She flung open the door, scooped up an identical scarlet envelope off the floor, and stomped over to Joe's bed.

'What time is it?' Joe croaked, rubbing his eyes.

'Daytime,' Becky replied. "Now get up!'

'What's the matter with you?'

'This.' Becky waved Joe's letter angrily. 'Uncle Percy and Will have gone to Medieval England without us.'

Joe bolted upright. 'What?'

'They've left. At some time in the night.'

Joe snatched the envelope from Becky's hand, ripped it open and began to read. As he did, his eyes bulged wide and he swore loudly. Crushing the letter into a ball, he pitched it to the floor and swore again. 'What are we going to do?'

'What can we do?'

Joe thought for a moment. 'We can go after them.'

'And how exactly can we do that?'

'I dunno,' Joe replied. 'But we can't let them do this. We can't just sit here and do nowt.' He shook his head with frustration. 'I can't believe them. We're not just passengers on this thing. If it wasn't for us we wouldn't have got the Golden Fleece, Pandora's Box or the Spear of Fate.' He leapt to the floor and kicked the bed leg hard. Trying to act like it hadn't hurt his foot, he grimaced, 'We need a time machine, and we need some coordinates to take us to Medieval England.' He hesitated, before his face flashed with an idea. 'Barbie … she's also a time machine. We'll get her to take us.'

'She's not here,' Becky replied. 'And I doubt she'd take us even if she were. She's a right goody two shoes.'

Joe fell silent again. 'Then we'll contact GITT headquarters, get them to put us in touch with Bruce Westbrook. I bet he'd take us in a heartbeat.'

'And where would we get the number? I don't think time travelling organisations are listed in the Yellow Pages next to truck hire. And I'm damn sure they don't have a Twitter page.'

Joe frowned at her. 'I bet you Maria or Jacob have a contact number somewhere.'

'Maria hates us travelling. There's no way she'd give us the number, even if she had one.'

Joe paced the room. His face ignited with another brainwave. 'What about the Magpie Inn?'

'What about it?'

'Reg Muckle was a time traveller.'

'He's dead. I doubt he'll be able to help us much.'

Joe ignored her sarcasm. 'I know, but what if we go to the Magpie Inn, break in and see if he's left a time machine or a portravella lying around somewhere?'

'Uncle Percy told me Reg's nephew's cleaned all his stuff out and sold the Magpie Inn. It's probably a Wacky Warehouse now. And it's not just about getting hold of a time machine, is it?'

Joe sank on to the bed. 'Then what d'you suggest?'

Becky exhaled deeply. 'I don't think there's anything we can do.'

'There has to be,' Joe replied desperately.

Just as Becky was about to suggest they think on it for a few hours, she remembered something from the night before. 'There are portravellas in the library. I saw a bunch of them on the writing desk.'

'Then what are we waiting for?' Joe said. 'Let's go and check them out.'

Within ten minutes they had washed, dressed and were powering up the stairs to the top floor. Reaching the landing, Becky strode up to the library door and turned the handle. It didn't budge. 'It's locked.'

'Damn,' Joe said.

Becky dropped to her knees and examined the keyhole. 'It's locked from the inside. The key's still in the lock.'

'Then how did he get out?'

'He's a time traveller, you div,' Becky said dismissively. 'He could've used one of those portravellas.'

Joe thought for a second. 'Can you blow the door off its hinges?'

'What?'

'Use your telekinesis. Hit it with a brain zap! Blow it off its hinges.'

'You have all the finesse of a burp.'

'Go on,' Joe urged. 'It's worth a try.'

'Uncle Percy would kill me.'

'Well he isn't here to kill anyone,' Joe snorted. 'He ran out on us … remember.'

But Joe had given Becky an idea. Crouching down again, her gaze found the key. She concentrated as hard as she could. Almost immediately, she felt the peculiar sensation of trickling water brush the crown of her head. The key quivered in the lock. Knowing she had full control of it, she rotated it three sixty degrees. Click! It had worked. She stood up, turned the handle and opened the door, before glancing back at an open-mouthed Joe. 'Now that's finesse,' she said.

'You could make a mint as a robber,' he said appreciatively.

Hesitantly, knowing full well Uncle Percy would be furious if he knew what she'd done, Becky entered Bowen library. She marched over to the writing desk, and saw the portravellas had gone. Her eyes found the desk drawer. She pulled its handle to find it locked.

'Do you reckon they're in there? Joe asked.

'Dunno.' Becky inhaled a deep breath. After a few seconds of thinking about what to do, she said in a gloomy voice, 'I really hope this isn't some priceless antique ... but let's face it, we both know it probably is.' She closed her eyes and focussed on the drawer. The watery sensation returned. She concentrated harder. At once, the drawer began to tremble violently. The table legs rattled the floor. Then– *crack* - the lock shattered and the drawer shot open. Opening her eyes, she scanned its contents: a stack of letter headed writing paper, a quill, a small bottle of peacock blue ink, and a portravella. Ignoring Joe's gasp of approval, she reached inside and extracted the portravella. She'd never seen one up close before. Made from some kind of heavy plastic, it resembled a giant calculator with a wrist strap and a small LED display at the top, beneath which were a succession of keys displaying the numbers zero through to nine.

Rotating it in her fingers, she saw four coloured buttons in green, red, blue and orange on the side. She pressed the green button. The LED display illuminated, revealing six blank boxes and the words Destination Code. A small bar, like a battery symbol on a mobile phone, flashed amber in the bottom right hand corner.

'It seems pretty straightforward,' Joe asked. 'We just need the six digit code.'

'I suppose,' Becky replied. 'But where are we going to get that?' She studied the portravella for a moment and then said, 'Joe, what are we doing?'

'We're up to no good,' Joe replied, grinning.

'Maybe we should just put it back.'

'Don't bottle it now,' Joe said. 'What if Will and Uncle Percy are in trouble and need our help? What if, even as we speak, Uncle Percy is strapped to some medieval torture device and getting his toes yanked off?'

'Err, shut up!'

'Seriously, could you sleep knowing they were hurt and you could've done something about it? Even worse, what if they never came back? What if you never saw Uncle Percy again? What if the Sheriff of Nottingham had his head impaled on a spike at Nottingham Castle?'

'I'll impale your head on a spike if you don't pack it in.'

But Joe's words had struck a chord. Becky's imagination went into overdrive; her imagination was assaulted with sickening images of an injured Uncle Percy and Will, each one more alarming than the last. 'How will we get the destination code then?'

'I dunno yet,' Joe said, surveying the bookshelves, each heaving with countless books, parchments and manuscripts.

'Maybe there's something here?' Maybe there's a time travelling manual or summat with the codes in?'

'You mean like a Time Travel for Dummies? That'd suit you.'

'Summat like that.'

Although Becky was highly skeptical they would have any success, she and Joe spent the next hour combing the library's vast collection. There were books on every conceivable subject, in numerous languages and dating from every imaginable era, but there was nothing that resembled a time travelling manual. As the hour passed, she couldn't help but feel they were on a wild goose chase.

Even Joe had lost all his enthusiasm and slumped on to a chair, head in hands. 'Okay, this is getting us nowhere,' he said miserably. 'What about Uncle Percy's safe?'

'What about it?'

'Well we know it's in the library, and he must keep something important in it. Maybe there's summat in there that can help us?'

Becky recalled the two occasions they had witnessed Uncle Percy open the library's wall safe. 'I'm not going to bust that open, too,' she said firmly. 'No, we should go and look for Barbie, she might be home now, and explain what's happened. Even if she won't take us, she might give us the destination code... I doubt it, but she might.'

At that moment, Joe leapt from the chair. 'I've got it!'

'Got what?'

Joe charged across the library floor and stopped abruptly at the bin. He sank to his knees and reached inside, groping around eagerly for something Becky couldn't see.

'What're you doing?' Becky asked, perplexed.

'Thank God Maria's isn't allowed in here to tidy up.'

'Seriously, why are you rooting through the bin? Are you hungry?'

'The lottery ticket,' Joe replied breathlessly. 'Three numbers were circled in green.' He extracted the shreds of ticket and began to reassemble them. Moments later, all the pieces were back in place, fashioning a coherent whole.

'13 – 19 – 39,' Joe said triumphantly. 'Six digits. It's got to be worth a try!'

Becky's heart leapt. Almost immediately, however, her delight turned into despair. 'Joe, we can't do this...'

'Why?'

'Because Emerson Drake gave us that ticket.'

'So?' Joe shrugged.

'So ask yourself - why would he do that? If you're right, if this is the destination code and not some phone number for his favourite curry house, then he would've only given it to us if he wants us there, at that time period. And if that's what he wants then you can be damn sure it can only be bad for everyone else. He's not exactly in the habit of doing us favours, that's for sure.'

'But –'

'We can't do what that nutter wants, Joe,' Becky said glumly. 'Maybe Drake has seen the future? Maybe he knew Uncle Percy wouldn't take us to Medieval England and he planted the ticket so we could get there without him? Either way, it doesn't matter. Doing what Drake wants would be wrong. It's as simple as that. And if it's good for Drake, if he's gone to so much trouble to make it happen, then you can be bloody sure it'll be disastrous for the rest of us.'

A fierce internal battle appeared to rage in Joe's head. 'I

don't care. Even if Drake thinks he's seen the future, that doesn't mean it can't be changed. We should be going on this trip. At the end of the day, we're a part of this. And we might be able to help. Again, what if something bad happens to Uncle Percy or Will, something we could have prevented if we were there? Also, we might be wrong … maybe this isn't the destination code? Who knows unless we try? Either way, it's worth the risk…'

Becky's head felt like a punch bag. On one level, she agreed with Joe. Despite Uncle Percy's intellectual brilliance, Will's fighting skills, there were things only she could do, things that had saved them from certain death in the past. But she still couldn't shake the feeling that following Drake's wishes, whatever they were, could have devastating consequences for all of them.

Joe, however, didn't appear to have any such reservations. 'Tell you what … we leave Barbie a letter … we tell her what we've done, where we've gone. If this isn't the destination code, if we end up in Ancient Rome or Cretaceous Crewe or somewhere equally off the mark, she can come and get us. No harm, no foul. Uncle Percy may not even have to know. What d'you reckon?'

It took some time before Becky found a reply. 'Okay,' she responded quietly. 'But if we're about to make the biggest mistake of all time, then all of this is on your head. You're getting the blame. All of it.'

'I can live with that,' Joe said.

'Let's just hope you don't die with it.'

Chapter 13

Destination Unknown

As the time passed, Becky felt ever more conflicted. One moment she was convinced she and Joe were doing the right thing - the next, they were embarking on the most foolhardy trip imaginable. There was, however, one thing she had no doubt about: Uncle Percy would be furious with them, regardless of how they tried to justify their actions or whatever the outcome. They had broken into his library, damaged his drawer, stolen his portravella, and were defying his express wishes by travelling to Medieval England using coordinates provided by Emerson Drake.

The more she thought about it, the more preposterous it seemed.

They couldn't even be certain they were coordinates at all.

Despite these concerns, Becky agreed to Joe's suggestion they leave at eleven that morning. They went down to breakfast to find Maria in a particularly breezy mood, humming cheerily as she served them scrambled eggs and hot buttered muffins. Becky was relieved to discover Maria and Jacob were leaving Bowen Hall for a day out with the Addlebury Townswomen's Guild, and, throughout breakfast, acted as naturally as she could, at pains to make sure that Maria – who seemed to have a sixth sense for detecting mischief – didn't discover their plans.

After breakfast, Becky and Joe hurried to the library, took some writing paper from the desk and composed a letter.

Dear Barbie,

We're doing something bonkers. Uncle Percy and Will have gone to Medieval England 2 look for something called the Sword of Ages and left us behind (Gits!). Anyway, we've got a portravella and are going to input these numbers into it as a destination code: 13 – 19 – 39. We're hoping they take us to Medieval England – we don't know where or when, but we're planning on finding Uncle Percy. If that's not the case and we end up in Iron Age Bolton, could you come and get us. Soz 2 dump this on you, but there's no one else we can ask.

Ta,

Becks and Joe

Xxx

PS. If Uncle Percy gets back before we find him, can you not mention any of this and come and get us anyway. If he finds out what we've done, he'll kill us!

Satisfied they had said all that needed to be said, Becky scribbled '**For Barbie**' on an envelope, slipped the letter inside, and she and Joe went to the Time Room where they slid it under the door.

An hour later, rain was falling hard from black clouds, splattering thick beads on to Becky's bedroom window. Inside the room, the air seemed unusually sticky and Becky gulped deep breaths to calm her nerves as she watched Joe circle the room, scribbling in a notebook as if making preparations for a camping trip.

'Now should we take a packed lunch?' Joe asked in all seriousness.

'You do know we're not going to Alton Towers,' Becky replied dully. 'Food is the last thing we should be worried about.'

'We don't know where we're going,' Joe replied bluntly. 'That's why we should take some grub.'

'Alright then,' Becky agreed. 'Maria and Jacob should've left by now so we can grab something from the kitchen.'

Joe nodded. 'What about clothes?'

'What about them?'

'You'll look outta place running round a castle in your Converse All Stars.' He paused. 'Where do you reckon Uncle Percy gets his stuff from?'

'I dunno, maybe he's got a costume cupboard, but if he has it's probably in the Time Room and I don't think I could break into there even if I tried.'

'Then let's go as we are and find clothes when we get there.'

'Fair enough.'

Becky went silent for a few seconds, knowing full well his reaction to her next words. 'Joe ... maybe this is a mistake.'

An ugly sneer spread on Joe's mouth. 'You're chickening out on me. I knew it ... I knew you would.'

'I'm not,' Becky shot back. 'I just think more can go wrong than right.'

'Like what?'

'I dunno. A billion things.'

Joe waved his hands dismissively. 'Nothing's gonna go wrong.'

'You can't be sure of that.'

'You can't be sure Uncle Percy and Will aren't being forced to eat each other's severed toes when we're sitting round here doing nothing…'

Becky couldn't argue with that.

They spent the next hour or so filling two backpacks with items they thought they might need: a torch, a box of matches, a first aid kit, a Swiss army knife they found in the kitchen drawer, and an assortment of food including a meat and potato pie, a loaf of bread, a hunk of cheese, four apples, and two large bottles of water.

They met up at eleven in Becky's bedroom. The rain outside was falling harder now and a snarling wind clattered the window frame.

Becky's stomach rolled in all directions as she stared at the portravella on her dressing table.

Joe looked at her, gripping his Joe-bow, a sword slipped into his belt. 'Go on, then,' he urged, an eager glimmer in his eye.

Striving to stop her hands trembling for fear Joe would see, Becky picked up the portravella, flicked the green button and watched the dial light up: Destination Code.

Joe slung the backpack across his shoulder. 'This is mad,' he grinned.

Becky didn't smile back. 'Yeah, it is.'

Joe raised the lottery ticket, which he had meticulously taped back to its original form. '13 – 19 – 39,' he said.

Becky curled the portavella across her wrist, fastened the strap and inputted the number 13 in the first box. With unsteady fingers, she typed 19 in the second box.

Solemn-faced, Joe took her arm. 'Here goes nothing,' he said.

For the first time, Becky detected a hint of uncertainty in his voice.

The moment Becky entered the final digit, the portavella vibrated softly. Fizzing light extended over her hand, zigzagging upward, covering her arm like a fiery tentacle. Then, in a silent blast, the light surrounded her, blinding her, cocooning her entire body in a shimmering orb. Joe's grip tightened as he roared, 'Here we goooooo!'

Becky said a silent prayer.

Then they vanished.

＊

The next instant, the smell of damp earth filled Becky's nostrils, and she heard the soft rustle of leaves wrestling a stiff breeze. Glancing round, she saw they had materialised in a forest, surrounded by honeysuckle bushes and tall birch trees, their lean silver trunks shining like totem poles.

'Well, we're certainly in England,' Joe said. 'It's freezin'. D'you reckon it's Sherwood Forest?'

'It could be anywhere, Joe. And any time…'

'It could be,' Joe replied in such a happy-go-lucky tone it made Becky want to slap him. 'But we're here now, so what we gonna do?'

'I thought you were in charge.'

'I ain't thought that far ahead,' Joe mumbled, scanning the area. 'I s'pose we should take a look around and – ' He stopped abruptly, his gaze locking on something in the distance. His face whitened. Then he swore loudly and charged off.

Flushed with a sudden panic, Becky shouted after him, "What is it?' Without waiting for a reply, she set off after him. It was only a few seconds before Joe slowed to a halt. Catching up with him, Becky saw something that made her feel sick.

Beryl, Uncle Percy's London Hackney cab, was upturned in

a flattened bush, its bodywork pulverised in a shambolic blend of dents, scratches and punctures. The driver's door had been ripped from its hinges and dangled high above them in the boughs of a nearby tree. Shattered plastic, wire, glass and metal littered the ground like glittering confetti.

Her blood turning to ice, Becky peered through the gap where the door had been. The car's interior had been similarly ravaged. The control panel had been smashed irreparably, leaving a chaotic mound of severed wires and cables. But there was no sign of Uncle Percy or Will.

'What the hell's happened?' Joe gasped.

Becky couldn't find any words. 'No idea.'

'At least we know Will and Uncle Percy are here,' Joe said, trying to sound as upbeat as he could, 'in this time period … somewhere.'

Becky was about to reply when, from somewhere in the distance, a shrill hissing sound split the silence, followed by a series of slow, heavy thuds, which echoed against the hard ground in a slow, steady rhythm.

'Are they … are they footsteps?' Joe panted, extending his Joe-Bow and pulling an arrow from his quiver.

Becky stared into the undergrowth, fearful of what she might see. The trees were older, thicker, their giant, gnarled trunks and low hanging branches blocking the way ahead. 'Dunno,' she replied hastily. 'But let's not hang around to find out…'

The thuds grew in volume, their frequency increasing. It was as if the trees themselves had come alive and were advancing with deadly intent.

Desperate to run, Becky found her legs had turned to stone. Then all went silent. Suddenly, the bushes ahead parted like

curtains, and an enormous reptilian head poked through –
scaly and orangey green with what were undoubtedly feathers
on its crown. The creature's jaws opened slightly as if in a
taunting smirk, flaunting tiny, saw-toothed teeth. Slowly, a
huge sickle-clawed foot pressed forward, and the creature
heaved its massive body into the light.

'It's a Velociraptor,' Joe gulped.

And amidst her paralysing terror, her utter disbelief, one
thought flashed through Becky's mind. When were they?

Chapter 14

Big Bad John

The Raptor sprang into the open, landing with such force it fractured the ground. It was enormous - much larger than Becky had seen in any film. Seething, its huge head tilted right; blood-red eyes peered down at Becky and Joe. Then it gave a thunderous roar.

Blind with terror, Becky felt her ear drums burst.

Joe fired an arrow into the Raptor's mouth.

The Raptor's jaws slammed together, shattering the arrow's shaft like a toothpick. In one swift movement, Joe had reloaded. He fired again, this time the arrow thumped into the Raptor's skull. The dinosaur didn't flinch.

Joe couldn't believe it.

And then, from their right, came a stomach-turning sound: more footsteps.

'RUN!' Becky screamed. She raced off, heart pounding.

Joe didn't hesitate. Catching up with Becky in seconds, he reloaded. Spinning round, he fired a shot into the Raptor's breast. It was then he saw two other Raptors join the first. 'There's three of them ...' he yelled.

Dodging tree after tree, Becky and Joe sprinted deeper into the forest. Glancing back, Becky could see the Raptors were gaining on them, devastating every tree that blocked their path. Then – thwack - her foot snagged a fallen branch. She fell hard, hurtling to the ground, barrelling over – once, twice –

before rolling to a standstill.

Joe skidded to a halt. 'Becks!'

Sensing triumph, the Raptors decelerated to a saunter, their eyes locked on their prey in a terrifying glare.

Becky knew they were dead.

Just then, she heard shouting. From high in the trees, voices bellowed, distracting the Raptors. And then arrows fogged the air, zipping toward the Raptors, each one hitting its target.

The Raptors barely noticed. Glancing upward, they roared in unison.

Then an amazing thought occurred to Becky: If there were humans, they couldn't be in Prehistoric times. It could only mean one thing.

'The Raptors, Joe,' Becky gasped. 'They're Cyrobots…'
And she remembered exactly how to stop a Cyrobot. 'Fire an arrow in their eyes… their right eyes…'

Joe pulled free an arrow, and fired at the nearest Raptor, piercing its eyeball. The Raptor stiffened, like a waxwork dummy. Joe reloaded, adjusted his aim and fired again. The second Raptor froze. Grinning, Joe turned to the final Raptor, winked at it and fired again. Direct hit. All three Raptors stood as still as statues.

Becky exhaled with relief.

All around, men leapt from the trees – a dozen men - hoods veiling their faces. One man towered above the others. He marched up to Becky and Joe with giant strides, before removing his hood.

Becky saw he was a handsome black man, as tall and sturdy as the trees themselves, with a welcoming face and deep brown eyes, which radiated kindness. To her surprise, he appeared as stunned as she was. The other men removed their hoods and were approaching the Raptors, prodding and poking, dumbfounded expressions on their faces.

'Good day to ye,' the man said in a deep, velvety voice.

'H-hello,' Becky said.

'Hi,' Joe managed.

The man nodded at the Raptors. 'And what manner of dragons are these?'

Becky looked at Joe. Neither knew what to say.

Joe thought it best to say something than nothing at all. 'We think they're Velociraptors.'

'I have never heard or seen such things in all my days,' the man said, shaking his head. 'And I have journeyed far and wide.'

'They're pretty rare,' Joe said weakly.

'Rare, indeed,' the black man replied, staring at the Raptors. 'What type of creature remains standing in death?'

Joe didn't know how to reply to that.

'Allow me to present myself - I am John Edmund Little.' The black man bowed. 'But most round these parts know me as Little John.' He waved at the men behind, who had moved away from the Raptors and gathered in line. 'And these are the virtuous men of Sherwood, merry and bold.'

Becky stifled a gasp. She was staring at the legendary Merry Men of Sherwood Forest. 'I'm Becky Mellor,' she spluttered. 'This is my brother, Joe.'

Little John's eyes narrowed as they met Joe's. 'Do we know each other, boy? Your face seems known to me.'

'Err, no,' Joe said.

'Your father, then?' Little John said. 'Perchance I know him?'

'Doubt it.'

Little John didn't look convinced. 'Well, your parentage aside, thou art as fine an archer as any I have seen. A true dragon slayer.'

'Cheers.'

'Now permit me to present my brothers in arms.' Little John pointed at the man closest, who was short and stout with ginger hair and scarlet cheeks that bordered a wide smile. 'This be Arthur Stutely - brawler, glutton, with a heart as fine as this here forest. Don't let his portly shape fool you … he's as quick as a roebuck and as strong as an ox in a scrap. Ain't that right, Arthur?'

'Aye, John.'

Little John pointed to the next in line, an extremely handsome man with tanned, flawless skin and a smile that could melt butter. 'And this be Alan A Dale - minstrel, poet, enchanter of fair maidens, and a warrior as good with a dagger as with his lute. Aye, Alan's a fine musician, but he can spear a gnat's arse from twenty yards with a blade. Do I speak the truth, Alan?'

'You always do, John,' Alan A Dale replied.

Next, Little John gestured to a young man with fair skin, bulbous eyes and large croissant-like ears. 'And this be the baby of the group, Aleric Fletcher – an upstart, with an unruly mouth that oft times earns him a clip around the ear for his cheek.'

Fletcher grinned at Becky and Joe. 'Good den to ye.'

'And the rest o' these rascals …' Little John pointed to each man in turn, 'be David Beale of Doncaster, Eldred Mulch, Arthur Berrymead, Michael Brundle, Kevin Costly, Bill Williams, Russell Crowfeet, and Errol Flint. A finer, more virtuous band of villains, scoundrels and thieves you could never wish to meet.' He gave a hearty laugh. 'They keep the breeze in Sherwood's trees and be the scourge of the Sheriff of Nottingham and that arrogant toad, King John. Don't you lads?'

The merry men nodded enthusiastically, many of them shouting an agreement.

Little John looked at Joe's clothes. 'Now what manner of garments are you wearing? I have seen naught like them even on the Crusades. Y'ain't Italians, are you?'

'No.' Becky shook her head. 'We're British.'

'Good,' John said with a grin. 'Them Italians may look as fair as a serving wench, but I ain't ever happened upon one that could wield a bow like you, boy. You must've had a grand tutor.'

'I did,' Joe smiled, knowing full well his next words would cause a stir. 'Will Shakelock…'

The smile left Little John's face. 'You know Will?'

Joe nodded. 'That's why we're here. We're looking for him. Is he with you?'

Little John looked dismayed. 'No, boy.'

Becky could tell from Little John's reaction there was more to the story. 'But you've seen him … recently?' she said.

'Aye,' Little John replied. 'Seen him and his silver-haired friend, Percy Halifax.'

'That's our Uncle Percy,' Joe said eagerly. 'Where are they now?'

Little John hesitated. 'They've been captured … captured by the Sheriff's men.'

'Captured?'

'Aye,' Little John replied. 'Two moons ago, from what we hear. They lodged with us for a few nights, and then said they had to depart for Alnwick Castle in Northumberland. They were keen to find our fat friar, Tuck, but he left us for Alnwick some time ago on matters of the cloth.'

'So where are they being kept?' Becky asked.

'In the dungeons of Nottingham Castle.'

'Then let's go and get them,' Joe said at once.

'That's where we're goin' now, boy. Futile though it may be…'

'Futile?' Joe said. 'Why?'

'Coz they're due to be hanged, drawn and quartered afore sunset….'

Chapter 15

Not in Nottingham

A bitter chill gripped Becky's heart. Hanged, drawn and quartered! 'So how do we get them out of these dungeons?' she asked, her voice barely audible.

Little John frowned. 'We cannot. Our spies inform us that twenty strong of the Sheriff's finest men guard them noon and night. And they are not unaided – a new evil has darkened the city of Nottingham – an evil in the guise of men, cold-hearted and brutal, who wear strange apparel and brandish weapons of such power to strike fear in Lucifer himself.'

'They're Associates,' Joe said coolly. 'We've encountered them before.' He glanced over at the Raptors. 'They would've brought those dragons with them.'

'Who are these Associates?' Little John asked.

'That's a long story,' Becky said. 'But you're right … they're pond scum and they're dangerous.'

'So if you can't get to the dungeons,' Joe asked, 'what're you planning to do?'

'No more than give our lives to save our friend,' Little John replied. 'Will and your uncle are to be executed in the market square. The Sheriff has fashioned gallows for all to watch. He wants a spectacle to rival Cleopatra's entrance to Rome. You see, many years back, afore Will's disappearance and that of the …' Little John stopped himself mid-sentence, glanced almost undetectably at the merry men, before continuing, 'Afore Will's disappearance, he were the Sheriff's nemesis. He made that fool Sheriff's life a living hell. And that of Prince John, as he were at the time, before the death of his brother, our rightful King, the Lionheart.'

'Richard the Lionheart?' Joe asked.

'Aye,' John replied. 'Anyway, if Will weren't already enough of a legend before he vanished, then after, he became one like no other. A legend that neither the Sheriff nor time could abate. The good folk of Nottingham adored Will above all, excepting God himself. And it were no surprise, not after what he gave them.'

'He stole from the rich and gave to the poor?' Becky said.

Little John smiled. 'Aye. I suppose there's truth to that. We all did. But he gave them more than coins or trinkets. Will Shakelock gave them hope. Hope this world could be a better place. He made them believe the Sheriff's dark ways, his insufferable taxes, his cruelty, could one day come to pass. And that's why the common folk adored him…'

'He's the best,' Joe said.

'Aye,' Little John replied. 'Ain't none finer. And the Sheriff'll be gloating like a cat with a slain pigeon now. He reckons spilling Will's guts all about Nottingham will show folk there ain't no point believing one man could change anything. And that's why he's forcing the good folk of the villages – men, women and bairns - for miles around to come and witness it all. That's why he's making a carnival of the whole affair – affording food and wine and ale for everyone. What he don't realise is there ain't no man in England loved more grandly than Will Shakelock. The people won't be there for merrymaking. They'll be there to say farewell to their champion, their hero…'

Joe nodded miserably. 'So what is your plan?'

'We'll offer a fight,' Little John replied without any trace of confidence in his voice. 'Until every man here has swallowed his last breath. But there ain't no other way it'll end. We can't hope to gain victory 'gainst the Sheriff's army. And we can't save Will. We've said farewell to our loved ones and we all thinks this is as good a day to die as any. Don't we lads?'

Each of the merry men nodded.

Joe thought hard for a few moments. 'Reckon I've got a better plan than that. One that might work. Me and Becks are coming with you.'

'Nay, lad,' Little John replied. 'This ain't yer day to die. We'll take you to our encampment in the forest. There are fine people there - my wife, Elisa, will feed and shelter ye.'

'No,' Becky and Joe said simultaneously.

'We've come for Uncle Percy and Will,' Becky said firmly. 'And we'll get them back.'

'But your just young 'uns,' Little John said kindly. 'And –'

'We may be young,' Joe interrupted. 'But we're different. Becks, show him what you can do.'

Becky nodded. She fixed her gaze on Little John, focusing hard.

In that instant, Little John's arms locked to his side, as if standing rigidly to attention. 'Blessed Mary!' he puffed.

Becky raised her head.

Little John's body rose steadily upward, his giant frame as stiff as plywood, except for his head, which shook wildly in protest. 'What're ye doin' to me?'

The merry men gave a collective gasp.

Little John was at least four feet in the air when he stopped suddenly, dangling like a marionette. 'Release me,' he bellowed.

'Do it, Becks,' Joe said calmly.

Becky gave a sharp nod. Little John descended slowly, his feet soon finding solid earth. Becky released him from her control. Stepping back, flustered, he shook his arms to prove he had command of his faculties once more. Then he stared wide-eyed at Becky.

'What manner of witchery was that?'

'I'm not a witch,' Becky replied dully, not wishing to spend time explaining something she didn't understand herself. 'It's just … something I can do.'

'Now, who's your best archer?' Joe asked.

Still in shock, Little John dipped his head toward Aleric Fletcher. 'Young Fletch…'

Joe scanned the area, before locking on a small hollow moulded in the trunk of a distant tree. Pointing over, he turned to Aleric Fletcher. 'D'you see that hole in the tree over there?'

'Aye,' Fletcher replied, squinting.

'Try and hit it…'

Fletcher raised his bow and drew an arrow from his quiver. Taking his time, he lined up his shot and fired. The arrow flew straight and true, but thumped into the trunk, an inch or so below the hole.

Joe didn't wait for Fletcher to lower his bow. In a flash, he had raised his Joe-bow, fixed an arrow and fired. The arrow cut the air, before, with a resounding thump, striking the hollow dead centre.

The merry men mumbled their appreciation.

Fletcher gulped. 'Fine shot.'

'I had a fine teacher,' Joe said flatly, glancing at Little John. 'And I'm gonna get him back. Whether you like it or not.'

A half-smile rounded Little John's mouth. 'Perchance we

could profit from your aid.' He turned to the merry men. 'Mayhap these young 'uns are the fortune we need, lads? Belike, we may not die of this day!'

Joe looked satisfied. 'Sorted. Then let's get going.'

Little John looked up at the sun. 'Aye, boy. Time is growing short.'

But something concerned Becky. 'So how do you plan on getting into the market square? Won't the Sheriff be expecting you?'

'In faith, that may be so,' Little John replied. 'But he's also demanding upward of two thousand folk from all 'round the Shire – Worksop, Blidworth, Edwinstowe, Mansfield – be in attendance. The Sheriff's men'll find it plenty testing to fix order. And we've set a few locals to hold his toadies distracted, just to give us leave to enter the square. Thereafter, only God and Saint Christopher can aid us …'

Within minutes, the group were heading into the forest, which thickened until only the tiniest flecks of grey cloud filtered through the branches above. Mulch and Arthur Berrymead had given Becky and Joe their cloaks and Little John, much to Becky's displeasure, had smeared their faces, hair and hands with mud. Although Becky didn't welcome being caked in dirt, she couldn't deny the result was effective – she and Joe could easily pass for peasants.

Despite the cheery banter of the merry men, Becky couldn't shake the feeling things would not end well. She wasn't about to say this to Joe, however, who looked more stone-faced and determined than ever.

'How big is the forest?' Joe asked Little John.

'As long and wide as the sea,' Little John replied. 'It covers most of the Shire. Tis why our camp has never been found, despite the Sheriff and King John's labours. 'Tis a Royal Forest, you see, ruled by the King's hand. At least, it were. For years it's been ours - the people's forest ... as it shud be. We tend her, and she, in turn, tends us ... the acorns and bark give us flour to make bread, the birds and animals give us meat, and the River Maun affords us fresh water that's as sweet as any wine. And furthermost, her trees offer safe haven from them that would see us harmed ...'

As they pressed on, Becky could see exactly what Little John meant. Sherwood Forest was enormous - vast, dark and sprawling.

After an hour or so, the forest began to thin, the ceaseless wall of trees morphing into open pastures and rambling fields of wheat. And then, from all around, people were joining the footpaths, dozens of people, their shoulders hunched, wearing joyless expressions as if trailing a funeral procession. Most wore dirty, stained rags, their gaunt, weathered faces grey and leathery from countless hours spent outdoors.

Joining the line, Becky watched the merry men silently acknowledge members of the crowd, before blending in seamlessly, hoods hiding their faces, their bows tucked beneath their cloaks. As one, the procession trudged up a hill.

Reaching the top, Becky's stomach flipped. In the distance, high atop a sandstone outcrop, an enormous castle overlooked a large market square, already bustling with people like ants in a nest. A stone wall, long and high, enclosed rows of narrow streets, thatched houses, taverns, and several churches and friaries.

Nottingham.

Becky looked down to see a line of villagers were passing through a great portcullis, ushered into the city grounds by armoured guards, clad in black cloaks and wielding large swords. She gulped nervously, before glancing at Joe, who looked as resolute as ever.

'Here goes nowt,' he muttered under his breath.

A short while later, Becky and Joe filed into line.

All the time, Becky's gaze was fixed below, not wishing the guards to glimpse the fear she felt certain flickered in her eyes. It was then she spotted Joe's trainers poking out from beneath his cloak.

'Your trainers,' she whispered, 'they're visible.'

'I know.' Joe stooped as low as he could without falling forward. 'But this flippin' cloak isn't long enough. If I get any lower I'll be rolling into Nottingham.'

As the queue diminished, Becky saw that the guards, their faces scornful and ugly, were stopping some of the villagers, patting them down and searching for weapons. Her heart sank. The merry men were heavily armed. Someone was certain to be caught.

Then, from behind, a thundering shout met her ears. Whipping round, she saw a brutal maelstrom of punches and kicks. Eight men she didn't recognise were slugging it out in a brawl. Knuckles crunched bone. Shrieks of pain echoed out. At once, guards raced from the gate, swords raised. As a guard seized one of the brawlers, an old woman stepped in, her warty, pockmarked face savage with rage.

'How darest ya slay Will Shakelock!' she screamed.

'Shurrup y'reeky hag!' the guard hollered back, struggling to hold the brawler who was desperate to return to the fight.

'Ee's a finer man than ye.' The woman hacked up a gobbet of phlegm. Then she spat it in the guards face.

The guard released the brawler and grabbed the woman

roughly. 'Ye toxic witch,' he roared, wiping his face. 'Yeh'll gerra thrashin' fer that.'

'Gerroff me yer stinkin' cur,' the old woman shrieked. 'Yer a sack o' goose crap and so's yer bootlickin' master...'

Astonished at the woman's courage, Becky was about to intervene when she felt a powerful hand grasp her arm. She glanced up to see Little John, his face and hair swathed in cloth, leaving only his eyes visible, which gleamed with satisfaction. 'Come with us,' he whispered. 'Old Imelda'll be all right. And them's her boys scrapping.'

Becky knew instantly the fight had been staged. She glanced ahead and saw the gates were now unmanned. Like a tidal wave, people rushed through, the merry men amongst them, safe and unchecked.

Becky raced after them, Joe at her side. Entering the city walls, she tailed the crowd, turning right into the market square. She stopped dead in her tracks. At least a thousand people had already gathered, not one of them smiling as they faced a high wooden stage, set upon which was a large set of gallows. Great tables heaving with untouched food and wine adorned the square's edges. The only ones who seemed to be rejoicing were the wealthy nobles, elegantly dressed and shaded from the elements beneath open marquees of multi-coloured silk.

Becky's gaze negotiated the marquees, before finding the one closest to the gallows. Inside, standing at a large oak table, was a skinny, bearded man, his face long and pointed like a rat. He wore a velvet surcoat and a dark purple cloak lined with fur, fastened at the shoulder by a silver brooch. He was smirking nastily and raising his goblet to someone on his left.

'That must be the Sheriff of Nottingham,' Joe said.

Becky was about to reply when the blood froze in her veins. A colossal man with cropped flaxen hair stood up, accepted the Sheriff's toast with an emotionless smile, before sitting down again.

Joe had noticed, too. 'I shudda guessed,' he mumbled. 'I knew we'd be running into Otto Kruger sooner or later.'

Chapter 16

The Rescuers

Becky knew she couldn't afford to think about Kruger. They had come with one thing in mind and one thing only: rescuing Uncle Percy and Will.

'So what is this great plan of yours?' Becky asked.

Joe explained it to her. Admittedly, it wasn't the greatest plan in the world, but it wasn't the worst either.

'So what d'you reckon?' Joe asked, after he'd finished.

'As it's the only idea we've got,' Becky replied, 'we don't have much choice.'

'Great,' Joe replied. 'I'll tell Little John.' He searched the area. Little John was easy to spot. Pushing through the mass of people, Joe pulled Little John close and whispered his plan. After Joe had finished, Little John nodded and left to inform the rest of the merry men.

Joe returned to Becky. 'We need to get to the front.'

Becky and Joe inched their way through the crowd.

All the while, Becky felt a rising sense of anxiety. The more she thought about it, the more things she knew could go wrong. Very wrong. Would her powers work? Could Joe really fulfil his part of the deal? The one thing she knew was if something did go wrong Will and Uncle Percy were dead for sure.

And that could not happen.

A long wall of the Sheriff's men stood side by side behind

125

heavy teardrop-shaped shields, about six feet from the stage. Heavy nasal helmets pitched their eyes into blackness. Becky and Joe agreed on a spot about thirty feet away from the platform, close enough to do what they had to do, but far enough away for them to be obscured by the rapidly growing crowd.

Becky's pulse was racing now. She glanced over to see Kruger conferring with three Associates in the marquee. As the minutes passed, the noise of the crowd grew, but it was not the sound of excitement, it was that of despair. Men and women wept openly, reassuring each other with gentle embraces. The mountain of food remained untouched.

A moment later, a loud drubbing sound filled the square. A young boy, his face expressionless, marched on to the stage, a snare drum hanging loosely from his neck by thick rope. Hefty drumsticks pounded skin in a slow rhythm, like a terrible metronome. Each blow muted the crowd further. Then, from the shadows of a dark tower behind the stage, a heavy stone door creaked open. From the gloom, a tall man stepped into daylight, his shoulder length silver hair tangled with dirt, sweat and blood. Uncle Percy looked down, frail and helpless. Will trailed him into the open, colossal guards on all sides, shielding him from clear view. Both men's hands were bound tightly behind their backs, their faces ravaged with fresh bruises, lacerations and blood.

Becky was in no doubt they'd been tortured.

A fury blazed within her, one that ignited every nerve in her body. She glanced over at the Sheriff, who was clapping wildly, his thin ugly smile extending from ear to ear. She had a sudden impulse to crush his skull like a paper cup. Glancing round, she could see what Little John meant. The square's flanks were lined with perhaps a hundred guards, each one looking as ferocious as the next. They outnumbered the merry men ten to one at least. It was then she glimpsed Arthur Berrymead, Russell Crowfeet, Aleric Fletcher and Bill Williams shuffling through the crowd, whispering something to some of the villagers, who responded with amazement, before nodding enthusiastically.

The executioner, a bear-like man with a flushed, sweaty face and greasy black hair, met Will and Uncle Percy and led them up the stage steps to the gallows, passing a wooden block and a huge axe, which glistened in the dusky light. Just then, the Sheriff of Nottingham sprang impatiently from his seat and marched to the platform, a euphoric glint in his beady eyes. He climbed the steps and stood at the front of the stage, his arms open wide.

The drumming stopped.

Silence gripped the square.

'Fair people of the Shire,' the Sheriff shouted. ''Tis a jubilant day. The scourge of Nottingham, William Shakelock, hath been captured, and justice shall be acted upon him this day for those he hath aggrieved - your Sheriff, your King, your country and your God. I gather many of ye deem William Shakelock a hero, and not the toad-spotted vermin, the cutpurse he is … A hero? Nay, methinks not. Doth a hero steal? Doth a hero kill? Doth a hero dishonour his Sheriff and his King? Nay, on my soul, today I claim a victory for English law … for the King's Law. And on this eventide, justice shall be delivered … a sweet, honeyed justice as would chill Judas' crypt.' And with a horse laugh, the Sheriff left the stage, where he was met with a scant smattering of applause from the nobles in their marquees. The crowd, on the other hand, made no sound whatsoever.

The drumming started again.

Becky's heart echoed its beat.

Uncle Percy was shoved to one of two nooses hanging from the gallows' highest beam, directly above a trap door set in the floor. The executioner fitted the noose around his neck, before doing the same with Will. A voice in the crowd shouted, 'God be wit' thee, Will.'

Another yelled, 'Yer spirit'll nay be forgotten.'

'You ready?' Joe asked Becky, keeping his Joe-bow low. He squeezed its grip and it lengthened in his hand.

Becky nodded her reply.

The drum sounded again, the tempo slowing like a time bomb ticking down to a catastrophic end.

Joe's eyes hardened. Still out of sight, he secured an arrow to his bowstring.

Pushing her nerves aside, Becky closed her eyes and focussed.

The drummer struck a final, decisive blow of his snare. The sound punctured the silence like a gunshot. Then the executioner pulled the leaver. The trapdoor shot open. Uncle Percy and Will plummeted simultaneously, their bodies falling no more than a few inches, when they came to an abrupt stop, suspended in mid-air, as if landing on an invisible ledge.

Gasps of disbelief echoed all around.

Suddenly, an arrow severed Will's rope. A second arrow followed almost immediately, slicing Uncle Percy's rope. In shock, their hands still bound behind their backs, Will and Uncle Percy leapt safely to the wooden platform beneath.

And then a number of things happened simultaneously. An ear-splitting crack rang out as the central pole of the Sheriff's marquee snapped in two, the heavy canvas collapsing on all those within. At the same time, the executioner scooped up the axe and charged at Will, swinging at his neck. Will ducked the blow. Then he flung himself at his attacker, head-butting him with a bone-splintering crunch. The executioner slumped to the ground, unconscious.

'Men of Sherwood,' Little John yelled. 'May your aim be true!'

Almost as a response to these words, the merry men were suddenly everywhere, bows raised. Arrows clouded the air, thumping into the guards, one after the other.

The crowd roared with delight. Through the chaos, Joe sprinted toward the stage, dodging villager after villager, his sword raised. The guards at the front were tumbling like dominos, arrows peppering their bodies, leaving a clear path to the stage. With a single bound, he leapt on the platform.

Will couldn't believe his eyes. 'In God's name!'

Joe didn't reply. Wasting no time, he sliced through Will's bonds, before doing the same for a dumbstruck Uncle Percy.

'Joe!' Uncle Percy panted. 'What're you doing here?'

'Saving your backside,' Joe replied, throwing the sword at Will who caught it.

'Where's Becky?' Uncle Percy asked.

Joe nodded at the marquees – more were collapsing, sealing their inhabitants inside. 'Doing her thing,' he grinned.

Will leapt from the stage. A guard charged at him. Like lightning, Will cut him down. Two more guards rushed at him like bulls, weapons raised. In a flash, they had fallen. More guards entered the fray. Like a terrible force of nature, Will fought every one of them, causing many in the crowd to scream with delight, until he was the only one standing. It was then a powerful hand pulled him back.

'We must flee!' Little John urged.

Will nodded. At that moment, the thunder of hooves filled the air. Alan A Dale, Arthur Stutely, Eldred Mulch, David Beale, and Kevin Costly galloped into the square on giant black horses, each of them clasping the reins of a second, rider-less horse. Alan A Dale drew to a halt before Will, and threw over the reins to his second horse. Will caught them and vaulted onto the horse's back. David Beale threw him a bow and quiver, and within seconds, Will was firing one shot after another at the guards. Then, through the pandemonium, he spied a giant figure heaving himself up from beneath the canvas of the Sheriff's collapsed marquee.

Otto Kruger stared at Will, his icy blue eyes seething.

A curious smile arched Will's lips. Then he steered the horse away, galloped up to Joe and pulled him on to his back.

At the same time, Kevin Costly drew up to Uncle Percy and threw over the reins to his second horse, which Uncle Percy caught and quickly mounted. Desperation in his eyes, he scanned the crowd, finally finding the one face he wished for more than any other. 'Becky!' Galloping over, he offered out his hand. 'Fancy seeing you here, young lady.'

Through watering eyes, Becky stared up at his face, which was almost unrecognisable from his injuries. She couldn't speak. Instead, she tendered her hand and Uncle Percy wrenched her up.

'Yahhh!' Uncle Percy shouted, when Becky was settled. His horse bolted off.

A wide gap had formed in the crowd and, after checking that every one of the merry men had straddled a horse, Will powered the convoy out of the square.

Becky gripped tightly to Uncle Percy's waist. Just before

they left, she glanced back at the chaos behind. Many of the Sheriff's guards lay dead on the ground, and those that were alive were struggling to contain the rampaging crowd, who were still playing their part in creating as much disturbance as they could.

Becky clung on to Uncle Percy for dear life, and, soon, the clamour from the square was replaced by the sound of a harsh wind thrashing leaves as the convoy headed into Sherwood Forest.

Daylight was fading fast and a silvery half-moon flashed through the cracks in the trees, but the group pressed on, deep into the belly of the forest. It was twenty minutes before Will steered them into a clearing, drew his horse to a halt and dismounted. Everyone followed suit.

Climbing down, Joe stretched his arms and exhaled loudly. 'That was some crazy stuff, eh, Will?'

Will ignored him. Marching over to the edge of the clearing, his back to all of them, he stared impassively into the blackness beyond.

Bewildered by Will's odd behaviour, Joe walked over to him and tapped his shoulder. 'Are y'alright, Will?'

Will didn't move.

'What's the matter, Will? Are you -'

Before Joe could finish, Will spun round.

Becky was startled by what she saw. Expecting to see relief in Will's eyes, even gratitude, she could see nothing but rage - a ferocious rage that seared Joe like a branding iron.

'What hath thou done, boy?' Will demanded.

'S - saved your life, I reckon,' Joe replied weakly.

'We did not need saving!'

'I – I don't understand.'

'I TOLD YOU NOT TO COME TO THIS TIME!'

'Why are you being like this?' Joe asked. 'We've just saved your life.'

'My life means nothing,' Will shot back, glaring at Joe, whose eyes were dampening. Will saw this and at once his fury gave way to compassion. In one movement, he heaved Joe into the most powerful embrace. ''Tis because I care for you, boy,' he said, his voice cracking. 'I care for you as a father cares for a son.'

'And I … I care for you,' Joe replied. 'That's why I had to come…'

Watching Will and Joe hold each other, Becky could scarcely breathe. But although the vision touched her beyond words, she also found herself craving answers to two simple questions: Once again, why had Will reacted in such a way? And what about Joe being here, in this time, filled him with such dread?

Chapter 17

Questions and Answers

After a few moments of silence, Little John stepped forward and gave a small cough. 'Will, we must leave if we're to see our encampment afore blackness chokes us.'

Will nodded. 'Aye, John.' He released Joe, and they returned to their horse. Everyone remounted and soon they were pressing once more into the forest.

As Becky held on to Uncle Percy, she couldn't stop thinking about Joe.

'I care for you as a father cares for a son.'

Melancholy and joy filled her in equal measure. She knew exactly what those words would have meant to him. Ever since their father's disappearance, he had been without any kind of role model, certainly not a male one, until Will Shakelock had entered his life. And in a very short space of time, Joe and Will had formed a solid, unbreakable bond. On more than one occasion, she had felt a touch of envy at their relationship, but more than anything she felt thrilled ... thrilled they had found each other.

The final gasp of day yielded to night. In the gloom, the forest assumed a sinister air. A cacophony of sounds met Becky's ears: tawny owls yodelled; bats fluttered above their heads; nightjars churred from the branches of tall oaks.

The party pushed on for a further twenty minutes, when, through the undergrowth, Becky glimpsed light. A campfire pitched coils of smoke upward like ghostly apparitions. At once, she felt giddy with excitement. They were approaching the merry men's camp. As Will led the group into a wide glade, shrieks of joy echoed all around. Figures hurried from the shadows – old men, women and children – and rushed eagerly toward the merry men, who dismounted and embraced their loved ones. Will, in particular, was singled out for extra attention, his horse besieged on all sides by well-wishers.

A tall, heavyset woman with full crimson cheeks stomped over to Little John, and shovelled him in her fleshy arms. 'Husband … Thank the Lord above there's still breath in your lungs.'

'Aye, wife,' Little John replied, kissing her forehead. 'But it ain't the Lord that deserves gramercy. 'Tis these young 'uns.' He motioned to Becky and Joe. 'Come hither.'

Becky and Joe walked over.

Little John curled his giant arms around their shoulders and pulled them close. 'Wife of mine, this be Becky and Joe, ' he said proudly. 'Kinfolk of Percy Halifax … and two of the grandest warriors to have ever graced these tormented lands. They made the Sheriff look like a brain-boiled dolt. The lad be as fine with a bow as our Will … and the lassie - in truth, she be as dangerous as a dozen Boudiccas. Becky, Joe, this here's me betta half, Elisa.'

'Hello,' Becky and Joe said simultaneously.

Elisa gave a deep bow. 'Then truly, Becky, Joe, I thank ye …' she said in a kindly voice. 'Thems of the Forest thank ye.'

'Err, no problem,' Joe replied.

Through the corner of her eye, Becky noticed Uncle Percy

whisper something in Will's ear.

Will nodded gravely and turned to the assembly. 'Friends,' he shouted, mounting a fallen tree trunk so he was visible to all. He waited for the commotion to fade. 'It saddens me, but we must all abandon this forest forthwith.'

The group fell silent.

'But why, Will?' someone shouted up.

Will looked grim. 'My return has brought a new species of monster to the forest, one that shall surely find us soon. These woods are not safe ...'

'They're ne'er safe, Will,' someone else spoke up. 'We've ne'er fled before.'

'This is different,' Will replied gravely. 'Dragons roam the land – three of them - dragons in the enemy's command. T'would take too long too illustrate, but for the care of all, we must leave.'

Little John laughed. 'Will, the dragons be gone. The boy vanquished them like a doused flame.'

Will looked shocked. 'Gone?'

'Aye,' Little John pointed at Joe. 'He slew them. All three of them ... I claim I never saw owt like it.'

Will smiled at Joe. 'You did?'

Joe nodded. 'They were only Cyrobots.'

Clearly impressed, Will faced the crowd again. 'Then it appears the forest is a haven once more.'

The gathering roared their approval, many of them glancing at Joe admiringly.

Becky took stock of her surroundings. In the hazy glow of the firelight, she could make out small wooden huts, some built at ground level but obscured behind thick foliage, others built high on the branches of the trees, their leaves concealing them from plain sight. A tree village. Astonished, she was about to tell Joe when she heard Uncle Percy's voice.

'Becky, may I have a word?' He turned and walked to the edge of the glade, out of earshot of the others. Becky followed.

'First of all,' Uncle Percy said. 'Thank you for saving our lives.'

Becky looked at him. Through his patchwork of injuries, she saw relief and gratitude.

'Tell that to Will,' Becky replied. 'He doesn't seem to agree with you.'

'Will's had a difficult time adjusting to being back here. Sometimes he's not quite himself…'

'But he's been acting weird since he heard about Morogh MacDougal's knife.'

'Because he knew the trail would lead us back here, to this time.'

'Okay,' Becky replied, 'but why's that such a big thing? No, there's definitely something more, something he's not telling us.' Her voice fell to an accusatory whisper. 'And neither are you.'

Uncle Percy looked awkward. He was about to say something when Becky interrupted.

' – And don't bother making something up just to make me feel better, because that's not fair.' Becky suppressed her welling anger. 'We both know you're keeping summat from us, and I'm going to have to accept that. But what I will say is that you'd throw a wobbly if we kept something from you.'

'I would try to understand.'

'Maybe … maybe not,' Becky replied tersely. 'Anyway, what did you want to talk to me about?

Uncle Percy hesitated for a moment. 'How did you get

here?'

'We used the numbers circled in green on the lottery tic -'

'I mean … literally,' Uncle Percy cut in. 'Please tell me Barbie brought you and is lurking around here somewhere?'

Becky looked down. 'We broke into the library and took a portravella out of your desk drawer.' She pulled up her sleeve. 'This one…'

Uncle Percy sank his head into his palms. 'Darn it!'

'I'm sorry we broke in but –'

'I don't care about that.'

'What is it then?'

'This portravella's Rectriator is broken. I intended to fix it when I got back.'

'What does that mean?' Becky asked.

'It means it can't return us to the twenty first century. For this particular portravella, this could only ever be a one-way trip.'

'Can you fix it?'

'Not here … no.'

Becky was panicking now. 'What about your other portravellas?'

'After Will and I were ambushed by the Utahraptors – '

'I thought they were Velociraptors?' Becky interrupted.

'Don't get misguided by Hollywood's depiction of Dinosauria. The Velociraptor was a small dinosaur, about the size of a large dog. No, the cyrobots you came across were Utahraptors – much bigger, much deadlier. Anyway, Will and I were ambushed by the Utahraptors and a group of Associates as we approached Beryl. Upon our capture the Associates took everything - my portravellas, my pagidizor - anything that could aid our return home. The only thing they didn't get was

Morogh McDougall's knife which I managed to drop in a mound of leaves once the attack started, so I suppose we should be thankful for small mercies.'

'So we're stuck here?'

'It certainly seems that way.'

But then something occurred to Becky. 'Not necessarily ... I left a note for Barbie saying if we didn't return with you then she should come and find us.'

Hope flashed in Uncle Percy's eyes. 'You did?'

'Yes. And I left her the coordinates.'

Uncle Percy smiled. 'Well done. That's certainly something. Furthermore, as long as Kruger and his thugs are still in this timeline, there's always a chance we can acquire a portravella one way or the other. Besides, I don't think they'll be going anywhere without the Sword of Ages.'

'So you definitely think it's here then?'

'They certainly believe it is.'

'How do you know that?'

'Let's just say, as my appearance suggests, that we were interrogated rather forcibly, and whilst we managed to remain tight-lipped, the interrogators were far from it.'

'What do they know?'

'They believe Morogh MacDougal hid the sword in Scotland, and, as Will said, they believe his two daggers hold the key to its location. They do not, however, seem to know anything about the riddles. What I do know is they're searching for Tuck. They know he's left Nottingham but have no idea where he's gone. Subsequently, the sooner we find him the better.'

'Little John said he's at a castle.'

'Yes,' Uncle Percy replied. 'Alnwick Castle in

Northumberland.'

'So we're going to Alnwick?'

'At first light. Of course, without a time machine it'll be a long trek.'

At that moment, Little John appeared, carrying two large wooden kegs and wearing a wide smile. 'Halifax,' he bellowed. 'We must toast your good fortune. Let's drink until we stain these trees with our puke!' He laughed.

'Charming,' Uncle Percy muttered under his breath.

Little John didn't hear him. 'So what say you?'

'I say a nice cup of Earl Grey wouldn't go amiss.'

'Earl of who?'

'Doesn't matter.'

Becky would always remember that evening as one of the best she'd ever had. Laughter shook the trees. Food was consumed until they were fit to burst. And the merry men told stories and sang ballads until their voices grew hoarse.

At midnight, Becky and Joe retired to Friar Tuck's empty cabin, which was on the ground level, because, according to Little John, 'There be no oak in Sherwood strong enuff to prop the friar's pudgy bulk.'

Becky climbed into her makeshift straw bed and pulled a blanket around her neck. At once, fractured images of the day's events peppered her thoughts. So much had happened in just a short space of time. Within minutes, Joe's soft snores purred in her ears. She lay there for what seemed like hours, wide-awake and alert. Deciding some fresh air might help her sleep, she got up, left the cabin and walked into night. All was silent, save for the machine gun taps of a distant Woodpecker and the faint sputter of the campfire. It was then she saw Little John sitting by the fire, staring absently into the embers and taking long swigs from a pewter flagon.

Becky stepped toward him. A twig snapped under her foot. In a flash, Little John drew from his waistband a dagger, which glowed in the firelight.

Flustered, Becky said, 'Little John, it's me … Becky.'

Little John lowered the dagger. 'I beg thy forgiveness, child.'

'That's okay,' Becky replied. 'Can't you sleep, either?'

'Sleep could never find me on a night such as this,' Little John replied, slurring his words slightly. 'And a finer one for havin' our Will back in our bosom… all thanks to you and your kin. Come hither, sit with me.'

Becky walked over and sat down. Little John raised the flagon and offered it over. 'Ale?'

'No, ta.'

'It will aid your sleep.'

'Still no, ta.'

Little John took another slug. 'Do as thou wilt.'

Silence washed over them for a few moments, before Becky spoke up, 'So how did you meet Will?'

'Ah, Will and me been acquainted for years,' Little John replied, a wistful smile arching his mouth. 'We first chanced upon each other as young 'uns in the archery tournaments at the local village fairs - Bingham, Thoresby, Kegworth, West Chillwell, Gotham … and many more across the Shire.'

Becky smiled. 'I'm guessing he won.'

Little John chortled. 'Every one of them. T'were none could match him. Still can't. Anyways, we weren't much older than thou when we left these shores for the Crusades…' He gave a weighty sigh, the dying flames making his face look older than his years. 'And a vain pursuit it were, too. I deem more wars have been fought in the name of God than any other cause … that and the folly of fool-born rich men. And therein lies the truth of warfare - the rich do the talking … the poor do the dying. The crusades were no different. In truth, King Richard were unlike most – a noble man, as skilled with a longsword as any, and as valiant in combat as the creature that bequeathed his name - Lionheart. Be that as it be, I always deemed the Crusades a reckless quest. What gives a man claim to thrust his faith on another is beyond my reckoning.'

'So why did you go?

'Promises made from them in power – the church, the landowners. And it ain't easy bein' of lowly stock in England, many don't live to any kind of age. I reckoned if I were to die young, might as well do it with the sun on my face beneath a foreign sky. By my thinking, Will's reasons were nobler than mine …'

'What were they?'

'He can answer that righter than I. But I do know many Englishmen are still living because of his involvement. Bettered all others in battle he did. Soon, his reputation flourished and he were summoned to the King's side. In time, Will grew more in the King's favour than any of his most trusted Knights. Thing was, as we were fighting in lands afar, Prince John were scheming to seize England for himself. Anyway, in time the King heard talk of this and sent Will home to expose the Prince's plotting. Me, Alan A Dale and Arthur Stutely journeyed with him. However, on our return to English shores, we found ourselves hunted like dogs. Prince John had fixed a reward for our heads. So, as wanted men, we took to the trees of Sherwood for sanctuary. In time, our merry band grew…'

Becky took a moment to process this. 'I see,' she replied.

Then she swallowed a deep breath as she readied her next question. 'Little John, can I ask you something?'

'Aye, lassie.'

'You saw Will earlier. He never loses his temper like that.'

''Tis true,' Little John nodded. 'He hath the gentlest of temperaments.'

'So why d'you think he reacted to Joe like that?'

Little John said nothing for some time, before his lips parted and a single word came out. 'Guilt...'

Becky wasn't expecting that. 'What do you mean guilt?'

'Will has seen much wickedness in his life, witnessed many horrors inflicted on those he cares for. He is, by nature, a protector, and wishes no more from life than to protect those he cherishes. I think he cherishes you and your kin.'

'But why guilt?'

'We were livin' for years in this forest, helpin' feed the people of the Shire, happening' to blunt Prince John's treasons, when word reached us King Richard wished Will to see him. Outta duty, Will left once more for foreign shores. The crusades had just ended in failure, and the King had returned to Europe to try and rebuild his rule. Problem was, he did not trust some of those that gave him council. Treachery was everywhere. When Will finally were by the King's side, the King gave him a ... a gift ...' Little John's voice stumbled to a halt.

'What gift?' Becky pressed.

'A baby.'

Becky stiffened with shock. 'A baby?'

'Aye. The King had fathered a son - Prince George ... the rightful heir to the throne. King Richard entrusted the baby's safekeepin' to Will, said he wanted George to be reared in

England, but in secret, as a commoner … far away from them who would see him harmed … until he were old enough to take the crown. Will agreed and returned to Sherwood. Tragically, the King were killed in a misfortune soon after in Châlus, France. By this time, Prince John had heard 'bout the baby and grew crazed with hunting him down.'

'What happened to the baby?'

'Prince John had success,' Little John replied miserably. 'The baby were found by the Sheriff's men, seized like a kestrel snatches a mouse, and were never seen again. I believe guilt fuelled Will's words to your brother – guilt at the death of the Prince he loved…'

Chapter 18

The Long Trek

It was then Becky realised just how little she knew about Will's past. At once, she wanted to sprint to his cabin, wake him and hold him until morning. Instead, she remained absolutely still, her breath forming silvery orbs in the chilled night air. 'How did it happen?' she asked quietly.

Little John took another slug from the flagon, froth lingering on his lips as he struggled to find the words. 'Prince George must've only been months old.' He gave a cheerless smile. 'A waggish rascal, he were. Ne'er a moment passed when there weren't a grin fixed to his face. And in passing over charge of the child, the King asked but one thing of Will, and that were every Sunday, if fortune allowed, he wanted the boy to attend church. And Will did his rightest to comply. Hindrance was, Will had a face known to all ... and the Sheriff's eyes were everywhere. But there were a buxom lass friendly with Alan A Dale from a nearby village, Adela Fernyhough her name were...'

'Each Sunday, Adela would take the baby to the Church of Saint Mary in Edwinstowe and pass him off as her own. Will would always chaperone them to Edwinstowe, but then stay hidden by the forest 'til she returned from the service. Anyhow, on this one Sunday, a swelterin' July morn it were... Adela didn't return. Will waited, but heard nowt. Bothered, Will went into Edwinstowe and found poor Adela's body on the village green. Poor girl'd been stabbed. The baby snatched.

He raked the village but to no avail. A villager declared he'd seen a band of the Sheriff's men attack the girl and seize the child. Will searched and searched the area for hours but nowt … The trail went as cold as the grave. Anyhow, by the time Will returned to us he were a changed man.'

'And he never found Prince George?'

'Nay.'

'So he could still be alive?'

Little John gave a glum shake of his head. 'Nay. There be no prospect, poor little scamp. Thenceforward, Will were a shadow of himself, didn't speak to a soul. Twas only days after that, he vanished for good. And we ne'er saw him for three summers, 'til he appeared with yer uncle.'

'And that was three years ago?'

'Aye.'

Little John's jaws tightened and his next words came out as a hiss. 'The Prince and the Sheriff have much to pay for. And one fair day they shall, if only for that little Prince who breathes nay more…'

*

Becky felt numb as she returned to the cabin. As she entered, torchlight wakened the room, sending long shadows against the timber walls.

'Where've you been?' Joe asked.

'Talking to Little John.' Becky replied, slumping onto her bed.

'Is everything okay?'

'Yep.' Becky hesitated. 'And no. Turn the light off, Joe, there's something I need to tell you…'

She spent the next ten minutes explaining all she had been told. Even in the darkness, she could feel Joe's shock emanating outward like a wall heater. After she had finished, the resultant silence threatened to choke them both.

'Will never told me any of that,' Joe managed finally.

'Why would he?' Becky replied. 'I bet he still feels awful.'

'I s'pose we finally have an answer to why he didn't want us here. Do you think we should mention to him that we know?'

'No. It's not our business. And it wouldn't make him feel any better.'

'Are you going to tell Uncle Percy?'

'I don't think so,' Becky replied. 'He'll probably know anyway. I think we should just keep it between ourselves.'

'Poor Will. How long ago did all this happen?'

'Three years or so.'

'But Will's been at Uncle Percy's much longer than that.'

'Yeah, but that's the weirdness of time travel, isn't it? They could've come back at any point. And just because Will left the camp, we don't know when he met up with Uncle Percy. It could've been years later.'

'I s'pose.'

Joe fell silent. Suddenly he let out a small gasp and said, 'Becks … Drake knew about the Prince.'

'What do you mean?'

'Remember the message on the back of the lottery ticket. 'For Harry, England and Saint George…' It's a bit of a coincidence the prince was called George, don't you reckon?'

Becky felt nauseous. 'Who's to say what he knows and what he doesn't…'

'I know,' Joe said insistently. 'And I know he knows…'

Becky found it almost impossible to sleep after that. She tossed and turned for what seemed like the entire night. She awoke with a start to the sound of the door groaning open.

Will entered, carrying two piles of clothes, which he laid on the floor. 'Here are garments for you both, Miss Becky,' he said. 'Did thou sleep well?'

'Yes,' Becky lied. 'Did you?'

'Like a man free of discord,' Will replied. 'I have missed these wood deeply.'

Joe awoke with a yawn. 'Well I didn't. It was like kipping on frozen steak.'

Will chuckled. 'Thou hath been too spoilt by luxuries, Joe. We are leaving forthwith. We must away afore the camp wakes.'

'Are the merry men coming with us?' Becky asked.

'No,' Will replied. 'This is one venture we must journey alone. Our farewells were said last night.' He hesitated. 'But I do wish to repeat my apologies for my temper of late. The reasons are complex but I assure thee both it shall not occur again.'

The previous night's revelations returned to Becky. 'It's not a problem,' she said gently.

'Ah we all get crabby sometimes,' Joe said. 'You wanna try livin' with my sister. I swear she was born with a shell and claws…'

A few moments later, Becky and Joe had packed their rucksacks and left the cabin. The first breath of daylight illuminated the village. Five horses, slender-limbed yet burly, stood parallel beside the ashes of the campfire, their bushy tails whipping left and right. Four of the horses wore polished leather saddles; the fifth, however, carried two large packs tied across its wide back, balanced evenly on both sides.

'Morning,' Uncle Percy said. 'Sleep well?'

'Not really.' Becky rubbed her eyes.

'Ah, I slept like the proverbial log,' Uncle Percy said. 'As Socrates once wrote, "He is richest who is content with the least, for content is the wealth of nature."'

'Yeah, well gimme a Premier Inn any day,' Becky muttered.

Uncle Percy, a sword dangling from his belt, approached the smallest of the five horses. Sturdy yet elegant, it had a sleek, sandy brown coat that gleamed like melted chocolate. He brushed his face against its muzzle and curled his fingers through its silken mane. 'This one's yours. Isn't she dazzling?' The horse flipped its head high and whinnied. 'Of course, Peggy would've made the journey somewhat quicker, but we're having to do it the old fashioned way.'

'And how far is it to Alnwick Castle?'

'It's a distance… approximately a hundred and seventy miles. So prepare yourself for a somewhat tender derrière.'

'How long will it take?'

'Two days, and that's if we make good time. Joe's not as experienced at riding as you so we'll have to take that into consideration. Will thinks we should arrive by nightfall tomorrow.'

'Does he know the way?'

'Apparently. He's been there a number of times before and there's a little surprise for you but I'll save that until tomorrow.'

'What kind of surprise?' Becky asked warily.

'You'll have to wait and see,' Uncle Percy grinned. 'Anyway, shall we skedaddle? I think it's best if we find Morogh MacDougal's dagger before we do anything.' He hunched over, cupped his hands and gestured for Becky to slip her foot inside. 'Allow me, M'lady…'

Clasping the horse's neck, Becky pushed herself on to the

horse's back and settled in to the saddle. She watched Joe, Uncle Percy and Will, who was now armed with a sword, bow and a quiver of arrows, do the same.

And then they set off. In a matter of seconds the camp had been camouflaged wholly by undergrowth. The group hurtled down a muddy trail flanked with trees, their writhing branches like gargoyle's fingers, reaching out and forming an archway ahead. The forest extended before them in brilliant colour, unnerving, mysterious, endless. Birds scattered overhead; red squirrels scuttled up moss-covered tree trunks thick with age.

Becky lifted her head into a cool north wind. She felt it lash her hair into disarray. She didn't mind one bit. She felt exhilarated.

It didn't take so long before they reached Beryl's battered shell.

Uncle Percy drew up his horse at the car and lowered his head. 'I'm sorry, Beryl, when all this is over I promise I'll return and fix you up as good as new.' Then he leapt down and walked north for twenty feet or so, reaching a small oak tree. 'Here's a nice slice of Sherwood trivia. Do you see this sapling here? Well, in our time, this tree still exists and is over eight hundred years old. It is also arguably the most famous tree in the world.'

'Really?' Joe said.

'Absolutely, it's known in our time as 'The Major Oak'.

'Why is it so famous?' Becky asked, intrigued.

'Legend has it that Robin Hood himself used to hide from the Sheriff of Nottingham's men in its hollow trunk.' He pointed at the sapling. 'But I doubt you'd fit in there at the moment, would you, Will?'

'I would not.' Will smiled. 'But then, as I have said before,

I am not Robin Hood. Perhaps the real life Robin was much smaller than I?'

Chuckling, Uncle Percy rummaged beneath a mound of leaves, before standing up, the dagger clasped tightly in his hand. 'We've finally caught a break,' he said. He slipped the dagger into his cloak and mounted his horse. 'Onward to Alnwick then …'

Passing through dell and dale, gorge and gulley, they pushed onward. Steadily, the forest thinned into wide stretches of open pasture, golden meadows and endless strip fields separated by hedgerows. For the first time since they arrived in Medieval England, Becky found herself at peace. There was something about the undulating motion as she rode, the hooves pounding the dewy ground, which made her forget the terrible affair of Prince George. And it occurred to her: even in the remotest parts of twenty first century England, there was always some marker of civilisation on the horizon, something that evinced so called progress – electrical pylons, motorways, cars zipping down country lanes, planes soaring overhead. Here, there was none of it. And she liked it.

She liked it very much.

Stopping for the odd break, they continued, the wind at their rear, urging them forward. Morning became afternoon, which, in turn, morphed into evening. Not once did they see anyone, save for the odd crofter working the field on ox-drawn ploughs, or small groups of workers harvesting crops.

Night arrived. Sequin-silver stars coated a midnight blue sky. They had been riding forever. Every inch of Becky's body was in pain. Her muscles burned, her joints stiff. She felt a swell of relief as Will drew his horse to a halt on the bank of a river. 'We shall make camp here… Miss Becky, Master Joe, if thou wouldst gather wood for a fire?' He turned to Uncle Percy. 'My friend, if you might erect shelter, I shall search for a meal.' He leapt to the ground, slung his bow and quiver across his back and walked off.

Becky dismounted, her feet welcoming the earth. She surveyed the area. The river, wide and fast flowing, sliced through the landscape like cheese wire. On the opposite side an otter's head poked through the glittering water, a flailing bream clamped securely in its powerful jaws.

Uncle Percy approached the packhorse, detached its load and knelt down, unravelling the contents within on the sandy ground: long sweeps of cotton, wooden poles of different sizes, rope and metal pegs. He looked up at a bemused Becky and Joe. 'It may not be your Premier Inn, Becky, but we have tents …'

Becky and Joe spent twenty minutes collecting firewood. On their return they were surprised to see Will had made it back before them. Four large trout lay on a cloth, surrounded by breads, tomatoes and fruits brought from the previous night's feast. Uncle Percy basted the fish in oil, salt and various herbs Will had found on his forage.

Becky and Joe stacked the wood high. Will set dried bark, sun-baked moss and twigs into the fire, and soon a ravenous flame was devouring all in its path. Will whittled a crude roasting rack, lined the fish parallel and began to cook. Twenty minutes later, they sat down to eat.

After the meal was over, Uncle Percy sat back with a contented smile and said, 'I don't mind telling you, William, but that was a supper fit for a King.'

'A supper for King John would involve arsenic,' Will replied darkly.

'I take your point,' Uncle Percy replied. He turned to Becky and Joe. 'Anyway you two, I believe it's customary to recite spine-chilling stories around a raging campfire? Do you know any good ones?'

Becky thought for a few moments. 'Not really,' she said, pausing before she spoke her next words. 'But I think you do.'

Uncle Percy looked taken aback. 'Really? Like what?'

'Why don't you tell us about Emerson Drake?'

The grin vanished from Uncle Percy's face. 'It's been a perfectly lovely evening, do we really want to ruin it talking about that fiend?'

'I think so,' Becky replied doggedly. 'We can't pretend he doesn't exist. And I think we've got a right to know why he's like he is ... after all, he's got our dad ... he's the reason we're all putting our lives on the line time and time again ...'

'Becks is right,' Joe said. 'Maybe you know something that'll help us beat him when it comes to it. Because he isn't going away, and neither are we. Do you know much about him?'

It took some time before Uncle Percy could find a reply. 'I believe I do, yes.'

'Go on then,' Becky urged. 'Tell us.'

Uncle Percy looked conflicted.

Will leaned into the fire, its reflection dancing in his eyes. 'They speak the truth, old friend. Their courage, their valour, their spirit hath earned them that right...'

'Very well,' Uncle Percy replied, hesitantly. 'But it's not a pleasant tale.'

Becky never thought for a moment it would be.

Chapter 19

From Boy to Maniac

Uncle Percy opened his mouth to speak but closed it again almost immediately. He did this a further three times before finally seeming satisfied with what he was about to say. 'Emerson Drake was born in 1961 to a Yorkshire industrialist, Herman Drake and his wife, Eleanor Drake. The Drake Family had for many years enjoyed a prosperous domination of the coal mining industry, primarily by exploiting their workforce in the cruellest of ways – poor wages, even worse working conditions. But nothing mattered to Herman Drake bar the pursuit of wealth and power. His immense wealth enabled him to hold sway over many in the British Government. He was a quite despicable man, cruel and bitter, with extreme right wing views. During the Second World War, although this was never made official, he was heavily involved in an organisation called The Right Club.'

'What's the Right Club?' Becky asked.

'They were a secret society headed by the Member of Parliament Archibald Ramsey. Highly unscrupulous, they were Pro-Nazi and very dangerous. I am, however, in no doubt that Herman Drake and not Archibald Ramsay was the real brain behind the movement, a puppet master par excellence, if you will. And during the war, The Right Club made its primary goal to destabilise Churchill's government and forge an alliance with Adolf Hitler. With this in mind, their aim was to assassinate

Winston Churchill.'

Becky was shocked. 'Really?'

'Really,' Uncle Percy replied. 'Of course, they failed, and many of those involved were sent to prison. Herman Drake, however, somehow eluded capture and even consolidated his power after the war had ended.'

'What was Drake's mum like?' Joe asked.

'An alcoholic,' Uncle Percy replied, 'and far more interested in Dior dresses than her newborn baby. She saw Emerson as a parasite, something that thwarted her efforts to socialise, entertain and shop. So yes, it's safe to say Emerson Drake was born into a somewhat dysfunctional family.'

'You sound sorry for him?' Becky asked.

'As a baby and a child ... absolutely. It's impossible not to be. And I'm afraid things were to get much worse for the young Emerson Drake. He was barely an infant when his parents were killed in a house fire. Anyway, he was sent to live with his Grandmother, Agnes Drake, in Whitby. And it was Agnes, I believe, that inflicted the lifelong psychological damage that would define Emerson forever.'

'What did she do?' Becky asked quietly.

'It's what she didn't do ... and that was to show him any love, affection or anything that could be described as innate human tenderness. Agnes Drake didn't have an ounce of feeling in her body for anyone or anything, with the exception of her three Norfolk Spaniels. There was certainly no love left for Emerson.'

'Good,' Joe said stubbornly.

Uncle Percy scowled. 'Hardly, Joe. No child deserves that.'

'He didn't have to turn into a scumbag just because he didn't have a cuddle every now and again, did he?'

'Perhaps not,' Uncle Percy replied. 'But that's very easy to say when you've been brought up surrounded by love and kindness. In retrospect, I don't believe Emerson had much of a chance. Nature and nurture were both very much against him. The other thing about Agnes Drake was that she was a religious fanatic and a true bigot. Religious extremism has always been an immensely destructive force, just look at some of the dreadful events that have occurred in your lifetime. For the most minor violations of her strict rules – spilling some orange juice, leaving a handprint on her polished silver - she would make Emerson recite the bible for hours on end. For more serious misdemeanors, she would beat him with it until he was black and blue. Often, she would take Emerson and her dogs for long walks along the cliffs overlooking the sea, and on many occasions threaten to push him off if he failed to meet her perversely high standards. You must remember he was only seven years of age…'

Becky didn't know what to say. 'She should've been locked up.'

'I agree,' Uncle Percy replied simply. 'But who knew? Abuse is always a terrible thing. And abuse of a small child, any kind of abuse, is the most deplorable thing in the world. Anyway, inevitably Emerson grew detached from the world. He couldn't form friendships. Instead, he immersed himself into scholarly pursuits. He had a natural ability for science and mathematics and that became his life. He never attended school. He had a long line of home tutors, who resigned very quickly when they realised what Agnes was like. In the end, he pretty much tutored himself. When he was eight years of age, one by one, Agnes' beloved dogs met with strange accidents. Over a six month period, all three died from seemingly natural causes or misfortunes around the house.'

'And he did it?' Joe asked.

'Im afraid so,' Uncle Percy replied. 'I can't be certain of his reasons … whether it was to punish her for the way she treated him, or whether he thought without the dogs around she would be compelled to offer him love and kindness, I can't be sure. Either way, it didn't work. If anything, she got worse.' He sighed deeply. 'And then one day, when they were out walking, it was Emerson who snapped and pushed the old lady over the cliffs. Agnes' corpse was found the very next day on the rocks below.'

Becky could barely speak. 'And what did the police say?'

'The police believed she took her own life.'

'How do you know all this?' Joe asked.

Uncle Percy filled his lungs with air. 'Shortly after I finished creating Barbie, I sent her back in time to compile an optohistophibic folio on Emerson's early life.'

'What's that?'

'Do you remember the optomediaphibic folio we watched about Israel Hands in Bowen Library … the one Barbie had compiled from digital sources?'

Becky and Joe nodded.

'An optohistophibic folio is an application within Barbie's circuitry that records first hand actual events, and doesn't use any secondary sources. To cut a long story short, Barbie travels back in time and, using her Invisiblator so she's never seen, records certain relevant events, then edits them into chronological order for a final Hologramophonic presentation. And that's how I know it was Emerson that pushed his Grandmother… I saw it with my own eyes.'

A chill swept through Becky. 'So what happened to him

after that?

'He was taken in by his distant uncle, Wilfred Hunt, and his wife, Emily. The Hunts were good people, kind people. But I think by this point there was no saving him. And the Hunts had a daughter, Melanie, whom they loved dearly. They did their best to treat Emerson with the same affection as Melanie, but as the years passed, Emerson grew fiercely jealous of her.' Uncle Percy wavered, momentarily unable to continue.

'What happened then?' Joe asked.

'Melanie was found drowned in a local lake,' Uncle Percy replied. 'Again, it looked like an unfortunate accident.'

Joe's face turned white. 'But Drake did it?'

Uncle Percy nodded. 'Yes. As you can imagine, the Hunts were devastated with grief, barely being able to function properly. I even went back and tried to stop Melanie's murder but the Omega Effect intervened. The Hunts still tried to raise Emerson as their own, but by this point he was beyond help. Later, as a young man, he went to Oxford University and that's where I met him.'

'So what was he like at Oxford?' Joe asked.

'To be honest, by then he was able to become two people – the public Emerson Drake, a charming, outwardly gregarious young man and the other - the one no one but him knew about - the cold, calculating monster within. Personally, he never liked me. I think deep down I always knew that. And that was partly because he envied my friendship with a girl we both knew, a girl that, although I was blind to it at the time, had something of a soft spot for me.'

Becky recalled their discussion the previous November when Uncle Percy told her about his tragic past. 'You mean Stephanie Calloway.'

'I do … yes.'

'Who's she?' Joe asked.

'She became my girlfriend, Joe.'

'You?' Joe said in a surprised tone. 'With a girlfriend?'

'Shocking, eh?' Uncle Percy replied with a doleful smile. 'Well, Emerson liked Stephanie very much. He made many attempts to woo her, but she rejected every one of his advances. Amazingly, she preferred me. To be frank, I'm surprised he let me live. Everything else he envied - Agnes' dogs, Melanie Hunt – well, they all seemed to come to a tragic demise…'

Joe leaned forward. 'So why do you think he –'

Joe's words were silenced by Uncle Percy's raised hand. 'Do you mind if we stop there, Joe. There really isn't much else to say and I think I've had enough talking about Emerson Drake for one night. Perhaps we should change the subject to one more in keeping with this lovely night, what do you say?'

But neither Becky nor Joe could offer a response. Uncle Percy did his best to steer the conversation to more jovial topics, but they all knew the evening was over.

What more could possibly be said?

*

An hour or so later, Becky and Joe lay in their tent, neither saying a word. Frogs croaked somewhere close by. The blackness drifted over them like a funeral shroud. The gruesome revelations about Drake had left them both feeling sick and appalled.

'So you feel sorry for him?' Joe asked finally.

Becky exhaled heavily, and considered her words before she spoke. 'As a baby, yep … course I do. I might loathe the man, but no one deserves to be brought up like that, even

Emerson Drake. Course, as an adult – well, we all make our choices in life, don't we? He chose to be a murderer. Maybe you can forgive him for knocking off his psychoid granny. But that's it! The rest is mindless, crazy murder. No matter how I feel about him as a child, I could never feel sorry for the man.'

Joe sat up on his elbows. 'Okay, I've got a question for you.' He stopped himself before continuing. 'You know what he's done, what he's capable of doing?'

'Go on.'

'Could you kill him?'

The words hung thick in the air.

'I don't wanna talk about it.'

'Seriously, could you kill him? Joe repeated. 'If killing him would stop all of this, could you, would you kill him?'

'This isn't Call of Combat 15, or whatever stupid game you're into on the Xbox one. This is someone's life you're talking about.'

'I know,' Joe replied. 'And I know very well it's not a game. But look at the man I'm talking about... he's a monster. I'm just asking if you could do it if it came to it?'

Becky thought hard for a few seconds. Finally, she said softly, 'I don't think I could kill anyone. I really don't. If I did then it wouldn't make me any better than them, would it? I want him arrested and locked up forever, that's it.'

'But what prison could hold him? He's much too clever to be just banged up in Strangeways. He'd get out. And then he'd kill again. Besides, the world doesn't even know about time travellers. To lock him up in a normal prison means the world would have to know about Time Travel. And no one wants that.'

'He could be dumped on a tiny island a million years ago,

like we did with George Chapman. Just left, with no time machine, no portravellas, no way of escaping. That's what I'd do.'

'So you'd like him to be stuck on a desert island, eating coconuts and workin' on his tan? Some punishment that'd be.'

Becky scowled. 'Well I don't think I could kill him…'

'I could,' Joe said without a trace of hesitation in his voice.

'That doesn't make you cool, you know?' Becky snapped back.

'I know,' Joe replied. 'But I could. And I wouldn't lose any sleep over it.'

'Then I suppose that's what makes us different. If I killed somebody, I don't think I'd sleep well again for the rest of my life …'

*

Becky woke to hear a light breeze licking the tent, its fabric fluttering like a moth in flight. She pushed herself vertical. At once, her muscles screamed with pain. The previous day's riding had taken its toll. She couldn't help but dread what was to come. Irritably, she thumped Joe awake, who groaned an obscenity, before rolling over and going back to sleep. Becky crawled outside to see a glittering coat of dew lay all around. Will stoked a newly built fire, set upon which was a tin pot filled with a brown mushy substance that bubbled and popped. To his right, Uncle Percy was folding up his tent. His eyes brightened when he saw Becky. 'Good morning, my dear,' he said cheerily.

'Morning,' Becky replied, getting to her feet, her face grimacing with pain.

'Are we suffering today, by any chance?'

'Just a bit,' Becky winced.

'A day in the saddle will do that to anyone. What you need is a dip in the river. It's rather bracing at first but you'll soon get used to it. It's worked wonders for my arthritis.'

Becky glanced over at the surging water. She shivered at the thought of it. 'I'd rather eat my own feet.'

Uncle Percy chuckled. 'I don't think that's necessary. And with regards to food, Will's preparing us a lovely breakfast of rye bread and pottage, which he assures me is a delicious soup of grains, turnips and celery.'

'Sounds scrummy...' Becky mumbled sarcastically.

After breakfast, they packed quickly and were soon on the road again. As the morning deepened, swirling cloud thickened overhead. By lunchtime, the sky had turned charcoal grey, leaving no one in any doubt a storm was brewing. By early evening, the heavens opened. Rain pelted down in sheets, turning the already rutted paths to sludge. A harsh wind howled, causing the trees to sway back and forth like pendulums. Their pace slowed, but they pressed on nonetheless.

As night began to fall, Becky could not have felt more miserable. Drenched to the skin, cold, and aching from toe to head, she wondered whether the journey would ever end. Then, as they came to the slope of a high hill, Will's upstretched hand ushered them to a standstill and they gathered in a circle.

'We have made fair time,' Will said. 'Alnwick Castle is just beyond this mount.'

Joe expressed his heartfelt thanks with a selection of rather choice words, which earned him a heated glare from Uncle Percy.

Will turned to Becky and Joe. 'But there is a certain matter of which you should be mindful. A matter you may well find unforeseen.'

Becky's recalled Uncle Percy's words: 'And there's a little surprise for you but I'll save that until tomorrow.' Her gaze found Uncle Percy. 'Is this the surprise you were on about?'

Uncle Percy grinned. 'Let Will finish.'

'Alnwick Castle is an eminent stronghold and belongs to esteemed nobles, the De Vesci family,' Will said. 'A friend of mine was wed to Edward De Vesci, a nobleman whom I discovered latterly was slain in Jerusalem. But this lady friend I have not seen for many a year, so I wish your behaviour to be courteous and not - ' he paused, '- roguish…'

Becky swapped a confused look with Joe. 'Why would we be roguish?'

'What does that even mean?' Joe asked.

A strange glint flashed in Will's eyes. 'Because my friend's wedded name is Marian De Vesci…'

'Maid Marian?' Becky breathed.

'Marian is a maid no longer,' Will replied simply. 'She is a Baroness now, and should be treated as such with grace and courteousness.'

Speechless, Becky glanced at Joe, who looked equally flabbergasted. 'We're gonna meet Maid –' Her words were cut short by an almighty BOOM, which shook the ground like an earthquake. It appeared to come from the other side of the hill. A flash of orange lit the sky.

'What the bloody hell was that?' Joe yelled.

Uncle Percy gulped. 'It - it sounded like a tank!'

Chapter 20

Siege

More sound came from beyond: gunfire, shouts, and screams.

Will pulled his horse right and galloped to the top of the hill. Everyone followed, stopping in a line. Not one of them could believe what they saw.

A giant castle rose from the landscape; built on raised earth, it was bordered by high walls and a deep trench, six feet wide. A smouldering crater, thirty feet wide, punctured the fronting wall. Dust thickened the air around the hole. Some distance away, a green Sherman tank inched forward, thin tendrils of smoke rising upward from a gun that had just been fired. Military jeeps zigzagged left and right, dodging flaming arrows, which rained down from archers on the castle's ramparts. Inside the jeeps, Associates fired back with machine guns. Alongside the Associates, sixty or so Knights, clad in cloaks of the deepest blue, raised their swords and shields and waited to attack.

Will's jaws tightened. 'King John's men.'

Just then, dozens of Alnwick Knights raced out from the breach in the wall. The King's men charged. Steel met steel in a thunderous clash.

Becky struggled to comprehend the chaos unfolding before her. Her horror increased when she saw a giant reptile step out from behind the tank, its skull elongated to a point at the cranial crest. It screeched hideously from a long toothless beak, before extending its fibrous wings and taking to the air. Then it flew toward the castle. 'What the hell is that?'

'It's a Pteranodon,' Uncle Percy replied, eyes wide with shock.

'There are Associates, King John's men, tanks and cyrobot dinosaurs?'

'The Pteranodon isn't strictly a dinosaur, it's a –'

'Oh, please, shut up!' Becky snapped.

'Point taken.' Uncle Percy glanced at Will, who looked as if his mind were wrestling a thousand thoughts. 'Now, Will, don't do anything. We need a strategy.'

Will glimpsed the blackening sky above. 'I have one.'

'What's that?' Joe asked.

Before anyone could stop him, Will had grabbed his horse's reins and was charging at the fray, pulling his bow from his shoulder.

'Darn it,' Uncle Percy uttered. 'Now, Joe, just –'

But Joe wasn't listening. With a 'YAH!' he forced his horse into a gallop, trailing Will into the battle.

'JOE ... YOU BAGHEAD!' Becky yelled, before turning to Uncle Percy. 'What can we do?' she asked frantically. 'They haven't got a chance.'

'We need to stop that tank! How powerful is your telekinesis?'

'I don't know.'

'Can you do something with the tank's gun before it fires again?'

Not wavering for a moment, Becky fixed her gaze on the tank, locking on the gun barrel. Feeling the hairs on her neck stand up, she focussed with every ounce of energy she had. She could do this. She had to do this. Concentrating hard, she imagined the barrel's contours, its texture, as if she were there alongside it, grasping it in her fingers. Immediately, the crown of her skull felt like it had been doused with water. Exhaling slowly, she focussed harder, willing the barrel to curl upward. She couldn't see whether it was working or not, but she knew deep down something was happening.

Just then, an explosion shattered the night. The gun barrel exploded in a dazzling fireball or orange and red, metal shards showering the field like blazing raindrops.

Uncle Percy's mouth fell open. 'Err, well done, Becky.' Then he pulled free his sword. 'Ah, well, the devil hates a coward.' He swallowed a huge breath. 'You stay here.' The instant the words left his mouth, he charged after Joe.

Head spinning, Becky didn't know what to do. She didn't have a weapon. And she couldn't use one if she had. But she had no intention of staying put and doing nothing. And besides, she was a living weapon. Clutching the reins tight, she leaned forward, squeezed the horse between her legs and held on for dear life. The horse set off like a bullet. Looking ahead, she saw Will in the midst of the battle, twisting and turning on his horse, firing a stream of arrows down at Associates, who were taken completely by surprise. One Jeep after another skidded to a standstill as its driver and passenger were cut down. Through the crook of her eye, she saw Uncle Percy leap from his horse, run over to a stationary jeep and drag out its wounded occupants, who slumped to the ground, writhing in pain. He jumped on to the driver's seat, powered up the jeep and sped off. Glancing round, he saw Becky and pulled the jeep parallel to her. 'Get in,' he shouted over the pandemonium.

Throwing her legs over, Becky pushed herself off the horse's back and jumped on to the passenger seat, landing safely.

'I thought I told you to wait,' Uncle Percy yelled, his head whipping left and right, searching out Joe.

'And miss all the fun stuff?' Becky shouted back sarcastically. Then, above the heads of the clashing Knights, she spied Joe. 'He's over there,' she yelled, pointing. As Uncle Percy steered the jeep in Joe's direction, her eyes were drawn upward. Fear gripped her. The Pteranodon had doubled back and was soaring toward Joe, its beak trained on him like a javelin. 'JOE,' she screamed at the top of her voice. 'LOOK UP!'

Joe heard her. Glancing up, he saw the Pteranodon. In a split second, he raised his Joe-bow. Barely having time to take aim, he released an arrow. THUMP. It pierced the Pteranodon's right eye – at once, all life deserted it, and it plunged into the earth in an explosion of dirt and mud. At this, Joe's horse reared in fright, throwing him off. Joe crashed to the ground.

Uncle Percy pulled the jeep to a halt beside him. 'Are you okay, Joe?'

Clutching his ribs in pain, Joe got to his feet, and groaned, 'Sound as a pound.'

'Stop being a wuss and get in the car!' Becky yelled.

As Joe clambered into the jeep, Uncle Percy scoured the battlefield. Spotting Will, he slammed his foot on the accelerator and powered off, colliding into one of the King's men on the way. 'Sorry, old chum,' he muttered. 'But you picked the wrong side.' Swerving through the battle, he screeched to a stop beside Will's horse. 'Get in the jeep, Will!'

Sweat glazing his face, Will looked down and shook his head. 'To the castle…' Without giving Uncle Percy a chance to respond, he galloped toward the wall, the ditch looming ahead. Tilting forward, he vaulted it in a graceful motion and disappeared through the hole.

At the same time, Uncle Percy turned the jeep about and rocketed off after Will. 'Err, hold on to something, please.'

'Like what? Becky yelled over the roar of the engine.

Uncle Percy gripped the wheel so hard his knuckles threatened to break through skin. 'Whatever you can!' Forcing the jeep to maximum speed, Uncle Percy trained the jeep at the ditch. A few seconds later, the ground disappeared from beneath them. They soared through the air. With a jolt, the jeep's front wheels smashed against solid ground and they bounced twice, nearly pitching Becky from her seat.

'That was excellent,' Joe whooped.

Becky's hair resembled a kitchen mop. 'Yeah, just brilliant,' she grumbled.

Uncle Percy steered them up a steep slope, through the hole and into the castle grounds, where they saw Will had dismounted and drawn his sword. A dozen or so of the King's men had already made it inside, and were fighting the Alnwick Knights who remained this side of the walls.

Will ran over to the jeep, when he suddenly stopped dead. He had heard something. Turning swiftly, his gaze locked on a swordfight between an Alnwick Knight and two of the King's men, one tall and lean, the other squat and burly. The Alnwick Knight was small in stature and wore a helmet that masked his entire face. The Alnwick Knight fought hard, skirting and blocking every swipe, but the King's men were bigger, stronger. Seizing the Knight's sword arm, the larger of the

King's men knocked him to the ground, before slamming his boot on the Knight's wrist, forcing him to release his sword. The Alnwick Knight gave a peculiarly high-pitched scream. Then, as one, the King's men raised their swords slowly, priming themselves for the kill.

Those few moments were all Will needed. At once, he was upon them. Lifting his sword high, he cut the taller man down, before thrusting a dagger into the belly of the other. In less than a second it was over.

Taking a deep breath, Will peered down at the Alnwick Knight, a whimsical smile curling on his mouth. 'Good E'en to thee, Lady Marian.'

Marian heaved off her helmet and cast it aside. Her frizzy, flaming red hair, parted at the centre, cascaded down her shoulders. 'Will Shakelock?' she gasped with disbelief.

'The very same,' Will bowed. His eyes gleamed like a man witnessing a sunset for the first time.

Marian was speechless. 'I – I held you to be dead?'

'Many have tried,' Will replied. 'But, as yet, all have failed.' Leaning over, he assisted Marian to her feet. 'It does me good to see you again.'

'And I … you.' Marian glanced at the two dead men. 'And I thank ye for my life.'

'Your life shall forever be assured if I am with you,' Will said softly.

Marian smiled. 'Why are you at Alnwick, Will?'

'I seek Tuck. Is he with you?'

Marian shook her head. 'Nay. He has journeyed to Wulvern House. The Lady Ann Moyer is sick. She doth not have long for this world.'

'The Lady Ann is dying?'

Marian nodded.

Will frowned. 'That saddens me. But we must depart for Wulvern forthwith. You must join me and my companions.'

'No, Will,' Marian replied. 'Can you not see all that proceeds? Alnwick is under attack by dark forces. The castle must be defended.'

Will's expression hardened. 'Marian ... Alnwick is lost. You speak the truth, dark forces do stir tonight. And their numbers will rise. More will come, wielding arms, in truth, you cannot comprehend.'

'Then I shall remain and die with this castle.'

'No, Marian,' Will said resolutely. 'You will be needed to help the De Vesci family repair all that will be. Alnwick can rise again. But if you dwell, all that can happen this night is your death. And that cannot be.' The light dulled in his eyes, but he held firm and spoke with complete sincerity. 'Have faith ... those that have caused this bloodshed will suffer for their wickedness. But not tonight. Do you trust me, Marian?'

'With all that I am.'

'Then you must journey with me and my friends, and we must depart now...'

Chapter 21

Under Loch and Key

Becky watched the conversation. She saw Marian nod twice, glance nervously at the jeep, before making hesitant steps toward them.

'That's Maid Marian,' Joe whispered in Becky's ear. 'How cool is this?'

'It would be if we weren't in the middle of a war zone!'

Will hurried Marian into the jeep. Climbing in beside Joe, her eyes scanned the strange vehicle, overwhelmed and frightened.

'Hiya,' Joe said to Marian, who was too bewildered to reply. Then, beyond the wall, sheets of scarlet light erupted across the night sky, followed by a devastating bang as if a meteor had crashed to earth, shaking the ground.

'What's that?' Joe shouted, his ears ringing.

'Reinforcements,' Uncle Percy replied grimly, powering up the jeep. 'By my reckoning, very big reinforcements.'

'Can't we just time zap out of here?' Joe said.

'The jeep's not a time machine.' Uncle Percy glanced at Will. 'Where's Tuck?'

'He's at Wulvern House. Many miles from here.'

'Do you know where that is?'

'Aye.'

'Then you're navigating.' Uncle Percy smiled at Marian. 'Good evening, Marian.' He spoke with urgency. 'I'm sure you have a thousand questions, which we will endeavor to answer in time. For now, be assured this vehicle is quite safe ... and so are you.' Not wasting another moment, he swung the jeep about, tyres screeching, and powered through the hole. Emerging on the other side, he braked suddenly. 'Blimey O' Reilly,' he gasped.

A giant cargo plane had materialised just beyond the battlefield, its tail doors open, exposing a wide ramp, which angled down to the ground. More jeeps raced out of the plane, two at a time. Through the flickering glare of headlights, Becky saw a man's gigantic silhouette march down the ramp, a rifle clasped beneath his arm. She recognised him at once. 'Kruger's here.'

'Then it's time we weren't.' Uncle Percy switched off the jeep's headlights, pitching them into almost complete darkness. Taking a sharp right along the wall, he accelerated to maximum speed, before powering them over the ditch. The jeep sped away from the battlefield, into the blackness beyond.

Becky glanced back. In the chaos, no one had noticed their escape. Within minutes, they had made it onto a tree-lined path. Satisfied they were not being followed, Uncle Percy switched the jeep's lights back on. 'Well, wasn't that eventful? Now, Will, where exactly are we going?'

Will told him. Then he turned to Marian and placed his hand on hers, which was trembling wildly. 'How fare thee?'

'Who were those with the King's men?' Marian asked in a low voice.

'They are from the future,' Will replied simply. 'And so are we.'

'The future?'

'Aye. Many years from now.' Will paused. 'Things change,

Marian. They have knowledge and skills you could not believe. They do not journey by horse, but by carriages such as this, carriages that can even soar as the Falcon soars ... they have weapons far beyond blade and barb, weapons that can lay waste to mountains. And there are some, like the dark forces you have witnessed this night, that will use such power for their own wicked ends.'

Marian listened carefully. 'And how know you this to be true?'

'I have lived amongst them for many a year ... in their time, and for much longer than it may appear. My home is with them now - with Percy Halifax ...' He pointed at Uncle Percy, before doing the same with Becky and Joe. 'And with Becky and Joe Mellor. These have become my kin, and I cherish them as ever I would my own blood...'

'But how can the future be in the now?'

'Many years hence, some can journey through time as you would journey from shire to shire. The years, the days, the hours are but pathways to hike as you would a muddy track.'

Seconds passed. Finally, Marian smiled and said, 'This is much to accept.'

'I concede that. But after all you have seen, you know I speak the truth.'

'You could only ever speak the truth, Will. So what, pray, do those future soldiers want with Alnwick?'

'They are not here for Alnwick. They seek Tuck. As we do.'

'Tuck?' Marian replied, surprised. 'Why Tuck?'

'He has custody of an object, one that may be known to you: MacDougal's dagger.'

'The ivory dagger?' Marian gasped. 'He hath shown it to me countless times and I've heard him voice its worth, but I believed him not.' She shook her head in disbelief. 'Alnwick hath been sacked for a dagger?'

'This dagger is a minor player in a grander production.'

'You speak in riddles, Will.'

'The soldiers believe the dagger will guide them to a sacred relic forged by God himself. And with all I've witnessed, I know there to be truth in that claim.'

'What relic?'

'It is known as the Sword of Ages,' Will replied. 'A sword that was present at the dawn of time, at the creation of all. A sword of such dominion it would imbue its wielder with greater power than even Alexander could dream.'

Marian was lost for words. 'And you believe this tale?'

Will exhaled heavily. 'I have seen much, Marian. Things you could not imagine unless witnessed with your own eyes. I know relics such as this do exist. I have observed their power for myself. And it is for that reason we are here … these future soldiers, and their depraved master – a man called Drake - must be stopped from wielding that power. For he is a true villain, and hath a thirst for evil that is unquenchable…'

It was approaching midnight when a great house emerged on the horizon, bordered by trees and wide lawns. Firelight flickered in the upstairs and downstairs windows. Uncle Percy steered the jeep into a thicket, hiding it from plain view, before glancing at Will and saying, 'Do you mind if I have a little word, William … in private?'

Will nodded. Climbing out, he trailed Uncle Percy into the shadows.

Becky opened the rear door and stepped out. She looked back at Marian, who looked as though she was about to be sick, before extending her hand. 'Let me help you out?'

Marian took Becky's hand and left the jeep as quickly as she could. 'So this is how you journey in this future of yours?'

'It's one way, I s'pose,' Becky replied. 'It's called a jeep.'

'Verily, I favour my carriage to be pulled by something with a mane, a heartbeat and four legs.'

'You get used to it.'

Marian smiled warmly and said, 'And you are Lady Becky?'

'Err, just Becky.'

'I am pleased to make your acquaintance, Becky,' Marian said. 'You are most beautiful.'

'I'm really not,' Becky blushed. 'But you are,' she said sincerely. 'You really are.'

'You are kind, child,' Marian replied with a curtsey. 'And you must be Sir Joe?'

'Yep,' Joe grinned. 'Sir Joe's good.'

'It's just Joe for him, too,' Becky said. 'His head's already as big as a bag of spuds.'

'Spuds?' Marian replied, confused.

'Potatoes,' Becky clarified.

'Ah,' Marian said. 'I ask you forgive my ignorance of your future sayings. In truth, my head whirls as a spinning wheel at these new events.'

'Nowt to apologise for,' Joe replied. 'I'd be well freaked if I were you.'

Marian clearly didn't understand him. 'Freaked?'

'Shocked,' Becky said.

'Ah, that I understand. Aye, I am shocked.'

At that moment, Will and Uncle Percy reappeared.

Although Uncle Percy wore a broad smile, Becky felt certain she could see deep concern in his eyes.

'Okay, everyone,' Uncle Percy said. 'Shall we see if we can

find Tuck?'

They set off toward the house.

'So whose place is this?' Joe asked Will.

'This is Wulvern House, the dwelling of Lady Ann Moyer – a very old and dear friend.'

'And how do you know her?'

'In my time at King Richard's court,' Will said. 'Her late husband, Lord Arthur Moyer, was a close confidante of Henry Plantagenet, Richard's father. Lord Arthur was a noble man with a gentle soul, and served the people of his manor with kindness and respect. A rare quality in the rich. Lady Ann and he were godparents to the young Richard, and in truth, were more a mother and father to him than his own...'

Up close, Becky thought Wulvern House as grand a building as she had seen. Painted in yellow and black, it had three floors, wide arched windows and a tall stone chimney.

Will approached the great oak door. Pushing it open, they entered an entrance hall, its walls decked with paintings and tapestries, most of which depicted religious scenes. A great fire illuminated the room on the north wall, pitching lengthy shadows onto a banquet table. The smell of roast pheasant coloured the air. At the far end of the hall, a steep staircase led to the rooms above.

Just then, an upstairs door burst open, followed by the rumble of heavy footsteps. 'Who's there?' a deep Scottish voice echoed through the hall.

A short fat man in a tattered cloak, as wide as he was tall, thundered down the stairs, wielding a short sword. His face was as round as a football with blazing red cheeks that could fry sausage. Friar Tuck descended three steps when, looking at the group below, he came to an abrupt halt. His mouth plunged open.

'Good e'en, old friend.'

Tuck's face exploded. 'Will Shakelock?' He hurdled the remaining steps three at a time and charged over to Will, slinging his chubby arms around him in a spine-shattering hug. 'Do mine eyes betray me?'

'They do not.'

'Heavens above, you are a fine sight.'

'As are you.'

Friar Tuck released Will. He turned his toward Marian, who smiled back at him. 'And Lady Marian?'

'Good e'en, fair friar,' Marian said.

'M'lady.' Tuck bowed.

'And these are my friends,' Will said. 'Percy Halifax and Becky and Joe Mellor.'

'Greetings to you all.' Tuck bowed at each of them in turn, before looking back at Will and saying, 'I believed you to be with God, my brother.'

'That time will come soon enough,' Will replied. His voice grew solemn. 'How is the Lady Ann?'

'She is fading,' Tuck replied. 'The Lady Caroline watches over her as she sleeps, but her time with us is short now. However, her benevolence has assured her a place at God's side.'

'That it has.'

'And what brings you all to Wulvern House?'

'You,' Will replied.

'Me?'

'We seek your knowledge, your counsel and your experience.'

Friar Tuck laughed heartily, his chin rippling like jelly.

'Och, you must be in grim circumstances if you seek my counsel.'

'We're searching for the Sword of Ages,' Uncle Percy said.

The words winded Tuck. 'The Sword of Ages?' he puffed. 'You're searching for the Holy Sword?'

'We are,' Uncle Percy replied. 'The problem is we barely know anything about it. We were hoping you might be able to illuminate us?'

'Aye… of course I can. The tale of Excalibur is legendary in my homeland.'

Becky could scarcely believe her ears: *Excalibur*.

Joe clearly felt the same way. 'Excalibur!' he gushed. 'The Sword of Ages is Excalibur?'

'Aye,' Tuck replied. 'But the Sword of Ages has had countless names through the ages: Caledfwlch, Claíomh Solais, the Sword of Peleus. Tis a weapon of matchless power that can conquer any foe. Legend claims it to be forged by God himself.'

'Of course!' Uncle Percy exclaimed, as though Tuck's words made something fall into place. He looked at Becky and Joe. 'Do you remember the bible passage said the Garden of Eden was guarded by a flaming sword?'

Becky and Joe nodded.

'Well, in numerous Arthurian myths, it was said Excalibur's steel was forged in dragon fire and that it had an unnaturally shimmering appearance – like celestial fire. A flaming sword, indeed.' He smiled. 'Who'd have thought that Excalibur, the Flaming Sword of Eden and The Sword of Ages are all one and the same? Isn't it intriguing how we keep finding the real-life origins of these famous legends?'

But Joe was much more interested in something else. 'So is

it true that Excalibur was King Arthur's sword?' he asked Tuck.

Tuck looked astounded. 'What does thou know of Artúr, laddie?'

'He was an English King, wasn't he?'

'Bah!' Tuck growled. 'Artúr were as English as I. He was a Scot – but he was ne'er a King. He was Prince Artúr mac Aedan, first son of Aidan, of Dalriada. It is said that Prince Artúr unearthed Excalibur in the vestiges of the Roman fort, Ad Vallum, in the Kingdom of Manann. With Excalibur by his side, he was victorious in countless battles, until a cutpurse stole the blade. Without its guard, Artúr was slain in the Battle of Miathi. The sword vanished for hundreds of years, until it was found in the Holy Land by a Knight of the First Crusade.'

'You mean Morogh MacDougal?'

Tuck looked impressed. 'You know of Morogh MacDougal, laddie? You have wisdom beyond your years. Aye, MacDougal was a great Scottish Knight, a virtuous Hospitaller, and a scholarly man.'

'So how did he find Excalibur?' Joe asked.

'It is said that Saint Andrew came to him in a vision during the Siege of Antioch, and gave him the path to Excalibur's resting place. MacDougal journeyed to the Dead Sea, where he found the ruins of a Church, founded by Saint Andrew himself. It was there he found the sword...'

'So what happened then?' Joe asked.

'In time, MacDougal saw the blade's influence over those it touched. And he grew to fear it, as the disbeliever fears death. And it was then he had a second vision from Saint Andrew – a vision that charged him to return to Scotland, to his home, his mighty castle on the banks of the Ness - '

'A castle on Loch Ness?' Uncle Percy interrupted. 'Do you mean Urquhart Castle?'

'I do, sire,' Tuck replied. 'Urquhart was his home.'

'What was the second vision about?' Joe asked.

'It commanded he hide Excalibur from the eyes of man because one day, a Prince, the son of a great King, would require its control to vanquish a great evil from the world. And so Morogh MacDougal hid the sword and crafted two daggers to point to its location, for the prince to find when that hour came.'

'And did a prince ever find it?' Joe asked.

'No, laddie,' Tuck replied. 'And as the years passed, the daggers vanished … separated, some say, across continents, never to be reunited.'

Will's eyes met Uncle Percy's. 'Perhaps it is time you showed my old friend the artefact that has brought us here.'

Looking uneasily at Will, Uncle Percy withdrew MacDougal's dagger. 'We thought you might know something about this.'

Tuck's eyes bulged. 'Ye gads!' he gasped. 'Can it be true?'

'It can and it is,' Uncle Percy replied.

Trembling, Tuck took the dagger. He could barely speak. 'Dost thou know what this is?'

'Not really,' Uncle Percy said. 'We were hoping you could tell us.'

Tuck wasn't listening. His eyes were fixed on the inscription.

As Tuck processed the words, Becky felt certain she saw fear line his face.

Will noticed, too. 'What is the matter, old friend?'

'I am just startled,' Tuck replied. 'I have speculated over

this dagger my whole life, to hold it is very special...'

'Will informs us that you have similar one?' Uncle Percy said.

'It never leaves my person,' Tuck replied, delving beneath his cloak and pulling out a second knife. He placed them side-by-side. The daggers were identical in almost every way, except for the Latin inscription on the blade.

'What does the text mean?' Becky asked, pointing at Tuck's dagger.

His expression still difficult to read, Tuck cleared his throat and began to speak.

> **'Solve the text of Symphosius**
> **Find the one with no one**
> **Then trail the Sword's light,**
> **To the place far from sun,**
> **And within that setting**
> **Beyond beast and man**
> **The Holy Sword waits**
> **For thy Royal hand...'**

'What's a Symphosius?' Joe asked Tuck.

'I have never known,' Tuck replied.

'Well I think I do,' Uncle Percy said. 'And I believe Symphosius is a 'who' and not a 'what'. He was a third century Christian author of riddles, about which almost nothing is known. His only known work is The Aenigmata, a collection of riddles written in Latin hexameters.'

'So we have to solve one of Symphosius' riddles?'

'It seems that way,' Uncle Percy replied.

'And what about the line: find the one with no one?' Becky

asked. 'I mean - that doesn't even make sense.'

'No ... it doesn't.' Uncle Percy frowned. 'Any thoughts Tuck?'

Tuck shook his head. 'In truth, the entire verse hath confounded me since I first held the blade.' His eyes found the second dagger. 'But with this other verse much has been revealed.' There was a dark nuance to his voice.

'D'you think so?' Joe asked keenly.

'I know it to be so, laddie,' Tuck said. He fixed Uncle Percy with a stare. 'And before I speak more I need to know who you are ... and why you seek the sword?'

Will, who had been silent thus far, reached out and placed his right hand firmly on Tuck's shoulder. 'Good friar,' he said. 'There are matters of which you have every right to know. And we shall tell you these in time, as we have told Marian. But you must understand we would not embark lightly on this quest. I cannot speak for MacDougal's prophecy, but a terrible evil does exist, and that same evil seeks this sword for its own harmful ends.' His following words were delivered in a slow, precise manner. 'And be assured, old friend, it is perchance a more terrible evil than this world has ever known, more malevolent than King John, more persuasive than the church of Rome, more powerful than Saladin and his Ayyubid armies. So you must trust me, Angus, as you have done so many times before ... my friends and I must secure the sword before our enemies do.'

Tuck appeared both shaken and astounded by Will's words. 'I do trust thee, Will ... more than any man alive. If you believe this threat be so great, then of course I shall tell thee all I know. But I must warn you, to seek the sword puts you in perils you dare not imagine. Sire, can you read Latin?'

'I get by,' Uncle Percy replied.

Tuck passed both daggers to Uncle Percy. 'Then please recite the verses as one.'

Uncle Percy nodded and began to speak.

'I leave, for thy finding,
O, future prince,
The fiery blade forged
With divine providence,
Tramp the land of my fathers,
To the shrine that I raised
In the steps of Columba
See my guide, held in glaze

Solve the text of Symphosius
Find the one with no one
Then trail the Sword's light,
To the place far from sun,
And within that chamber
Beyond beast and man
The Holy Sword waits
For thy Royal hand…'

After he had finished, Uncle Percy stared at Tuck and said, 'The Land of my fathers … a shrine … Saint Columba … Am I right in thinking we're looking for a church or a monastery in Scotland?'

'I deem it so,' Tuck replied. 'And there can be only one that befits this verse.'

'Which one?'

'Saint Cuthbert's at Abriachan,' Tuck replied. ''Tis a short trek from Urquhart Castle.'

'And why that one?'

'Because Saint Columba founded the first ever church raised at Abriachan.'

Uncle Percy didn't look convinced. 'But didn't Saint Columba establish over three hundred churches across Scotland?'

'He did, sire. But Saint Cuthbert's is the only one with –'

It was if a light bulb flicked on in Uncle Percy's head. ' - A stained glass window depicting Saint Andrew.'

'Aye, sire.'

'I don't get it,' Becky said, confused. 'How did you know that?'

'The riddle,' Uncle Percy replied. 'It says 'See my guide, held in glaze'. Saint Andrew was MacDougal's guide to the location of sword. Add this to 'held in glaze' and it suggests his image adorns a window.'

'Great,' Joe said triumphantly. 'Then we know where to start. Let's get to Saint Cuthbert's. We can figure out the rest later -'

'No,' Tuck interrupted forcefully. 'Abriachan is a perilous place, laddie, and the church had been long abandoned because of - ' He stopped mid sentence as if unable to continue.

'Go on,' Becky insisted.

'- Because of the evil that patrols the Ness' black waters from Saint Augustus to Drumnadrochit to Inverness.'

'What do you mean "evil"?' Joe asked.

'The tale goes that when MacDougal found Excalibur in the Holy Land, he stole it from the guard of a great dragon ... a creature birthed in the very depths of hell, a beast at home on the land as in the water: The Kraken - '

Uncle Percy made an audible groan.

'What's a Kraken?' Joe asked.

'It's a mythical sea monster, Joe,' Uncle Percy replied flatly.

'Why are these things always guarded by bloody great monsters?' Joe said loudly. 'Just for once, couldn't they be guarded by chickens?'

'Please, Tuck, continue …' Uncle Percy said.

'It is said that in stealing the blade,' Tuck said, 'MacDougal incurred the Kraken's wrath so greatly the beast swam across the known seas, tramped deserts and mountains, in a hunt for the blade it lost. It took upward of two summers but the Kraken found MacDougal, and in revenge for the theft, laid siege to Urquhart Castle, slaying everyone and everything within its ramparts, including MacDougal himself. The Kraken left Urquhart in ruins and it has ne'er been inhabited to this day.'

'And what happened to the sword?' Becky asked.

'No one knows,' Tuck replied. 'It had been long hidden afore the Kraken appeared in the Loch. But many still believe the monster haunts the waters of the Ness to this day, hunting for the blade it lost.'

And then something occurred to Becky. 'Hang on, so you're saying the Kraken is the Loch Ness monster? That's just brilliant.' Her eyes pierced Uncle Percy like daggers. 'Did you hear that? Nessie's real … and she eats people. Whoopee doo!'

Chapter 22

Revelation and Revulsion

'Now, now, Becky,' Uncle Percy said, trying to sound as upbeat as he could. 'We don't know this Kraken is real. After all, the good friar only mentions it in terms of legend.'

'Gimme a break,' Becky replied with a snort. 'Look at our track record: Hydras, Zombies, Harpies, Mummies, Sea Serpents, and a dirty great Sphinx. I think it's probably fair to say Nessie is a twenty headed killing machine as big as a KFC drive through.'

'And so what?' Joe shrugged. 'We've beaten monsters before.'

Becky scowled at him. 'You know, one day, when summat massive bites your legs off, don't start blarting when you're writhing about on the floor like a slug.'

Joe was about to respond when an upstairs door creaked open. A middle-aged woman in a lilac taffeta dress appeared at the top of the stairs, her dark hair hidden beneath a pearl-white wimple. She glanced down with surprise at the group. 'Fair friar... I understand Wulvern House has visitors?'

'It does, Lady Caroline, forgive our noise. Will Shakelock is here and hath brought with him stirring tidings.'

'Will Shakelock?' Lady Caroline said, shocked.

'Indeed, Lady Caroline.' Will bowed.

'It does me well to see you, Will.'

'And I you,' Will replied. 'I am regretful if we woke you.'

'Truly, I was not sleeping,' Lady Caroline replied. 'But the Lady Ann hath wakened. She heard children's voices and requests she may receive them in her chambers. It hath been many years since she the strains of youth have been heard in the halls of Wulvern House.'

Uncle Percy looked strangely flushed. He glanced at Will. 'I don't think that's a good idea.'

Becky was surprised by his words. 'What do you mean?'

'Lady Ann is sick,' Uncle Percy replied. 'It may be infectious.'

'She is without sickness,' Tuck said. 'She is merely passing over to our maker's keeping. Truly, it would benefit her to see the faces of children for a final time.'

'I'm not so sure,' Uncle Percy said.

Becky scowled at Uncle Percy. What was the matter with him? 'Don't be daft,' she said. 'We'll see her. Won't we, Joe?'

'Course we will,' Joe agreed.

'That is good of thee,' Tuck said. 'Come ... I shall make the introductions.'

Turk turned and approached the stairs. Becky and Joe followed. Reaching the first floor, Tuck entered a doorway. Following him inside, Becky and Joe found themselves in a large room with a high ceiling, criss-crossed by thick oak beams. A fire crackled in the corner, illuminating a large bed, lying in which was a woman, about seventy years of age, her silver hair rolling over a velvet pillow. Her eyes were kind and gentle, her skin crinkly like the bark of an ancient tree.

'M'lady,' Tuck said gently. 'How be you?'

'Breath still dwells in my body, Tuck,' Lady Ann said, struggling to find the energy to speak. 'But my time on this earth grows short.'

'The place to which you now journey, M'lady, is a far happier one than this earth. You will be hailed by Saint Peter with open arms like an old friend.'

'Thank you, friar.' Lady Ann glanced at Becky and Joe. 'And who are these that come to my house this night?'

'Old friends,' Will said, walking over to her and kneeling at her bedside. He took her hand.

An incredulous smile formed on Lady Ann's mouth. 'Will Shakelock?'

'Aye, M'lady.'

'Can this be true?'

'It can, Lady Ann.'

'I am blessed to see you before I die.'

'And I am honoured to be seen.'

'And these children … they are with you?'

'They are,' Will replied. 'This is Becky and Joe Mellor.'

Lady Ann raised an unsteady hand, beckoning Becky over. 'Please, child, come closer. Permit an old woman to see your face.'

Becky walked over to the bed. 'Hello, Lady Ann.'

'Greetings, Becky,' Lady Ann said, smiling. 'Child, you are as fair a maiden as any my eyes have seen.'

'Thank you.'

'And there is a boy with you?'

'Yes. My brother.' Becky nodded for Joe to join her.

As Joe walked into the light, something unexpected happened. Lady Ann's eyes widened. She couldn't speak. 'Do mine eyes deceive me?' she panted. 'Hath my time arrived? Art thou an angel?'

Joe didn't know what to say.

'You are beside me again … Richard!'

'Err, I'm sorry,' Joe replied. 'I'm not –'

Lady Ann didn't appear to hear him. Tears were trickling down her cheeks now. 'Oh, Richard, you look as strong as the mighty oak …'

'I'm sorry, Lady Ann,' Joe said. 'I'm not Richard. I'm –'

Recognition flared in Lady Ann's eyes. 'Truly, my fading eyes betray me. Forgive me … you are George … Prince George.' She gulped a mouthful of air. 'You are your father's match in every way – your stature, your locks, your eyes.'

'Lady Ann, this boy is named Joe,' Tuck said.

'This boy is named George,' Lady Ann insisted, her voice frail but steady. 'And he is our Prince. He is the late King's son, and I would know him any place, for he is the double of the boy I raised like a mother. Oh, I am joyful to have lived long enough to see this day. Come hither, George, take my hand.'

Joe didn't know what to do. Slowly, he leaned over and slipped his hand in hers.

'Bless you, George,' Lady Ann said, lips quivering. 'I wish you to have something of mine, something I have held dear for an age. Lady Caroline … I beg ye, pass me my locket.' She pointed at a golden object coiled on the dresser.

Lady Caroline walked over and picked up the locket. Then she approached the bed and placed it in Lady Ann's hands.

'This is yours now,' Lady Ann said to Joe. Her fingers fumbled at the clasp. She opened it to reveal a portrait within. She passed it over to Joe.

Joe took the locket. Looking down at the portrait, his face dropped. Bewildered, he whispered, 'I don't get it.'

Becky stared at the portrait. To her astonishment, she saw

an image that could easily have been Joe. Her mind spiralled into overdrive. She looked over at Uncle Percy for answers, something that would explain all that was happening, but saw nothing but deep sadness etched on his face.

'Will?' Joe said, his voice weak. 'What's going on?'

Will didn't reply.

'I praise the Lord to have seen this night,' Lady Ann said. 'George, you must leave me now. I am weary. But If I am taken in my slumber, know this ... I shall watch o'er you from the heavens and protect you with my very soul...'

The group left the room in silence.

Gathering downstairs, everyone looked at each other, not one of them daring to say anything. Finally, it was Joe who spoke.

'Is it true?' he asked Will. 'This picture... it's me. I mean ... it looks just like me. Is this my real father?' His expression became grave. 'Is this what all your freakiness has been about?'

Will's eyes met Joe's. He was about to reply when Uncle Percy's voice filled the air. 'Please, Will,' he begged. 'This will change –'

'No, Percy,' Will cut him down. 'The truth must out now.' He turned to face Joe. 'Lady Ann speaks true. You are King Richard's son, George.'

Tears gathered in Becky's eyes. 'I – I don't understand.' The moment the words left her mouth, Drake's words flashed into her mind.

Lies surround you - surround both of you ... a web of glorious lies, and you have no idea. You just live quite happily, content in your ignorance, blissfully unaware of the truth, unwitting pawns in someone else's game, blindly trusting those you really shouldn't trust...'

'I do, Becks,' Joe said, the strength returning to his voice. 'It means I'm not your brother. I mean, at least not by blood. Am I, Will?'

'No,' Will replied. 'You are not…'

Chapter 23

The Point of No Return

Becky watched Will lower his head. She waited in vain for a smile to confirm this was some kind of perverse joke. But it never came. Never before had mere words scorched her so deeply. Never before had so many emotions threatened to tear her apart.

Uncle Percy turned slowly to Marian, sighing heavily. 'Marian, do you think the four of us could speak privately? Perhaps you could take Tuck upstairs and explain who we are and where we've come from.'

'Aye,' Marian replied. 'Come hither, friar,' she said, leading a confused Tuck back upstairs.

Uncle Percy nodded at the banquet table. 'Perhaps we should sit down?'

For the rest of her life, Becky would never remember walking over to the table. As Joe sat beside her, she took his trembling hand in hers.

'I'm so sorry you had to find out like this,' Uncle Percy said. 'And this is a very long story ... one that will be difficult to tell and still more difficult to hear. It is a story of great sadness and boundless love.'

Becky's steely gaze found Uncle Percy. She could barely stomach the sight of him. 'How dare you,' she hissed. 'How dare both of you.'

'Please, Becky,' Uncle Percy replied desperately. 'Listen to what we have to say. Obviously, you have every right to loathe us now, but I hope we can explain everything. Yes, life as we have known it has changed forever. But that doesn't mean we can't rebuild … rebuild trust and goodwill.'

'I don't want to rebuild anything,' Becky said. 'As far as I'm concerned you can both go to –'

'Becks,' Joe interrupted, squeezing her hand. 'Let them say what they've gotta say.' He glanced at Will. 'So this is why you never wanted me in Medieval England? This is the reason you freaked whenever I mentioned it?'

'Aye,' Will replied. 'The risk of discovering that which you now know was too great.'

Joe gave an impassive nod. 'Fair enough. So come on then … who am I?'

'You were born George Plantagenet, son of King Richard, in St. Céré, France,' Will replied. 'Mercifully, the Crusades were at an end, and he had returned to Europe to start anew. Sadly, your mother, Helene, passed away of pneumonia a short time after you were born. Her passing devastated your father. And more darkness was to surround him. Prince John had grown powerful in the King's absence and wanted him dead, and any other with a claim to that throne - and that meant you. Prince John's agents were all around, and the King knew not whom to trust. Fearing deeply for your life, the King requested I take you back to England and raise you away from court, away from prominence, until he could return and restore his influence. Sadly, the King died shortly after. But the word about you spread like wildfire. Prince John had treated his subjects with such disdain, they were eager for you to be Richard's successor. This enraged Prince John, and he sent his emissaries across England to hunt you down.'

'We know all of this,' Joe replied. 'Little John told Becky everything. He said that King Richard asked you to take George – ' He hesitated. '- I mean me to church every week and it was on one of those trips that George was killed by the Sheriff's men.'

'Aye, to this day that is what John believes,' Will replied. 'But that is not the truth of it. On the day of note, I did indeed escort you to a church in Edwinstowe, accompanied by a young maiden, Adela Fernyhough. Fair Adela took you to the service, whilst I waited in the forest for your return. But return she did not. Fearful, I rode into Edwinstowe and found her slain body on the village green. I learnt from the villagers the Sheriff's men had assailed her and taken you with them. I tracked them down, and found you alive. Knowing I had no time to gather assistance, I attempted to ambush them alone, but their numbers were too great, more than thirty. I was captured.' He flashed Uncle Percy a weak smile. 'That is when your uncle appeared in the time machine, Bertha, and saved my life.'

'What were you doing there?' Joe asked Uncle Percy.

'It was just coincidence,' Uncle Percy replied. 'Malcolm Everidge was showing me the delights of Sherwood Forest, when we came across the Sheriff's men. We saw them brutalise Will, using you as part of their torture.'

'What do you mean 'me'?' Joe asked.

'They held a knife to your throat and you can imagine the rest,' Uncle Percy said gravely. 'You were just a baby, Joe. There was no way I could stand by and watch that, regardless of the consequences. I felt compelled to intervene.'

Will looked at Joe. 'And we both live today because of your uncle's deeds. Then we fled to the future, to Bowen Hall…'

'And what happened then?' Joe asked.

'Will explained to me who you were,' Uncle Percy said. 'The dangers you were in. We both knew you would be found and killed if I'd have left you in your time, so Will asked if I could give you a home, away from the violence that would surely follow you. I said I would. Anyway, I gave him a choice: He could live with us in the twenty first century or stay in his time.'

'I returned to Sherwood Forest to consider his offer,' Will said. 'I remained there for days, but my understanding of the world had altered evermore. I had no wish to stay. I wanted my home to be close to you, lest you needed my aid. Your uncle had given me a pagidizor and stated if I desired to live in the future, I use it. And so it was ... I left my time and forged a new home at Bowen Hall. The rest you know...'

'So how did I end up with my mum and dad? I mean ... the Mellor's.'

'They're still your mum and dad, Joe,' Uncle Percy insisted. 'Never doubt that for a second. They love you as if you were their own flesh and blood.'

'I know,' Joe replied quietly. 'But how did I end up with them?'

Uncle Percy's brow furrowed. 'What I'm about to tell you is very painful.' He inhaled deeply. 'Just after all of this happened, your mother lost a baby. She'd been seven months pregnant.'

Becky gasped.

'And there were complications,' Uncle Percy continued. 'She was a very sick lady and in a coma for quite some time.' His eyes turned to Joe. 'Anyway, upon hearing about you, John rushed to Bowen Hall. He fell in love with you at first sight. He pleaded with us to let him raise you as his own.'

'And I consented,' Will said. 'It was right you had a family. A true family. And I am eternally thankful that John and Catherine gave you the home I never could. They are your parents. And finer parents could not be wished for...'

'But what about Mum?' Joe said. 'You can't just turn up with a baby from nowhere.'

Uncle Percy swallowed. 'Your mother doesn't know you're not hers....'

The words shattered the air like an explosion.

'B - but that's impossible,' Becky panted. 'She must know.'

'Your father made the decision to memorase the last few months of her life. And I agreed with him. All the pain she had suffered, the terrible memories vanished in an instant. All she knew was that she had a beautiful baby boy. She didn't question anything.' He turned to Joe. 'You were the light of her life. And you still are...'

Joe didn't say a word.

'You may be enraged at our actions,' Will added. 'But our rulings were made out of love and a yearning for your welfare and protection...'

Joe was shaking now. 'Is there any more I should know?'

'No,' Will replied. 'That is your tale.'

Suddenly, Joe stood up with a jolt. 'I can't get my head around this...' He raced across the floor, through the door and into the night.

'I should go and see him,' Uncle Percy said, rising from his chair.

'No,' Becky snapped. 'You've done enough damage. I'll go.' She leapt from her chair and raced outside. Hurriedly, she scanned the area. She saw Joe disappear behind the house. 'Joe... Wait!' she shouted, charging after him. Trailing him, she saw he had stopped, his back facing her. 'Joe?' she said softly, approaching him.

Joe swivelled round. 'I'm not Joe!' he yelled at her, tears flowing down his face. 'Call me George!'

Desperately trying to suppress her own tears, Becky didn't respond. Instead, she marched over and threw her arms around him. Heaving him close, she forced his head into her shoulders and held him like she had never held anyone before. 'Listen to me,' she whispered in his ear. 'You are Joe. You just are. And you're my brother. I don't care whether we're blood related or not. We're closer than that. I love you more than anything or anyone on this planet. Do you understand me?'

Joe didn't reply.

'I said do you understand me?' Becky repeated, more forcefully this time.

'Y-yeah.'

'Good,' Becky replied. 'And besides, you must be my brother because I hate you with all of the appropriate hatred a sister should have for a brother.'

Through the tears, Joe forced a smile. 'I hate you, too.'

Becky smiled back at him. 'Now that's better.'

Joe mopped his eyes. 'But Becks, this changes everything...'

'It changes nothing,' Becky replied. 'Mum and Dad love you. Nothing changes.'

'I don't mean that,' Joe replied. 'I mean that Drake knows about all of this.'

'Maybe he did. Maybe he arranged to get us here because he knew it could wreck our family, that's the kind of scumbag he is, but we're not gonna let that happen ... are we?'

'No,' Joe replied. 'But that's not what I mean. Think back

196

to what Tuck said: MacDougal had a prophecy that – '

'Oh, come on, let's not start believing in daft prophecies now.'

'Just listen to me,' Joe pushed. 'MacDougal's prophecy was that a Prince was to find Excalibur and use it to rid the world of a great evil. Well, that's me, Becks … I'm the son of a King … I'm a Prince. But if Drake knows the future, and let's face it, we're only here because of him, then maybe the prophecy's wrong. Maybe I don't rid the world of evil at all. Maybe I make things a whole lot worse…'

Chapter 24

The King's Speech

That's a hell of a lot of 'maybes', Joe,' Becky said. 'And who cares? We haven't a clue what Drake knows or doesn't know. And you know how brain mashing this time travel thing is - whatever he thinks he knows could change anyway.' She sighed. 'Let's just deal with what we do know. And that's we've just had our heads done in by a pretty big revelation. The question is, how're we going to deal with it?'

'It's not for 'we' to deal with,' Joe replied bluntly. 'I'll just have to handle it. And I will ... in time. I say we forget about it for now. Let's concentrate on finding this sword, and then figure out some way to get back home. Nowt else matters...'

'Fine,' Becky said. 'So are you okay?'

'Course I'm not,' Joe replied. 'But what can I do? It is what it is.'

Becky nodded. 'It is,' she said softly. 'Do you want to go back inside?'

'In a bit,' Joe replied. 'Just give me a minute to clear my head.'

Becky wrapped her hands around his face. Softly, she whispered, 'I do love you, bro.' Then she leaned in and kissed his cheek. Not waiting for a reply, she turned and went back to the house. Entering, she saw Will and Uncle Percy standing anxiously by the fire.

'Did you find him?' Uncle Percy asked.

'Yes.'

'Then where is he?'

'He just needs a moment on his own.'

'Is he okay?'

'What do you think? You've just torn his life apart. But yeah, all things considered, I think he's coping pretty well.'

'And how about you?'

'It doesn't matter about me.'

'It really does, Becky.'

Becky took a moment to respond. 'If Joe's got the strength to be fine with it, then I can find it, too. Besides, if you hadn't done what you'd done he'd have been killed and I never would have met him. And despite the irrelevant matter of a bit of blood, he's my brother, and I can't imagine life without him. So I suppose I should feel thankful … and, given time, I probably will…'

'And that's what makes you the special person you are,' Uncle Percy said. 'I am truly sorry about everything, but there was no way of making this public without crushing a lot of hearts.'

'I don't s'pose there was,' Becky replied honestly. 'But Mum must never find out. It would destroy her.'

Uncle Percy shook his head. 'She won't.'

Just then, Joe entered the entrance hall. 'Okay, that's it,' he announced in a loud, resolute voice that filled the room. 'I've had my little blartin' session. And it won't happen again.' He looked over at Uncle Percy and Will. 'I don't blame you. And I'm not angry … it's just – well, it's a lot to take in and I might need some time to get my head around it…'

'We understand,' Will replied.

'Of course, Joe,' Uncle Percy said. 'Take as long as you

need.'

'Then let's forget about it.'

'Tis forgotten,' Will said. 'But if there is any you wish to hear of your real father then – '

'I have a real father,' Joe replied steadily. 'His name's John Mellor and he's been banged up somewhere in history by Emerson Drake. And one day I'm gonna get him back. But for now, all I care about is finding Excalibur. I'll cope with everything else in my own time and in my own way, but for now it's all about that sword ...'

Becky had never felt prouder of Joe in her life.

*

Tuck and Marian returned a short while later. Ashen-faced and quivering, Tuck was so overawed by all Marian had told him, that he surveyed the group as if they were beings from another planet. Then he disappeared into an adjacent room, only to return with a barrel of honey mead under his arm and a silver goblet. In quick succession, he downed three full goblets of mead, before his face burned as bright as a small sun and he finally found his voice. From then on, question upon question tumbled from his mouth. Uncle Percy and Will did their best to keep up, answering honestly, whilst still retaining a definite air of caution and restraint. By the time Tuck had finished his interrogation everyone was in good spirits, the novelty of their situation having faded, replaced by the jovial chatter of old and trusted friends.

Midnight had long passed when an unsteady Tuck escorted Becky and Joe to an upstairs bedchamber. Illuminated by tallow candles, the room was damp and cool, with a heavy wooden bed large enough for three people, enclosed by linen hangings of mint green. Becky climbed onto the bed.

'I never knew King Richard beyond his station as my sovereign,' Tuck slurred at Joe, his mead-fumed breath capable of stripping paint. 'But from what reached my ears, from paupers to peers, he held as virtuous a character as any man in this world or the next...'

From his blank expression it was clear Joe had no intention of discussing the matter further. 'Cheers for that, Tuck,' he said, taking the friar's arm and leading him to the door. 'We're a bit shattered, so we'll see you in the morning. Make sure you don't fall down the stairs.'

'Aye, my fair prince.' Tuck patted Joe's hand and stumbled out the room.

Joe hadn't even made it to the bed when a chorus of loud bangs and a single loud shriek sounded below.

'I did warn him,' Joe said, shaking his head.

'You don't think he's hurt, do you?'

'Nah,' Joe replied. 'With all that padding, I'm surprised he didn't bounce right back up here.'

Becky smiled. She watched Joe join her on the bed. 'Anyway, how're you feeling ... my fair prince?'

'I'm okay,' Joe replied. But if you call me that again I swear you won't be...'

'Why?' Becky replied playfully. 'Will you send me to the tallest tower in the tallest castle and have my head cut off?'

'I just might...' Joe paused, and for the first time in hours a twinkle flashed in his eye. 'Actually, maybe I should stop stressing about all of this and just go with it. After all, with King Richard gone, I'm next in line to the throne of England. Maybe I should be King ... it could be a right giggle.'

'A giggle?' Becky snorted. 'How could it possibly be a giggle?'

Joe looked deadly serious. 'Yeah, think about it ... I could do whatever I wanted and no one could stop me.'

'And what would you want to do?'

'Dunno,' Joe replied, thinking hard for a moment. 'If I fancied a holiday, I could just raise an army, invade Spain, seize a castle with a private beach and there you go ... free all-inclusive accommodation.'

'I think some people might have a problem with that,' Becky said.

'Who?'

'Err, the Spanish.'

'It'd only be for a few weeks.'

'Doesn't matter ... working on your tan would probably start a massive war!'

Joe flicked his hand dismissively. 'I doubt it.'

'That's what tends to happen when one country invades another.'

'Well there are lots of other things I'd do if I were King.'

'Like what?'

'Err, make it a two day school week.'

'It's the twelfth century. I don't think they have schools.'

'Even better,' Joe replied. 'I'd ban sprouts, runner beans, rhubarb, and carrot sticks.'

Becky laughed. 'What's wrong with carrot sticks?'

'I don't like carrot sticks,' Joe replied. 'I'd also make Meat and Potato Pie the national dish.' His brow creased as he continued, 'I'd ban rugby, detentions, chavs, salted popcorn, power walking, novelty slippers, traffic wardens, bullies, bobble hats and beards. Oh, and I'd make sure all Man United supporters were put in stocks for everyone to throw rotten veg at.'

'Again, it's the twelfth century, Joe. Football hasn't been invented yet.'

'Then I'd invent it,' Joe replied. 'I'd also invent skateboards, hot dogs, mars bars, microwavable rice and wotsits.'

'Microwavable rice?' Becky spluttered. 'There's no electricity, never mind microwave ovens.'

'I'd invent electricity.'

'And how would you go about that?'

Joe opened his mouth to reply, but closed it again almost immediately. 'I've not really thought it through.'

'You do say.'

'Anyway, with all these ace ideas I'd definitely go down in history as the best king ever.'

'Or the dumbest.'

'Perhaps,' Joe grinned. 'But either way I'd be remembered.'

'And probably murdered about a week into your glorious reign.'

'Maybe,' Joe yawned. 'Well, I need some sleep, so night night, peasant.'

'Good night, Prince Charmless.'

Joe turned over and closed his eyes.

Becky stood up and extinguished the candles before returning to bed. It didn't take long before Joe's snores vanquished all other sound. She turned over and stared at him. A ribbon of silvery moonlight fell on his face. She had a sudden urge to hold him, to kiss him – he'd been so fearless, so courageous - but she knew if he awoke she would never hear the end of it. Instead, she just lay there in silence, watching his chest rise and fall in a steady rhythm, all the while unable to shake the feeling more trouble lurked just around the corner.

And if that were the case, if trouble did find them again, there was one thing she felt certain about: she and Joe would deal with it together, unified as one, inseparable to the end.

As a brother and sister should ...

Chapter 25

Dreams Never End

The next thing Becky knew her surroundings had changed.

She was walking down a narrow footpath in the dead of night, rain hammering the ground, forming deep puddles that gleamed gold, reflecting light from a single streetlamp. A ruthless wind wrestled the trees that flanked the roadside. She felt alone, frightened, until a soft voice met her ears.

'Not far to the car now, Becky.'

Feeling a hand squeeze hers, Becky glanced up to see her mother smiling down at her. 'Yes, mummy,' she replied in a high-pitched voice that didn't quite seem her own.

'And your father's on his way.' Mrs Mellor sighed. 'I don't know, why do we always seem to break down when I'm driving? I must be cursed.'

'You're unlucky, and – '

A stomach-churning roar cut short Becky's words. Horror-struck, Becky looked back. Two silvery orbs materialised through the blackness. She was in no doubt about it: they were eyes. The monster had found them again.

'Mummy … RUN!' she screamed.

They ran.

Terror flooding her, Becky glanced back again. A giant black cat, as big as a car, was powering towards them, its toxic breath thickening the air in clouds.

At once, Becky knew they didn't stand a chance.

With a further roar, the cat's jaws stretched open, its curved teeth gleaming like barbed steel. And then, claws extended, it pounced …

Becky screamed.

Suddenly, her body was shaking wildly. Hands gripped her shoulders, followed by the sound of another voice.

'Becky … Wake up!'

Becky's eyes shot open. Leaping up with a start, her face damp with sweat, she saw Joe staring back at her, alarmed.

'You had a nightmare,' he said. 'Are you okay?'

'Yeah,' Becky said, calming herself.

'What was it about?' Joe said. 'You were well freaked.'

'It's just this weird dream I get every now and again,' Becky replied. 'I've had it a few times this year. Mum and me are being attacked by a monster - this massive black cat – and, well, that's it really. It's not like a normal dream though … it's always so real.'

Joe gave an empty smile. 'We're a right couple of basket cases, aren't we?'

'I s'pose so,' Becky replied. 'What time d'you think it is?'

'Dunno, two … three.'

'Then we'd better get some more sleep,' Becky said. 'Something tells me we're going to need it.'

'Okay,' Joe replied. 'But gimme a shout if Hello Kitty attacks you again.'

Becky curled up beneath the blanket. 'My hero…' she mumbled.

Becky woke to find the bedroom bathed in the first rays of morning. At once, all the previous night's revelations returned to her. She felt nauseous. Sitting up, she saw Joe was already out of bed. Searching his face, she saw dark circles beneath his eyes, the whites of which were inflamed. She knew straightaway he'd barely slept. 'Hiya.'

'Hi.'

'Did you actually get any sleep?'

'Not much.'

Just then, two sharp knocks rattled the door. Uncle Percy walked in. 'Good morning, all.'

Becky could see from the lifeless pallor of Uncle Percy's skin that Joe wasn't the only one suffering from lack of sleep.

'We're leaving for Scotland in about half an hour,' Uncle Percy said.

'How's Lady Anne?' Becky asked.

'She's still with us, if that's what you mean,' Uncle Percy replied. 'Please don't feel too sad for her. She's lived a very good life, she's well loved, and she's ready for what's to follow.'

'Are Tuck and Marian coming to Scotland?' Becky asked.

'Tuck's joining us,' Uncle Percy replied. 'Marian's staying here with Lady Anne.' His eyes found Joe's. 'And how are you today, young man?'

'Sound.' Joe's blunted tone made it clear he had no wish to discuss the night before.

'Very well,' Uncle Percy said. 'I'll see you downstairs.' And with that, he turned and left the room.

Becky climbed out of bed. She pulled a comb from her pocket and began to untangle her hair. 'I feel rank,' she said. 'What I wouldn't give for a hot bath, a face pack and some conditioner.'

'You're such a girl.'

Becky gaped at him, bewildered. 'And is that supposed to be an insult or are you just demonstrating your powers of observation?'

Joe changed the subject quickly. 'I'm starving.'

'Great comeback,' Becky said sarcastically. 'But I must admit I'm – ' Just then, a strange, familiar sensation swept the crown of her skull.

A sensation she'd not experienced for some time.

And then the scene before her changed again. No longer was she in the bedroom at Wulvern House, she was somewhere different entirely.

And furthermore she knew it wasn't a dream.

She was wide-awake.

This was really happening.

Jungle surrounded her on all sides. Great trees speared the sky, their branches ringing with the discordant chatter of monkeys. Sweat clung to her body like glue, making it difficult to move. To her right, she heard an eager voice.

'We must be close!' Joe gasped, pointing ahead.

Bewildered, Becky trailed his finger. What she saw made her jaw plunge to her collarbone. A giant golden statue of a king sitting on a lavish throne surfaced from the thick undergrowth. The king wore an ornate headdress, his eyes gazing down with awe at an object cupped in his hands.

Another voice floated on the heavy air. 'I think you're right, Joe.'

Becky glanced left to see Uncle Percy dabbing his brow with a silk handkerchief, a wide smile curled on his mouth.

'Is that – is that solid gold?' Joe asked, nodding at the statue.

'Unquestionably,' Uncle Percy replied.

Becky heard Joe's voice again. But this time it seemed distant, far away … and it wasn't just him speaking – he was shouting. And he sounded terrified.

'UNCLE PERCY ... WILL ... IT'S BECKY! GET UP HERE NOW!'

As the words bounced off the insides of Becky's skull, the jungle, the statue vanished, replaced by the bedroom at Wulvern House and the sight of Joe's anxious face.

'Becks, are you okay?' Joe asked, his voice shaking.

'Err, yeah.'

'What the hell's going on?' Joe said, studying her closely. 'You had one of those weird moments again. Your eyes went white, your skin changed. It was just like when you first got your googly powers.'

Becky didn't have time to reply when Uncle Percy and Will burst through the door.

'What is it, Joe?' Uncle Percy asked, anxiously.

'It's nothing.'

'But we heard you shouting.'

'Everything's okay now,' Joe replied. 'It was Becky. Remember how she used to freak out when she first got her powers ... how she turned into that demon witch type thingy with creepy white eyes and pale skin? Well ... she just did it again.'

Uncle Percy looked stunned. He stared anxiously at Becky. 'You did?'

'He's exaggerating,' Becky replied.

'I bloody well am not,' Joe replied resolutely. 'You looked like something in a horror movie. A zombie queen or summat...'

'I did not look like a zombie queen.'

'You didn't see yourself,' Joe replied. 'Seriously, Uncle Percy, she was the ugliest thing I've ever seen.'

'Err, shut your gob!' Becky barked. She turned to Uncle

Percy, her eyes pleading for sympathy. 'Something happened … something strange. I did have one of those … moments.'

'Was it your telekinesis?'

'No, it was something else.' Becky paused. She struggled to mouth the next words. 'I saw something … I can't explain it.'

'What did you see?'

'We were in a jungle,' Becky replied. 'Like the one they use in 'I'm a Celebrity.''

'I'm a celebrity what?' Uncle Percy asked, clearly with no idea to what she was talking about.

'It's a TV show. It doesn't matter,' Becky replied. 'But it was a really dense jungle, like the ones on documentaries about the Amazon rainforest.'

Uncle Percy nodded. 'Okay, so who was in the jungle?'

'I only saw you, Joe and me. It only lasted a few seconds. Anyway, we were in this jungle and we came across this massive golden statue … a statue of a king or something. I think he was sitting on a throne and holding something. I'm not sure what. But that was it really. Then suddenly it all disappeared and I was back here … with Joe.'

Uncle Percy glanced at Will and the two of them shared a strange look.

'Uncle Percy,' Becky said in a quiet voice. 'What's happening to me?'

Uncle Percy looked miserable. 'Nothing I don't think has happened before, Becky.'

'What do you mean?'

'If you want my honest opinion,' Uncle Percy replied with a sigh. 'I think you've seen the future…'

Chapter 26

Past, Present and Future

'What do you mean "seen the future?"' Becky panted.

'I mean precisely that,' Uncle Percy replied. 'Unless I'm very much mistaken, we find ourselves in that jungle standing before that golden statue at some point in the near future. I think you've had a premonition of sorts.'

'What are you saying?'

'I think it's entirely possible that, along with your telekinesis, you're developing another power – that of precognition.'

'Precognition?'

'The ability to see the future.'

Becky looked over at Joe, who looked equally shaken. 'What?' she spluttered. 'Why d'you say that? I have one little episode and suddenly I'm Mystic Meg?'

Uncle Percy looked dispirited. 'It's not just the one little episode though, is it?'

'It is. I think I'd know if I'd had one before.'

'What about that incident in King Minos' throne room last summer?' Uncle Percy said. 'You claimed to see a hooded man in the far room, and you were adamant it was me. However, no one else saw him … do you remember?'

'Yes,' Becky replied. 'And I was right. It was you.'

'Yes. I was on my way to rescue Pegasus. However, and bear with me because this explanation is quite complex, I think the vision you had of me wasn't one occurring in that present. And that's the reason Joe, Will or I didn't see what you saw. I believe what you saw was a vision of me in the future. Forty seven minutes into the future to be precise.'

In truth, Becky had forgotten all about the strange incident in King Minos' throne room, but there was something about Uncle Percy's logic that made her think he might be right. 'How can you be so exact?'

'Because that's how far ahead I set my portavella to give me enough time to do what I had to do to rescue Pegasus,' Uncle Percy replied. 'Think about it, it's just not feasible I would set it to the moment we were standing in the throne room - I could've easily been captured at any time. No, I purposely set it forty-seven minutes later, because I knew by that point King Minos and his guards would've proceeded to the Central Court to prepare for the opening of Daedalus' Gate.' He threw her a sympathetic smile. 'I'm sorry, Becky, but I'm certain I'm right.' He fell silent. 'And there's something else … '

'What?' Becky asked, suddenly worried.

'Let's just say your vision doesn't exactly surprise me.'

'What do you mean?'

Uncle Percy sat down next to her on the bed. His face looked drawn and weary. 'I've never told you this … but I knew someone who developed telekinetic powers as you have. Some time later, she too experienced precognitive imageries.'

Becky was stunned to silence. 'Who was she?' she asked in a whisper.

'Do you remember I once told you about a tutor of mine and the inventor of the first time machine, Henry Locket – well, it was Henry's wife, Hilary. A truly kind and gentle lady.'

'Do you think I could talk to her?' Becky asked. 'I mean,

maybe she can help me get my head around all of this.'

'I'm afraid Hilary passed away a long time ago.'

'We could go back in time and see her. I mean, when we get back to our time.'

'I don't think that would be a good idea,' Uncle Percy replied. 'The fact is Hilary was always - shall we say … uncomfortable with her gifts.'

'I know how she felt,' Becky replied. She paused before speaking in a fragile voice, 'I don't want to see the future, Uncle Percy. That scares me more than anything else I can think of. And I'm already a freak, I can't handle getting freakier.'

Uncle Percy slid his hand into Becky's. 'You're not a freak, my dear. You're exceptional.'

'But I don't want to be exceptional,' Becky replied. 'I want to be normal.'

But Joe had had enough. 'Are you bloody kidding me?' he blustered. 'This is the best news we've had in ages. Stop being such a mardy bum, Becks.'

'Not now, Joe,' Uncle Percy said firmly.

But Joe wasn't stopping for anyone. 'Can't you see just how cool this is? We're gonna be sooooo rich… Like Jay-Z rich. Just imagine - you have one of these freaky visions about the winning numbers on the national lottery and we're laughing all the way to the bank. And then there's the Euromillions, the footie, horse racing, boxing - we can bet on all of them … and we'll win … everytime!'

Uncle Percy scowled at him and said in a sharp voice, 'Joe – for once, could you try and show some sympathy for the feelings of others.'

'I'll do that when I've got my Ferrari!'

Becky frowned at Joe, who had begun to do a dance. Slowly, her lips arched into a smile. Before she knew it, she was laughing.

'That's better.' Joe grinned at Becky. He stopped dancing and said, 'Now are you gonna look on the bright side of this? Let's face it, your weird vision has already given us some ace news.'

'What's that?'

'If we end up in some remote jungle in the future, we can't be stuck in Medieval England forever, so that's a result, isn't it?'

Becky nodded. 'I s'pose.'

'And what did we look like?'

'What's that got to do with anything?'

'Did we look about the same age as we are now?'

'I think so.'

'Then that means not only will we make it back safely, but we'll make it back pretty soon. Another result!'

Uncle Percy looked impressed. 'Excellent reasoning, Joe.'

'Thanks,' Joe said. 'But I'm still all about that Ferrari.'

Just then, a worrying thought struck Becky. She turned to Uncle Percy. 'But there's something else you should know - Drake knew I might develop this new power.'

Uncle Percy's eyes narrowed. 'Why do you say that?'

'At Christmas, when you left us to plant those squid bombs in Memphis, the Butterby cyrobot asked me if I'd developed any more gifts. As we now know, that was Drake asking the question and not Butterby. So did Drake know about Hilary's powers?'

'Yes,' Uncle Percy replied.

Becky nodded. She mulled this over for a few seconds,

before coming to the conclusion it didn't matter one way or the other. 'I've said it before,' she said. 'There's no point worrying about what he does or doesn't know, so as Joe said last night, let's concentrate on getting this sword, and finding a way back home.'

'Quite right, sis,' Joe agreed.

'So are you going to be okay with this?' Uncle Percy asked.

'What choice do I have?' Becky replied honestly. 'I can't change it, so I'll just have to deal with it whatever way I can.' She fixed Uncle Percy with a firm stare. 'But I would like to know why it's happening to me.'

'Wouldn't we all …' Uncle Percy muttered.

Chapter 27

The Road to Urquhart

They were packed and ready to depart within ten minutes. They said their farewells to Lady Ann and Lady Caroline, before gathering in the courtyard to say goodbye to Marian. Becky noticed Marian seemed unusually troubled to see them leave, although she did her best to conceal this behind a mask of smiles.

But it was only when she and Will hugged that Becky understood why.

Their embrace lasted barely ten seconds, but it was one unlike any Becky had seen before. Will and Marian held each other in silence with such raw, unfettered emotion, their bodies locked as one, absorbed in each other, the rest of the world seemed to be disappearing around them. Becky felt embarrassed to watch, not because of anything inappropriate, but because the tenderness of the embrace was so pure, so revealing it made her feel like she was intruding on the most special of moments. And she knew at once whatever feelings Will had for Marian were returned a dozen-fold.

Will was the first to break off. He turned and walked away, not once looking back. As everyone followed him, Marian seized Uncle Percy's arm and said in a small voice, 'Sire, I beg thee take good care of Will. I pray to be with him again soon.'

'I shall try, Lady Marian.'

Seeing the jeep for the first time, Tuck's legs threatened to buckle. 'By God's bones,' he said. ''Tis a carriage fashioned by Saint Eligius himself.'

'Believe me,' Joe said, just loud enough for Uncle Percy to hear. 'It's got nowt on the Ferrari I'm gonna get.' He aided Tuck on to the backseat and sat next to him, trailed by Becky. A few moments later, Uncle Percy started the engine, swung the jeep about and drove off.

They were barely a mile from Wulvern House when something occurred to Becky. 'Uncle Percy, shouldn't we ditch the jeep, get some horses and ride to Scotland?'

'Why?'

'What if Kruger and the Associates have an Alto Radar? Even if they didn't see us leave at Alnwick Castle, they'll know we were there and that one of their jeeps is missing. Won't an Alto-Radar tell them exactly where we are?'

'It would,' Uncle Percy replied, 'and that very fact crossed my mind. Indeed, last night I struggled to sleep worrying myself about it. In the end, I stayed awake and watched the horizon for signs of Associate activity. But I didn't see any. The fact is, Alto-Radars are not standard issue in many time machines and most TTs tend to install them for cautionary reasons - being spotted by the casual onlooker, that kind of thing. Most TTs go to great lengths to respect the verisimilitude of whatever time period they visit. Well, I doubt Emerson Drake or Otto Kruger give a tinker's cuss who sees them, regardless of the time period. Subsequently, I doubt they'd have Alto-Radars installed in their time machines. Who knows? When all's said and done, we have a choice: we can drive to Abriachan in a matter of hours, or travel by horse and have it take days.' His lips tightened into a line. 'And I'm not convinced we have that much time.'

By nine in the morning, the sky was the colour of milk. Considering there were very few paths that resembled anything like a normal road, they were making good time. Even Tuck had come to terms with travelling by jeep, and it didn't take long before he announced in a loud, booming voice they were in Scotland. Energised by this, he asked Joe something that had seemingly been playing on his mind.

'My prince, I understand it is not my place, but shall you return to this time, force the claim of king and take the land that is rightfully yours?'

'No,' Joe said curtly. 'And stop calling me a prince. I'm not a prince, I'm not a king, I'm not a Sith Lord, and my name's not George - it's Joe ... Joe Mellor ... and I live in Wythenshawe, Manchester in the twenty first century with my mum and weirdo sister, and that's that. End of story. D'you understand?'

'But my liege –'

'But nowt!' Joe interjected. 'I'm not your liege. I don't even know what that means. And I don't want to talk about any of it anymore. End of!'

Becky spent the next hour watching the scenery pass in a blur. She had never been to Scotland before and was astonished by the harsh, unforgiving splendour of the countryside. A light rain had started to fall, covering the fields like varnish. Rolling hills of purple heather painted the skyline and a gentle mist clung to the glens, which were carpeted with yellow bracken.

It was three hours into the journey when Becky saw a stretch of water extend before them, carving the landscape in two. *Loch Ness.*

She had seen countless pictures of it in magazines and

books, but nothing could have prepared her for its magnitude or beauty. A virulent wind whipped the water into angry swells, which battered the shoreline relentlessly. And then she gasped with surprise. Set on a rocky peninsula on the north shore, the silhouette of a huge castle dominated the horizon, looming imposingly over the Loch.

'Urquhart Castle!' Tuck said darkly. 'As damnable a place as Abbadon.'

Uncle Percy turned the wheel and steered them away from it. 'Don't worry, Angus, that's as close as we'll be getting to it.'

'What're you doing?' Joe asked, dismayed. 'Aren't we going to check it out?'

'Why would we, Joe?' Uncle Percy replied. 'This isn't exactly a sightseeing tour.'

'I know that,' Joe replied. 'But I don't wanna visit Medieval Scotland and not take a gander at Morogh MacDougal's castle.' He pointed at the castle. 'I mean, look at it … it's very cool…'

Uncle Percy exchanged a look with Will. In an instant they understood each other perfectly. Joe had been through the most traumatic twenty-four hours - the least they could do was grant his request.

'Of course we can, young man,' Uncle Percy replied, smiling. 'And you're quite right – we should always spare a few moments to appreciate the world around us.' He glanced back at Tuck. 'Apologies, Angus, but we're popping over to Urquhart.' He steered the jeep in the direction of the castle. 'As a matter of fact, Joe, even in our time there's a legend that claims the Loch Ness monster inhabits a cave beneath Urquhart Castle…'

The moment his words were out there it was clear Uncle Percy regretted it. And the uncomfortable silence that followed made it apparent everyone felt the same way.

*

From a distance, Urquhart Castle looked like an imposing and impregnable fortress, an outstanding specimen of medieval craftsmanship and construction. However, on close inspection, it was clear it was a desolate, eerie, empty shell, overgrown with moss and brambles, which gripped the crumbling walls.

Uncle Percy brought the jeep to a halt to the right of a lowered drawbridge.

'Wow,' Joe said, looking around. 'What a dump!'

'It has been a century since human voices have echoed in these walls,' Tuck said, his usually crimson face whitish and pale. 'This is a cursed place. And we should not be here...' Fear in his eyes, he pulled free his sword.

Everyone left the jeep and made their way over the drawbridge into a wide courtyard, choked with weeds, many of them three feet high.

Joe glanced at Becky. 'You sure this isn't the jungle from your freaky vision?'

'No,' Becky replied, before looking over at the high walls opposite. A raven was studying them from a turret, its jet-black eyes following their every move.

'Not exactly the Disney Castle, is it?' Joe muttered to Becky.

Becky and Joe walked across the courtyard, through an archway, and stopped at a wide breach in the wall that led down to the water's edge.

Looking out over the Loch, Becky's eyes were drawn to what she thought was a fallen tree washed up on the rocks below. As her eyes locked on it, she nearly threw up. At least thirty seagulls were tearing the flesh from the corpse of a black and white whale, perhaps twenty-five feet long and five tonnes in weight.

'Flippin' 'eck!' Joe puffed, before shouting back, 'Uncle Percy. Will. Come and look at this!'

Hearing the panic in Joe's voice, Uncle Percy, Will and Tuck sprinted over, drawing their swords as they ran.

Reaching Joe, Uncle Percy's mouth tumbled open. 'Oh my word!' he gulped.

'It's a Killer Whale, isn't it?' Joe asked.

'Erm, it was,' Uncle Percy replied.

'What's a Killer Whale doing in Loch Ness?'

Uncle Percy took a second to compose himself. 'Err, the Loch is connected to the North Sea via the River Ness, so it's not surprising one could enter the Loch.'

'It could've got here by bus for all I care,' Becky said. 'Shouldn't we focus on what killed it? I mean just from its name I'm guessing a Killer Whale is pretty much at the top of its food chain, right?'

'You could say that,' Uncle Percy replied flatly.

'And it's pretty safe to say it didn't die from eating a bad prawn, did it?'

'Probably not.'

'Tis the Kraken's doing,' Tuck said, his hand tightening around his sword. 'The great beast still exists.'

'Let's not jump to conclusions, shall we?' Uncle Percy said.

'No, let's leap to them,' Becky replied, her voice rising. 'And what was it you said about a legend that it lived in a cave beneath the castle?'

'Okay … tour's over!' Uncle Percy said decisively. 'Everyone back to the jeep…'

No one disagreed with him.

Chapter 28

The Fallen of Ascalon

As one, they raced back to the jeep, and within minutes were tearing away at a breakneck speed. The further they got from Urquhart Castle, the more Becky began to feel at ease. She had seen too many bizarre and terrifying creatures over the last nine months to doubt anything other than the Kraken's existence, and if the legend did prove correct, if it did indeed inhabit a cave beneath Urquhart, then the further they were away from there the better.

As they pushed on, the weather took a turn for the worse, and soon booming claps of thunder and wispy streaks of lightning accompanied the rain that had plagued them for most of the day.

Soaked through to her skin and feeling miserable, Becky pulled her hood around her face and watched Uncle Percy power them up a steep incline to a plateau overlooking the Loch. It was then she saw a small stone church. Constructed from large, grey stone blocks, Saint Cuthbert's was composed of a curved apse, a thatched nave with pointed lancet windows and a high rounded tower. Rows of gravestones rose from the damp ground at angles, fencing the church like an attacking army.

'That's a lot of gravestones for a tiny church,' Joe said.

'Saint Cuthbert's is the last resting place of the *hundred*,' Tuck said solemnly.

'The hundred?' Joe replied. 'What d'you mean?'

'Morogh MacDougal's brothers in arms,' Tuck replied. 'Beneath this sacred ground, the same ground that once welcomed Saint Columba, lie the bones of a hundred of the bravest Hospitallers slain at the Battle of Ascalon. It is said that MacDougal wished his comrades to be buried in this sacred ground and not where they fell in the barren desert, and so he brought their bodies home with him on his return from the Crusades. Then he rebuilt the crumbling Saint Cuthbert's as a shrine to his fallen colleagues.' He motioned toward the gravestones. 'Tis even said he carved the inscriptions himself out of respect for his fallen brethren.'

'That's a very touching story,' Uncle Percy said, pulling the jeep to a halt.

'MacDougal was the noblest of Knights,' Tuck replied.

Uncle Percy stepped out of the jeep, everyone following close behind.

Staring out over the black water, the snow-tipped mountains and the sweeping glens, Becky felt as far from civilisation as could be. Even Wulvern House seemed a world away, in another time, another place. She also felt a swelling sense of apprehension. Were they close to finding the Sword of Ages? Could it really be here, at this abandoned church in the middle of nowhere? Did Kruger know they were here? And was the Kraken real and a genuine threat? The one thing she knew for certain was that every time they came close to finding an Eden Relic they were pitched into the most dangerous of situations. Would this time be any different?

Just then, her eyes fell on a nearby gravestone. Curiously, there were no actual words on it. Instead, a symbol was carved ornately into the sandstone. It was the eight pointed cross she recognised as the symbol of the Knight's Hospitaller, and just below that, so tiny it could easily be missed, a black bird, its wings extended. She scanned a second gravestone. The Hospitaller symbol was also there, but the black bird had been replaced by what looked like a ship's anchor. Finally, her gaze found a third headstone. She crouched down and leaned in for a closer look. Again, the Hospitaller symbol was present, but this time it sat above the figure of an animal covered in spines. Intrigued, she stood up as Uncle Percy appeared at her shoulder.

'I wonder if Morogh MacDougal really did carve all of those symbols himself?' he said, his outstretched hand fanning the cemetery. 'Now that would be a great deal of work.'

'It would,' Becky replied, before pointing at the headstone she'd just been studying. 'What do the symbols beneath the Hospitaller cross mean?'

'I don't know,' Uncle Percy replied, studying the headstone. 'Perhaps they're a pictogram identifying the characteristics of that particular Knight.'

'So that Knight had the characteristics of a hedgehog?'

Uncle Percy chuckled. 'Who knows? Hedgehogs are renown for being amongst the most deadly of the animal kingdom, not to mention gallant in the company of lady hedgehogs.'

'Really?' Becky said, surprised.

'No, not really,' Uncle Percy said with a playful smile. 'But I do know the name for a baby Hedgehog is a Hoglet, a term I do find most agreeable.'

'A Hoglet?' Becky laughed. 'Yeah, I like that, too.'

'Good,' Uncle Percy said. 'Now shall we go and see what secrets lie within Saint Cuthbert's hallowed walls? For the first time we may be on the verge of finding an Eden relic without being in an immeasurable amount of mortal danger.' Turning on his back foot, he set off for the church, trailed by Tuck, Will and finally Joe.

Becky followed them up a footpath, through a stone archway to a studded timber door, obscured by shimmering cobwebs. Uncle Percy wiped away the webbing, turned a heavy iron handle and pushed open the door.

Nerves flooded Becky as she entered the church. Inside, swirling clouds of dust clogged the air and the stench of dry rot clawed at her nose. Facing right, she saw an elaborate font and an octagonal pillar with a cross within a circle etched into the stone. Then she turned about and her eyes widened. Set into the far wall was a spectacular stained glass window, as impressive as any she'd seen in a cathedral, depicting a fair haired, bearded man, his head encircled by a shimmering halo. Saint Andrew's arm was curled around the shoulder of a young boy who was holding five loaves of bread and two fish.

In silence, the group walked as one toward the window, their footsteps echoing against the tiled floor. As they advanced, Becky could make out a series of Latin words in glittering gold letters at the base of the window.

Servo domum domino, sed rursus servor ab ipso

'So is this it?' Joe asked Uncle Percy, excitedly. 'Is this one of Symphosius' riddles?'

'Not as such,' Uncle Percy replied. 'It's perhaps a line from one of them, but by no means is it the whole thing.'

'What does it say?' Becky asked.

Uncle Percy took a moment to interpret the text. 'Correct

me if I'm wrong, Angus, but I believe it says, 'I keep the Master's House, the Master keeps me, too.'

Tuck nodded his agreement. 'Aye, that is my reading, too.'

'Doesn't sound much of a riddle,' Joe said.

'It isn't in itself,' Uncle Percy replied. 'A complete riddle by Symphosius would have been written in tercets.'

Joe snorted loudly. 'Like we know what that means!'

'Stanzas of three lines in length,' Uncle Percy said. 'This is clearly just one of three.' He turned and scanned the area, before a satisfied look crossed his face. 'And over there we have a second.' He marched over to a much smaller window on the east wall of the nave, which also contained a Latin phrase.

Virtutes magnas de viribus offero parvis

'So what does it mean?' Becky asked.

'I believe it says something like - 'Great Deeds with little strength I do.'

'Okay,' Becky replied, mulling it over. 'Well that could be pretty much anything.'

'Yes it could.'

Suddenly Joe's voice rang out. 'Over here!' he shouted from the other side of the nave. He was standing beside a third window, the smallest of the three. The window contained another sequence of Latin words.

Pando domos clausas, iterum sed claudo patentes

Uncle Percy walked over and read it, before taking a moment to ensure his translation was correct. 'This one says "I close the open, open the closed for you.""'

'That's it then,' Joe said eagerly. 'Three lines.' He looked to Uncle Percy. 'What were they all again?'

Uncle Percy cleared his throat before saying,

> **'Great Deeds with Little Strength I do**
> **I close the open, open the closed for you**
> **I keep the Master's House, the Master keeps me, too.'**

Tapping his fingers on his chin, he began to pace, mumbling the riddle to himself again and again.

'Is the answer a Door?' Becky suggested. 'A door opens and closes, and you have them in houses.'

Although Uncle Percy didn't respond immediately, her words seemed to trigger something within him. He came to a halt and a triumphant smile formed on his mouth. 'You're nearly right, Becky,' he said. 'The answer's a Key.'

Becky knew he was right. 'So we have to find a key?'

'It seems that way,' Uncle Percy replied. 'What was the inscription on your dagger again, Angus?'

Tuck began to speak.

> **'Solve the text of Symphosius**
> **Find the one with no one**
> **Then trail the Sword's light,**
> **To the place far from sun,**
> **And within that chamber**
> **Beyond beast and man**
> **The Holy Sword waits**
> **For thy Royal hand…'**

227

'So *'the one with no one'* is a key?' Joe said.

'Perhaps,' Uncle Percy replied.

Becky looked out over the church. 'And d'you think there's a key somewhere in here, maybe buried under something?'

'I really don't know,' Uncle Percy replied. He looked at Tuck. 'Angus, if MacDougal wanted us to find an actual key would you have any idea what it could open?'

'Nay. I do not.'

Uncle Percy gave a deep sigh. 'Well perhaps if we find the key itself then it may shed some light on what it's supposed to open. Either way, I suppose we get looking for a key…'

They began searching Saint Cuthbert's inside and out. Minutes turned into hours, every nook and cranny was checked, every stone was scrutinised thoroughly. They found nothing. After a frustrating search no one was in any doubt it was a lost cause.

'It's not here,' Joe said irritably, as they all gathered around the font. 'And unless we start ripping the place apart brick by brick we're not gonna find a thing …' He shook his head with exasperation. 'Find the one with no one. What the hell's that got to do with a key? Stupid damn riddles… I'm sick of them.'

But the moment the words left Joe's mouth, something occurred to Becky. 'God, we're so thick.'

Everyone stared at her.

'What d'you mean?' Joe asked.

'Forget the key thing for a moment,' Becky said. 'Find the one with no one. It's a grave. MacDougal was referring to a grave. One of the graves is empty. It's got no one in it.'

Uncle Percy cast her an appreciative smile. 'That does sound plausible.'

'But which one?' Joe fired at her. 'There are a hundred

graves out there!'

'How should I know?'

But Uncle Percy's face had changed. 'Angus, to your knowledge was anyone else ever buried at Saint Cuthbert's - I mean, other than the hundred Hospitaller Knights?'

'No,' Tuck replied. 'MacDougal claimed this ground for the fallen at Ascalon and for them alone.'

Uncle Percy glanced at Becky, his eyes twinkling. 'There are a hundred riddles in Symphosius' Aenigmata. One hundred graves. One hundred riddles.'

'Really?' Becky said, intrigued. Something was dawning on her, too. 'And what about the answers to those riddles? What kind of things were they?'

Uncle Percy and Becky shared a knowing smile. It was clear to them both they shared the same thought. 'It's a long time since I've read them, but the answers were essentially quite ordinary, everyday objects … or animals.'

Becky's smile widened. 'And was one of those animals a Hedgehog?'

'Yes,' Uncle Percy replied, reaching out and squeezing Becky's hand. 'I do believe it was.'

Watching Becky and Uncle Percy, Joe found himself getting irritated by their smugness. 'What're you two gabbin' on about Hedgehogs for? D'you know summat I don't?'

'A Hoglet knows things you don't,' Becky replied, grinning at Uncle Percy.

'Uh?' Joe grunted. 'What's a Hoglet?'

'Just let the grown ups talk,' Becky added.

Joe was about to snap back at her when Uncle Percy addressed the group. 'This intelligent young woman has solved a century old riddle,' he said. 'Morogh MacDougal's riddle, to be precise.'

Joe looked flabbergasted. 'Has she?'

'She has indeed,' Uncle Percy replied. 'You see, earlier today, Becky noticed each headstone outside sported a different pictogram on it, just below the Hospitaller's eight pointed cross. And I'm willing to bet my left kidney that one of those pictograms will be a key ...'

Chapter 29

The Chamber

Everyone hurried out quickly to find the rain had stopped. Whichever way they turned gravestones surrounded them like rotten teeth, stained and crooked. Soon, they were combing the grounds of Saint Cuthbert's, weaving from stone to stone, stopping just long enough to examine the markings before moving swiftly on.

All the while, Becky reeled with anticipation. On each stone, she saw a different pictogram - a flower, a mouse, a frog, a chain, a bull, a hammer, a wolf – but no key. It was less than five minutes, however, when she heard Tuck bellowing the following words with delight. 'Tis here!'

Becky looked at him. He was standing at the far edge of the churchyard, near a slope that plunged sharply to the water a hundred feet below. She sprinted over, careful not to slip on the muddy earth. Joe, Uncle Percy and Will did the same. In seconds, they were all standing beside Tuck, whose plump finger pointed down at the grave furthest from the church.

Becky stared at the headstone. Tuck was right. Carved elegantly into the sandstone was the unmistakable form of a key.

'So this is it?' Joe said to Uncle Percy. 'D'you reckon Excalibur's buried here?'

'It could be, Joe – that, or we're left holding a century old Hospitaller's skeleton with absolutely no idea as what to do next. Either way, I don't suppose we'll know unless we get digging.' He pulled free his sword and slammed the point into the ground, ploughing up the top layer of earth. Will, Tuck and Joe followed suit.

Becky watched as the four of them loosened the topsoil, and sank to their knees, scooping up fat hunks of dirt with their hands and flinging it to the side.

'What I wouldn't give for my trusty Molivator now,' Uncle Percy mumbled.

His hands black with dirt, Joe glanced up at Becky. 'Are you just gonna stand there like a lemon or help?'

Becky folded her arms. 'To be honest, I thought I'd do some lemon standing for a bit.'

'You are such a girl!'

'Again, not the most penetrating of insults, Joe.' But seeing the sweat on Uncle Percy's brow, Becky felt guilty. With a disapproving tut, she crouched down and set to work.

In no time at all, the earth was piled high around them. They had burrowed almost three feet down when Will struck something with his sword. A dull metallic clank sounded. Everyone froze.

Becky peered down. Through a thin veil of soil she saw the glint of steel. Was it Excalibur? Her heart raced faster. Will crouched down, wiped away the soil and heaved a large object into the open. It was a kite shield, painted black with a large white cross adorning its midpoint.

Joe gulped. 'It's a Hospitaller shield!'

Becky peered down. Two further kite shields were set flat into the earth like a trapdoor, one overlapping the other. A tiny crack between them revealed a sliver of soft white light.

'*Then trail the sword's light*,' Tuck breathed, echoing

MacDougal's riddle.

Hurling the shield aside, Will removed the other two revealing a hole, two feet wide, cut into the ground. A rickety ladder led to a tunnel below, its vaulted limestone walls brightened partially by the unseen light source. Ignoring the ladder, he vaulted down, landing deftly against the hard floor. Raising his sword slowly, he veered right and stared at the path ahead. The tunnel snaked down to a sharp bend, behind which the light glowed with even greater intensity.

'I must see,' Tuck said impatiently. He squeezed his huge bulk through the gap and scrambled down, undeniably nimble for a man of his girth and weight.

Uncle Percy turned to Becky and Joe. 'Now I don't suppose there's any chance you might wait up here is there?'

Becky contemplated this for a moment. 'We will,' she replied sincerely. 'If that's what you want.'

'You will?'

'Nah, not really.' Becky cast him the same playful smile he'd used on her earlier that day.

'Don't be such a mug,' Joe scoffed. 'As if we're gonna miss out on the cool stuff?' He entered the hole and disappeared from sight.

Still grinning, Becky traced Joe's steps and descended the ladder. Her smile quickly vanished, however, when she was struck by a sobering thought. They were approaching the Sword of Ages, the fourth Eden Relic, and her experience with the other three taught her this was the point when things became dangerous. Extremely dangerous.

Moments later, Uncle Percy joined them at the base of the ladder. 'Well everyone, there's no reason to believe we're in any danger but – ' He withdrew his sword. '- Better safe than sorry.'

Joe and Will raised their bows. Tuck drew his sword. Then, Will leading the way, they set off down the tunnel, no one daring to breathe. They advanced a hundred metres or so when they approached the bend. As one, they turned the corner and were bombarded by a sudden rush of light.

Becky shielded her eyes with her hands. When they adjusted, she saw the tunnel merged into a sprawling cavern, half submerged beneath the waters of the Loch, and on the far wall, glowing as bright as any star, was a sword, buried to its golden hilt in the oil-black rock.

'The Holy Sword,' Tuck gasped. He sank to his knees and began to pray.

'So the Arthurian legend really did have some truth to it,' Uncle Percy said, a childlike quality to his voice. 'Excalibur was the Sword in the Stone. How wonderful.'

As captivated as the others, Becky couldn't tear her gaze from the sword, or the light that radiated from it. That soon changed when she heard the anxiety in Joe's voice.

'Yeah, it all looks fantastic, but has anyone seen the ground?'

Becky looked down. At once, her awe transformed into revulsion. The cavern floor was littered with the bones of countless animals — seals, bears, deer, wild boars, wolves - stripped of flesh and scattered all about like a sickening white carpet. Her hand shot to her mouth. Her terror escalated further when she saw a mound of human skulls. 'What is this place?' she spluttered.

'Haven't you figured it out yet?' Joe whispered back. 'The Kraken doesn't live under Urquhart Castle - it lives here, and we're standing smack bang in its dining room.'

Becky glanced at Uncle Percy. 'We've got to get out of here …now!'

Uncle Percy nodded. 'I could not agree more.'

'Not without Excalibur we're not,' Joe said, his eyes finding the sword. 'I'll get it.' He took two cautious steps forward. Bones cracked beneath his feet, their sound shattering the silence. He came to a sudden halt as if fearful the noise would awaken the dead around him. 'Ah, sod it!' And he broke into a run. Soon the piercing sound of snapping bones filled the cavern.

Becky glanced fearfully at the water, which was as smooth as glass, before looking back to Joe, who was only a few feet from the sword now.

Reaching Excalibur, Joe seized its grip with both hands. He pulled hard. It didn't budge. Slamming his foot against the wall, he leaned back and pulled again using his full bodyweight. 'Come on …' he strained. Again, it didn't move.

Becky's eyes returned to the water. A thin ripple appeared, extending into a single, wide circle. 'Err, Joe …' she said, panic flooding her. To her horror, she saw more ripples break the surface, forming small waves, which extended ever outward. 'Joe,' she repeated, louder this time. 'Get back here!'

Joe barely registered her words when a tentacle shot out and flew at him. It curled twice around his waist, squeezing hard, threatening to break his spine. He yelled in agony. Becky screamed.

Will didn't waver. He raised his bow and fired. The arrow pierced the tentacle, showering syrup-like blood on the bones below. With astonishing strength, the tentacle launched Joe through the air. He landed hard, shattering the rib cage of a long dead bear, his face showered in fragments of bone. Then

235

the tentacle shot back in the water.

Becky was about to race to Joe's aid, when the Loch's surface bubbled wildly as if at boiling point. Then, in a colossal explosion of water, the Kraken leapt out, landing on the bank before them.

It was the strangest, most terrifying beast any of them had ever seen.

Chapter 30

The Kraken Wakes

The Kraken made an ear-shattering screech, its long jaws widening to reveal three sets of ragged fangs, glazed in drool, jutting out in all directions. Two bloodshot green eyes with vertical slit-shaped pupils glared at them.

Becky was disabled with fear. It was unlike anything she'd seen before. Four short, heavy legs with webbed feet supported a long armour-plated body peppered with large holes, from which dozens of serpentine tentacles thrashed the air, each seemingly with a mind of its own. It had a tree-trunk thick tail, ridged and powerful, that supported a large curved caudal fin.

The Kraken glanced over at Excalibur, as if to confirm it was still there, before refocusing on its quarry, sizing them up. The tentacles moved gracefully like a conductor directing an orchestra, in hypnotic swirls, and then … they shot out like bullets, each one targeting a different foe.

Uncle Percy snapped from his daze. He brought his sword down on the one attacking him, severing it in a spurt of blood.

Becky, however, had no sword. In a flash, a tentacle had seized her neck, its mighty grip cutting off her oxygen, choking the very life from her. Uncle Percy raced over, and thrust his sword deep into its leathery skin. The tentacle uncoiled itself and flew back to its hole.

Clawing at her neck as if to check the tentacle had gone,

237

Becky swallowed as much air as she could. 'Thanks,' she coughed.

At speed, The Kraken marched forward a step and lunged at Tuck, jaws snapping. Tuck ducked the bite and swung his sword high, plunging the blade into its snout. 'Be gone, swine of Satan!' he shouted jubilantly. His victory, however, was short-lived. A tentacle sped toward him and seized his waist, hoisting him aloft, before pitching him against the cavern wall, which he struck with a terrible crunch, slumping to the ground, barely conscious.

Will was firing arrow after arrow, aiming for the Kraken's eyes, but its twisting head and the mass of tentacles that surrounded it, prevented his having a clear shot.

Becky knew they had no chance in a straight fight. The Kraken was too large, too powerful, every fibre of its being built for devastation and slaughter. The perfect killing machine. But then, shimmering through the chaos, she spied Excalibur, and just like that she knew what to do. 'JOE,' she yelled so loudly it shredded her lungs. 'GET EXCALIBUR!'

Joe was about to join the fight when he heard Becky's voice over the battle. 'IT'S STUCK IN THE WALL,' he shouted back. 'I CAN'T BUDGE IT,'

'BUT I CAN!'

Without hesitation, Joe raced back to Excalibur, grasping its hilt with both hands.

At the same time, Becky's eyes locked on the sword. Almost immediately, Excalibur's blade quivered as if the rock itself had been struck by a tremor. With a loud *craaacck*, shards of rock fell away, showering the ground, releasing the sword from its bind. Joe withdrew the blade with ease. Entranced for a moment, he turned the blade over. Its shimmering reflection blinded him. He squeezed the grip, an odd sensation charged up his arm, feeding his body. He felt invincible, unbeatable ... he could not be defeated. The sword would not allow it. Teeth gritted, he turned to face the Kraken, which was battling Uncle Percy and Will. Then he charged, Excalibur held high, ready for the fight of his life.

Tentacle after tentacle attacked. He severed each and every one of them, blood thickening the air, drenching him. The Kraken abandoned its battle with Uncle Percy and Will, sensing a greater threat. It sprang at Joe, jaws wide-open.

Joe veered right, and with a huge leap vaulted on to the Kraken's back. He raised Excalibur aloft and sank the blade downward, slicing through the thick armour plating like a laser through metal, into its body.

The Kraken shrieked, its great head twisting wildly. Then it lost all strength in its legs and flopped to the ground.

Joe felt the Kraken gulp its final breath, before it grew still. Satisfied the Kraken was dead, he withdrew Excalibur and jumped to the ground, aware all eyes were fixed upon him.

Becky's expression shifted from terror to joy. She walked over to Joe and flung her arms around his neck. 'My hero,' she teased.

'Bog off,' Joe grinned.

Uncle Percy patted his arm. 'Thank you, Joe. You were extraordinary.'

'It's the sword,' Joe replied. 'It makes you - I dunno – it makes you invincible.'

'If history confirms anything it's that no one is invincible,' Uncle Percy replied. 'But thank you again. You've saved all our lives.'

'You fought well, boy,' Will said proudly.

Tuck staggered over, his face flecked with blood. 'He fought like a true King.'

Joe frowned. 'Let's not start that again, eh?'

'Forgive me,' Tuck replied. 'But you have bested the Kraken. You have freed this land from an evil that has haunted it for so long.' He stared awestruck at the sword. 'And Excalibur is yours. The prophecy has come true.'

'I don't know about any prophecies,' Joe said. 'But the sword isn't mine.' He looked at Uncle Percy. 'We're getting rid of it, right?'

'Yes, Joe,' Uncle Percy replied. 'As soon as we get home.' He walked over to the dead Kraken, clearly intrigued.

Becky appeared at his shoulder. 'I hate to say it but that thing makes Debbie Crabtree look like Beyoncé.'

'I can't speak for Ms Beyoncé, but I have to agree it's not the prettiest of creatures, is it? Still, it's one of the most extraordinary animals I've ever seen.'

'Is it from Atlantis?'

'Perhaps,' Uncle Percy replied. 'Or it could be a very distant, considerably larger relative of Metriorhynchus.' When he saw Becky's blank expression, he said, 'A type of crocodile from the late Jurassic period.'

'Did that have tentacles?'

'No,' Uncle Percy replied. 'Frankly, I've never seen anything quite like those before. It really is a remarkable creature.'

'Remarkably ugly,' Becky replied. 'Now can we get out of here?'

'We can and we should.'

Just then, Joe joined them, offering Excalibur to Uncle Percy. 'D'you wanna take this?'

'Why don't you look after it for the moment? After all, the

last time I handled an Eden Relic wasn't one of my favourite experiences. And besides, you did pull the sword from the stone.' He smiled. 'Shall we make tracks?'

'Hang on,' Becky said, suddenly concerned. 'When the Spear of Fate was first removed from Atlantis it made the whole island sink into the ocean.' She scanned the cavern. 'Maybe we shouldn't take the sword from here until we've got a portravella or something? You know, just in case we need to make a quick getaway.'

'Are you saying Scotland will sink if we take it?' Joe said sarcastically.

'No,' Becky snapped back. 'My point is we don't know what'll happen if we remove it. Maybe it's better to be safe than sorry. I mean, we're the only ones who know it's here so we don't have to worry about anyone else getting it.'

Joe snorted. He was about to press the matter further when Uncle Percy raised his hand to stop him. 'That's a very salient point, Becky,' he said with a kindly smile. 'To be honest, each of the Eden Relics appears to react differently in different situations. I suggest we try taking it with us and see what happens. We can always return it should we notice any unusual activity.'

'Like Glasgow falling into the sea?' Joe grinned.

In responding, Becky used at least three swear words she'd never used before. Even Uncle Percy couldn't bring himself to reprimand her.

*

A short while later Joe led the group up the tunnel, Excalibur's misty light brightening the way ahead. One by one they climbed the ladder to the outside world. It was then Becky asked Uncle Percy the inevitable question. 'So what're the plans now?'

'Well,' he replied. 'I think the best thing we can do is return to Wulvern House. From there, we can consider what to do next. I know it'll be dangerous, but somehow we need to find the Associates and acquire either a Portravella or a time machine. Alternatively, we can –' Glancing over Becky's shoulder, the blood seeped from his face. 'Oh, no,' he begged. 'Please, no!'

Panicking, Becky asked, 'What is it?'

Uncle Percy didn't respond. He closed his eyes, unable or unwilling to process what he had seen. 'Will, Tuck ... come with me,' he said. His eyes locked on Becky and Joe. 'STAY - HERE!' He raced off in the direction of the church, swiftly followed by Will and Tuck.

'What's going on?' Joe said.

'Dunno,' Becky replied, confused. 'But I don't think it's going to be good...'

'Well I'm not just standing here,' Joe said, and he set off after the others.

Becky wasn't about to stay on her own. Charging after Joe, she watched Uncle Percy come to a halt on the opposite side of a moss-tipped headstone. He crouched down, leaned toward the stone and extended his hand to touch something she couldn't quite see. Will and Tuck had joined him, their baffled expressions supplanted by dismay and rage.

Nearing the grave, Becky glimpsed a patch of lilac taffeta fluttering in the light breeze. She stopped abruptly. She'd seen the material before – Lady Caroline's dress.

Seeing their approach, Uncle Percy stood up straight and marched over, gesturing for them to move no further. 'Becky, Joe, turn around and walk away, please. You don't need to see this.'

'It's Lady Caroline, isn't it?' Becky said.

'Yes.'

'Is she dead?'

'Yes.'

'But I – I don't understand,' Becky said.

Out of the blue the rumbling of hooves rent the silence. A cavalcade of horses emerged from behind the church, ridden by dozens of knights wearing the colours of King John. Two jeeps filled with Associates trailed the procession.

Even from this distance she could see the hateful smile on Otto Kruger's mouth.

Chapter 31

Surrender

King John's knights formed a wide circle around them, their giant horses snorting and sputtering, nostrils flared, blocking any gap and making an impenetrable wall. The knights stared down through the horizontal slits in their barrel helmets, their chainmail glistening. In one great movement, they lifted their swords.

Becky swallowed. She looked at Uncle Percy, but his expression told her everything she needed to know. If they fought back, they would be defeated – and that meant certain death. She glanced at Will, who appeared engaged in a bitter internal struggle, part raring to fight, part resigned to the fact it would be suicidal. Only Joe demonstrated a flicker of hope, training Excalibur at the knight closest to him, almost willing the knight to make the first move.

'Put that down,' Becky said to him. 'We've lost.'

'We've got Excalibur,' Joe replied. 'We can do this.'

'Don't be a wally.'

'Trust me, Becks,' Joe replied. 'I'm the one holding it. It's got powers we haven't seen yet. I can feel it. And I know we can't lose.'

'I'm afraid we can, Joe,' Uncle Percy said. 'And for the moment we have.'

Otto Kruger climbed out of the jeep. He smoothed the

creases from his tailored black suit and adjusted his tie. Then he gathered an assault rifle from the back seat of the jeep and strolled over. His immense frame moved gracefully like a tiger homing in on its prey. As his eyes met Will's, he gave a low chuckle before turning to Uncle Percy. 'Good evening, Percy Halifax.'

Uncle Percy wasn't about to engage in small talk. 'Why did you have to kill Lady Caroline?'

Kruger's face showed no emotion one way or the other. 'I didn't have to kill her. It served no purpose. But it is important you understand that people will get hurt or worse when you interfere in our affairs – a factor you really should consider before you embark on these quests. Besides, I'm certain you will not object so much when I tell you it was she who informed us of your whereabouts.' His cruel grin broadened. 'She gave up this location the moment I freed Lady Anne of the burden of life.'

Loathing blazed in Uncle Percy's eyes. 'May God forgive you.'

Kruger laughed. 'As we say in my homeland, *Gott ist immer mit den stärksten Bataillonen.*' His silver hand gestured at the wall of knights. 'God is always with the strongest battalion.'

'Yeah, well, ' Uncle Percy replied. 'As we say in my homeland, 'Up yours!'

'Where's Marian?' Will said, urgently.

Kruger stared at Will. 'She is in safe hands, groundsman. Whether those hands remain so depends entirely on you. I am here for the sword. You give it to me, then perhaps you will see her again.'

'You're not having it,' Joe said.

'You will change your mind.' Kruger buried the rifle's butt

in his shoulder and aimed at Tuck. 'Shall we begin with the fat cleric?'

Becky was about to use her powers on the rifle, when a stiff gust of wind blew back her hair, hindering her concentration. The temperature plummeted. An orb of light appeared equidistant between Tuck and Kruger. It expanded outward, vibrant, bedazzling light, spellbinding in every way. With a loud *crack* it exploded, sending jagged branches of light in all directions, before disappearing, leaving a small shimmering figure in its stead.

Barbie stood there, hands on hips. 'Oh, finally,' she said, searching for Uncle Percy, who looked both astonished and elated in equal measure. 'Sir, the Omega Effect is behaving most unpredictably – quite different from anything I've seen or heard of before. You simply would not believe the amount of times I've tried to join you all, but I've barely been able to get close, never mind intervene. Still, I'm pleased to see it's finally lifted.' She turned and looked at Kruger. 'Oh, it's you ….'

Overcoming his surprise, Kruger turned the rifle on Barbie and fired a torrent of shots into her. After five or so seconds, he stopped.

'Oh, stop that you silly psychopath,' Barbie said. 'For heaven's sake, are you blind as well as stupid? I'm an Electroic Cognivated Gynoid, so what precisely do you expect your bullets to do, other than leave the odd dent?' She tapped her head twice as if to prove her point. 'Still, what you won't know about me is I have a magnetised deresistor built into the palm of my right hand. It won't work on your arm, but -' She raised her tiny hand. Straight away, an orange glow ignited her palm. '- It will almost certainly work on your toy.'

To Kruger's astonishment, the gun flew from his hand,

soared through the air. Barbie caught it and crushed it in her tiny fingers as if it were paper, before hurling it aside. 'Stupid guns,' she said. 'Anyway, Mister Kruger, precisely nine minutes ago I saw you and your companions arrive behind Saint Cuthbert's while my architect and his family were below ground. Now, although I was some distance away, it was clear you would never let them leave this place without a fight …' She paused. 'So I brought you one...'

Her eyes glowed white. At that moment, balls of light appeared all around like flickering stars, ballooning in size, before a thunderous *boooom* shattered the air. From nowhere, men appeared on horseback, some bearing swords, others with bows and arrows.

Becky's heart leapt.

The merry men attacked the jeeps first, sending arrow upon arrow at them, striking the Associates before they had chance to use their modern weapons. Barbie had instructed them well.

Kruger's chest swelled with fury. With astonishing speed, he sprinted over to Arthur Berrymead, wrenched him from his horse, and punched his face with a bone-shattering crunch, knocking him out cold. He turned swiftly and did the same with Eldred Mulch.

Michael Brundle steered his horse toward Kruger, swung his broadsword high, then brought it down, targeting Kruger's neck. With cat-like reflexes, Kruger caught the sword in his metal hand, pulled Brundle from his horse and in one powerful movement, slammed his fist down on Brundle's skull, who fell in an unconscious heap. Then he scooped up Brundle's sword, his eyes scanning the battlefield for Will.

Terror surged through Becky. Kruger was swifter, stronger, more terrible than she'd seen him before, than she'd seen anyone before.

The merry men turned their attentions to the King's men, who were ill prepared for such a quick and ferocious attack. Wearing no armour to weigh them down, the merry men were much faster and deadlier. Aleric Fletcher was the most lethal of them all. He had abandoned his horse and was weaving between King John's men, locating breaches in their armour and, with unerring accuracy, shooting arrows into the gaps, only moving on when sure the knight could be a threat no more.

Will, Joe, Uncle Percy and Tuck had also entered the fray.

Joe, in particular, was an unstoppable force. Taking on two knights at a time, Excalibur's enchanted blade sliced through steel like scissors through thread, leaving every blade it struck in pieces. Barbie, too, had every intention of doing her bit, flying overhead, speeding from knight to knight, smashing her fist down on as many helmets as she could.

Becky surveyed the chaos. Despite being outnumbered, she was in no doubt they were winning. It was then, amidst this chaos, she saw Will and Kruger approach each other. To her astonishment, Will leaned in and whispered something, which sent Kruger into a wild frenzy. He rushed at Will, arcing his sword high. Will pivoted, sidestepped the blow, and thrust forward in a counterattack. Kruger, faster than when they had fought previously, ducked the assault. More blows were traded, blades clanging. Each man launched strike after strike, with nothing penetrating the other's defences, but after a while there was no doubt that it was Will who was tiring.

In that instant, Becky knew she had to help. Images of Kruger's atrocities flooded her mind – the murder of Lady Caroline and Lady Anne, of Maria and Jacob's family, of

Captain Briggs and the crew of the Mary Celeste, and of the countless others across so many time periods. Forget what she'd said to Joe - Kruger had to be stopped, and if it meant his death, then so be it.

She could end Otto Kruger.

She focussed on Kruger. Concentrating all her energies, blocking everything else from her mind, she visualised him in every way. Immediately, the watery sensation swept the crown of her head, before permeating her eyes, when -

BOOOOOM!

An almighty explosion ripped Saint Cuthbert's church apart, forming a colossal ball of flame, smoke and dust. The ground shuddered violently, sending shockwaves all about. Horses whinnied in fright, rearing on their hind legs, hurling their riders to the ground, before bolting off in all directions.

Becky's ears screamed in pain.

The battle stopped at once. Disorientated, everyone stared at the deep crater formed where the church had once stood. Then, from deep within the heavy cloud, streaks of crimson light illuminated the swirling dust and ash. As the dust settled, a figure stumbled into view - a woman, her sky blue dress torn to shreds, her head tilted down as if in shame, hiding her face from the world.

Marian looked up. Her eyes were blotchy and swollen, her cheeks daubed with blood and tears. Almost immediately, a tall, slender man followed her into the open, his hand gripping a pistol that was aimed at her head.

'Now that's how to make an entrance,' Emerson Drake said.

Chapter 32

The Road's End

Drake kept walking until clear of the bombsite, Marian never more than a metre ahead. He surveyed the gaping mouths before him, his eyes searching out Uncle Percy. Identifying him, he gestured for Marian to stop. 'Percy, did you know that fiery creation of mine – I call it an Artax-bomb - has been buried beneath Saint Cuthbert's since the Pliocene Epoch? Can you believe it's remained both stable and operational after all that time?'

Uncle Percy didn't respond.

'Seriously,' Drake continued. 'That's over five million years with no impact on functionality. Even the great Percy Halifax must forsake his usual envy and accept I've created a remarkable little device.'

Uncle Percy remained expressionless.

'No, well, never mind.' Drake shrugged. 'Frankly, I had no intention of being here today, but it seems my presence is necessary. I really do need this particular Eden Relic. And besides, it has given me the opportunity to do a trial run with the Artax technology for my future endeavors.'

Uncle Percy's eyes narrowed at these words.

Drake nodded at Excalibur. 'Congratulations on finding the Sword of Ages, by the way. My Associates really didn't have much idea as to its location, and I've been far too busy with other things to do the legwork. I'd give you a round of applause but, as you can see, I'm holding a Beretta M1934 and I don't want to accidentally fire a bullet into Marian's cranium. Actually, as a keen historian, Percy, you may be interested to know this is the very same pistol used to assassinate someone you've met and liked very much - Mohandas Ghandi - so it already has an excellent pedigree for terminating the virtuous…'

'Go to hell, Emerson!'

'Oh, I've been there. I didn't care for it much.' Drake's grin threatened to cover his entire face. 'Hello again, Rebecca … Joe… Or should I say George?'

'It's Joe,' Joe snapped back.

'Very well,' Drake replied, acting surprised. 'But I would've thought you may prefer your birth name, particularly after the way you've played such a significant part in the history of this country.'

When Joe returned a confused look, Drake continued, 'It just so happens your recent skirmish with the Kraken - yes, I did a short time trip and found out all about that - laid the real-life foundations for the Saint George and the Dragon legend. You can't quite lay claim to being the original Saint George - he was a fourth century Christian Martyr - but certainly your story and his merge over time and become the rousing fable we all know and love. And as Saint George is the Patron Saint of England, I should've thought it would rouse some patriotic fervour in you?'

Joe wasn't interested at all. 'I couldn't give a flying -'

'Ah, but you really should,' Drake interrupted. 'All we can hope for in our short time on this earth is to make our mark in some way and you've certainly done that. Still, I can understand if you're not quite yourself at the moment. It can't be easy discovering your life has been a series of deceits by people claiming to care for you. I can't imagine how that makes you feel.'

'Not as bad as you must've felt when you pushed Granny off that cliff.'

Drake looked startled, but regained his composure almost immediately. 'To be honest, I didn't feel bad about that at all ... far from it. My darling Grandmother wasn't exactly the gentlest of souls. Frankly, she was a hateful, vindictive woman who deserved everything she got. I often wonder what she was thinking in those last few seconds as she plunged to her death ... I do hope it was of me.'

'And what about Melanie Hunt?' Joe added.

This time, rage blazed in Drake's eyes, as if Joe had touched on a matter buried for some time. 'Melanie was a pimple on the skin of this world,' he said, punctuating each word with venom. 'And if you say her name again there will be serious consequences.' He waited for a moment, allowed an insincere smile to round his lips and then turned to Becky. 'Now, Rebecca, what's this about a potential boyfriend? Dan Hardman, is it? I can't deny he's a handsome chap, but is he good enough for you? Would you like me to investigate into the way he behaves around women? You can never be too careful – good looks and charm are seldom signs of fine character. And besides I do feel somewhat responsible for you getting together in the first place.'

'We're not together,' Becky snapped back. 'And you just keep away from him, and anyone else I know.' She fought back a powerful desire to squash Drake's head like a lemon. 'Just put that gun down, give Marian to us and leave before you or anyone else gets hurt. You do know what I can do, don't you?'

'I know a lot more about you than you think,' Drake jeered. 'I also know I've planted a second Artax-bomb just below where you're all standing.' He withdrew a gadget from his pocket and raised it for all to see. 'This detonator can decide whether we all live or die. And with that in mind - I don't want anyone trying anything rash … no ridiculous heroics, no futile gestures of bravery. No one even moves until my business here is done. After all, we don't want anyone getting hurt in any crossfire.' He stepped closer to Marian and cocked the gun. 'What say you, Will?'

'Let Marian go,' Will said, desperation in his voice. 'It's me you want.'

'You?' Drake scoffed. 'Frankly, I don't give a damn about you. But I do want the sword.' He turned to Joe. 'So, boy, will you give it to me? Or am I to be the one to exterminate the legendary Maid Marian?'

Joe didn't respond.

'Pass over the sword, Joe,' Will urged.

For the first time since they had met, Joe saw an emotion on Will's face he'd not seen before: fear. 'But, Will, it's an Eden Relic. Drake can't get hold of an Eden Relic.'

'Please, Joe,' Will said. 'Marian cannot be harmed. If I mean anything to you, then give Drake the sword now. That is how it must be. I cannot say more. Do you have faith in me?

'Course I do, but -'

'Then he must take the sword,' Will said. He glanced at Drake. 'If we give you Excalibur you will leave this place now … Do you agree?'

'I am here for the sword,' Drake replied. 'Nothing else matters.'

'And there will be no more violence against my friends on

this day?'

'I give you my word.'

'The word of a liar means nothing,' Will replied. 'But I do know on this occasion you will keep it.'

Drake pondered these words with suspicion. 'How do you know?'

A curious expression flashed on Will's face. 'Pass over Excalibur, Joe.'

Joe couldn't bring himself to do it. He stared at Uncle Percy, who appeared conflicted, as if two powerful ideas were tearing him in opposite directions, neither leading him to an acceptable outcome. 'Uncle Percy?'

Uncle Percy ignored him. 'Are you sure, Will?' There was the strangest tone to his voice.

'There is no doubt in my mind,' Will replied. 'Percy, we have discussed this at length and you promised to keep your word.'

Becky stared at Uncle Percy, confused. *Keep his word about what?*

'I know what I said,' Uncle Percy said in a small voice.

'Then do as you promised.'

Uncle Percy looked broken. 'Please, Joe, do as Will says. Give up the sword.'

As far as Joe was concerned, Uncle Percy's words were the final nail in the coffin. Every ounce of defiance left him. As Will approached him, he handed over Excalibur, offering no resistance, his head swirling with a mixture of betrayal and a deep-rooted anger that their efforts had been for nothing.

Will saw that Joe was furious. 'All is not as it seems, Joe,' he whispered. 'Whatever comes to pass, Joe, you must not get involved. I have a wider plan that will make everything right.'

'A plan?' Joe said. 'What plan?'

But Will had turned away. Excalibur gleaming brightly in his hands, he walked over to Drake.

'What did he say?' Becky asked.

'He's got a plan,' Joe whispered. 'I knew he would.'

Becky watched Will come to a halt four feet away from Drake. For a fleeting moment, she thought he was going to kill Drake there and then. But he didn't move a muscle. Instead, he waited for Drake to point the gun away from Marian, before raising Excalibur high and plunging it deep into the soft earth. 'Excalibur is yours.' He took three steps back. 'Now release Marian.'

Drake never once took his eyes from the sword. He motioned for Marian to join Will. She dashed into his arms.

'Marian.' Will cupped her face with his palms. 'Marian … please stand with Joe.'

'I'm not leaving your side.'

'Do as I ask,' Will replied. 'I beg thee.'

Grudgingly, Marian kissed his cheek, and then walked over to Joe, who looked more confused with each passing second.

'What the hell's going on?' Joe said to Becky. 'Why's Will just standing there?'

Becky couldn't find an answer.

Drake pocketed the pistol. Then he reached down and drew the sword from the ground. Curling Excalibur in his fingers, he stared mesmerised at the glittering blade, his eyes gliding over every contour, every detail, like a father exploring his newborn child for the first time. 'It is everything I dreamed it would be,' he breathed. Then his face changed. His mouth twisted into a sneer. 'You know,' he hissed so quietly only Will could hear. 'I was telling the truth. For reasons of my own, I do need your extended family unharmed. They won't suffer any more violence today.'

'Good,' Will replied.

'But I didn't say anything about you …'

Will didn't flinch. 'Do with me what you will. I shall not object.'

'Interesting.' The ghost of a smile curled on Drake's mouth. 'You see, recently I made a promise to Mister Kruger … And I always keep my promises.'

Will remained impassive.

'Shall we see what he has to say about the matter?' Drake shouted over to Kruger, 'OTTO … JOIN US!'

Becky watched as Kruger set off to join Drake. 'This isn't good, Joe.'

'It'll be okay,' Joe whispered back. 'Will said it would. Just get ready to fight if he gives the signal.'

In twenty long strides, Kruger was standing beside Drake, his chilling gaze fixed on Will, watchful, waiting for a reason to strike. 'Yes, sir?'

'Otto,' Drake said. 'It is time I honoured my promise. Shakelock's fate is now in your hands. Apparently, he says we can do with him as we will. He will not object…'

'Really?' Kruger said, surprised. 'And if I choose to kill you, groundsman, then you would let that happen before your woman, your family, your friends … What kind of a man would do that?'

To Kruger's frustration, a serene expression appeared on Will's face. 'A man content in the belief that is as it should be.' It was Will's turn to smile. 'But know this … you have never bested me in battle. And you never shall. Now do what you must …' He raised his arms wide.

'What's he doing?' Becky asked Joe. 'When's this plan going to –' She glanced at Uncle Percy, and saw his eyes were dampening. In that moment, she knew instinctively what was about to happen. Her eyes flicked back to Will, desperate to use her powers somehow. By the time she saw the flash of metal in Kruger's hand, it was too late.

Otto Kruger sank his service dagger deep into Will's stomach, twisting it, knowing full well there was no way of surviving the strike.

Refusing to show any pain, Will collapsed to his knees, before slumping forward. He landed face down on the ground, blood pooling around him.

'WILLLLLLL!' Joe screamed. Fuelled with rage, he charged at Kruger.

Uncle Percy leapt in his path, flinging his arms around Joe's body, using all his strength to hold him back. 'No, Joe! This is what Will wanted. This had to happen…'

Joe wasn't listening. 'Let me go!' he yelled, kicking out like a wild animal. 'LET ME GO!'

Uncle Percy's grip intensified, clamping Joe powerfully to his chest, as if believing the mere act could lessen Joe's pain. Within seconds, Joe stopped struggling, his rage replaced by grief. The tears exploded from his eyes.

At the same time, a silent scream blared in Becky's head, never finding its way to her mouth. Distraught, Marian had already raced to Will's side, and was softly stroking his long hair, sharing words no one but they would ever hear.

In a horrified daze, Uncle Percy, Becky and Joe walked over. As they reached Will, Marian peered up at Uncle Percy through inflamed eyes. 'He wishes to speak to you.'

Uncle Percy fell to his knees. 'Yes, my dear Will?'

'Closer,' Will managed.

Uncle Percy leaned in, his ear an inch from Will's mouth. Will whispered something, which Uncle Percy responded to with a look of surprise and a nod. 'Of course, old friend.' His voice cracked. 'I shall…'

Will was fading now, the colour rapidly leaving his face. Straining, he turned his head toward Joe. 'C-come, boy.'

Joe sank to the ground and gathered Will's hand in his. 'Don't go,' he pleaded. 'Please, Will, don't leave me …'

'I shall never leave you,' Will exhaled. He strained a smile. 'I need you to live a worthy life, Joe, a life at the behest of no one but yourself, and I need you to be the protector now. Protect your uncle, your sister, all at Bowen Hall. Do that for me…'

'I will.'

'I - I am truly honoured to have known you -' Will swallowed a breath. ' - And to have loved you, Joe Mellor …' And with those words having just left his mouth, Will Shakelock closed his eyes for the final time and died.

Chapter 33

Farewell to a Friend

Becky's world collapsed. She didn't even notice Drake type six digits on his portravella and grasp Kruger's arm. Within seconds, their bodies were enfolded in dazzling light and, surveying the outpourings of brief with pitiless smiles, they disappeared.

Becky didn't care. Nothing mattered anymore. She stood immobile for an age, a living statue, her brain incapable of telling her body to move, her eyes to weep, her mouth to scream. A small part of her mind, the part that somehow clung to reality despite the pain, half expected a future Uncle Percy to appear at any moment and somehow reverse all that had happened, saving Will's life and reclaiming Excalibur in the process. It didn't happen. No one came.

One by one, the merry men shuffled forward in disbelief, surrounding their fallen comrade, heads down. A distraught Tuck administered a short prayer, his words disrupted by spluttering breaths.

Becky's eyes found Joe's. He was staring vacantly into space, his face displaying no emotion, whatsoever – no sadness, no anger, no sorrow … nothing. The tears had stopped. His body had shut down like a toy with a drained battery. She was about to hug him when he emerged from his trance, his eyes finding Uncle Percy, anger spreading slowly across his face.

'Come with me,' Joe snarled, keeping his voice down as best he could. He seized Uncle Percy's arm and dragged him away at pace.

Becky was speechless. She followed them, walking as quickly as she could.

When they reached what Joe considered an acceptable distance from the others, he swivelled round to Uncle Percy, jaws clenched and roared, 'You knew, didn't you? You knew he was going to die here … today!' He mopped the tears pooling in his eyes.

'No.' Uncle Percy shook his head. 'I didn't. I swear.'

'Then what was all that about a promise?'

Uncle Percy fought to manage his own grief, whilst maintaining his composure for the sake of Becky and Joe. 'Will told me there would come a moment on this trip when I'd have to do something that went against every instinct I had - a moment when I had to follow his wishes to the letter, whether I agreed with them or not. He said he would make it clear when that moment had arrived.' He reached out to place his hand on Joe's shoulder. 'I'm sorry, Joe, but –'

Still angry, Joe slapped the hand away. 'Don't touch me!'

Uncle Percy nodded sadly.

'When did Will say all of this?' Becky asked quietly.

Uncle Percy inhaled deeply. 'The night you showed me the lottery ticket I knew we had to travel to Medieval England without you. I visited Will at his tree house and we agreed to leave immediately. It was then he told me something significant would happen at some point on this trip. Something I might consider to be a bad thing, but that was necessary for the wellbeing of everyone in the future.'

'Do you think he knew he was going to die?' Becky asked.

Uncle Percy was struggling to keep it together. 'In retrospect, yes I do. But he gave me no indication at the time it would be anything like that. I would have never agreed if I'd have known, whatever the repercussions.'

'But how could he have known?' Joe asked.

'I'm not sure,' Uncle Percy replied. 'He wouldn't tell me more than I've told you. He kept it all vague, and begged me not to pursue the matter. He said I had to trust him. And of course I did...'

Joe wasn't satisfied. 'Yeah, well ... we're going back in time to try and change all of this.'

'We can't, Joe,' Uncle Percy said miserably. 'I gave my word.'

'Who cares about your stupid word?' Joe snapped.

'He did. And he insisted matters run their course, that one day I would understand why. And out of respect for our beloved friend, we shall honour that request...'

'But I don't want to,' Joe replied, trembling.

'I know,' Uncle Percy said emptily. 'And I know there's nothing I can say that can possibly make this better ... for any of us.'

Joe's face cracked. 'I - I just want him back,' he whispered. Shoulders shaking, he began to weep uncontrollably.

'I know you do.' Uncle Percy pulled Joe into an embrace. 'We all do ...'

Seeing this, Becky felt like her heart had been torn from her chest. She flung her arms around them both and squeezed with every bit of strength she could muster. And then, standing there, the three of them allowed their tears to mix as one.

*

By the time they returned to the others, a peach slice moon had appeared in the sky. Following a short discussion, it was the general consensus Will be buried in Sherwood Forest, and when Uncle Percy recounted the tale of the Major Oak and Will's connection with the legend of Robin Hood, it was decided he should be laid to rest there the following day. Against the better judgment of some of the merry men, it was decided the surviving knights of King John should be released unharmed. One after another, Barbie memorased each and every one of them, ensuring not one of them could recall the events of the last few days.

Upon their return to Sherwood Forest, Becky and Joe skulked around in a daze. They spent the evening ambling the woods until darkness fell, before returning to the camp where they sat beside the campfire with the merry men, listening to them tell stories about Will's life. More tears were shed, sad songs sung and laughter shared. It was a poignant but magnificent celebration of a life well lived.

The next morning, Becky awoke to the sound of red squirrels playing in the trees. Before she had even opened her eyes, the horror of the previous day crashed over her. Her pillow was still damp from the tears spilt overnight. She left the tree hut and inhaled the fresh air, which was as crisp as lettuce. The sky was a canopy of the richest blue, cloudless and never-ending, and despite her grief she acknowledged there couldn't be a more beautiful day for a funeral.

At noon, everyone gathered on the edge of the camp. Will's body had been wrapped in a green linen shroud and placed in an oak coffin, which Eldred Mulch and Arthur Berrymead had crafted during the night, whittling scenes from Will's lifetime on the wood like the panels of a comic book.

As the midday sun reached its apex, the procession set off slowly. Aleric Fletcher led the way, brandishing a wooden cross. Tuck followed close behind, wielding a bronze thurible before him, suspended on a single chain, which perfumed the air as it swayed left and right. Behind him, the coffin bearers - Little John, Arthur Stutely, Uncle Percy and Joe – held Will's coffin firmly to their shoulders.

Becky and Marian, her face screened behind a lace veil, came next, their hands entwined as one, with the remaining merry men and their families bringing up the rear.

As they walked, Becky saw the most remarkable thing … something that moved her beyond words. Hundreds of people, perhaps thousands, were emerging from the shadows of the trees – men, women and children - flanking the path ahead on both sides, each clasping a candle that flickered in the dark forest. Somehow word of Will's death had travelled far and wide, and the people of Nottinghamshire had turned out in force to lament the passing of their champion. For the first time in what seemed like forever, a smile found its way on to Becky's face.

Within twenty minutes they had passed Beryl's ravaged shell, and were standing beside an already dug grave beside the sapling that would one day be known throughout the world as The Major Oak.

Becky stood graveside, barely able to comprehend what life would be like without Will. Since their first meeting, her life had changed forever. She had journeyed in time, battled an array of the most fantastical foes, encountered some of the very best and worst specimens of humankind, and throughout Will had been ever present, protecting her and Joe, a shining example of courage and decency in a strange and often violent world. But now he had gone.

He was a memory.

*

The service itself lasted no more than twenty minutes. Tuck recited three passages in Latin from a hand painted bible; Alan A Dale performed a ballad so melodious it silenced the birds in the trees; and both Uncle Percy and Little John delivered such heartfelt eulogies their words were barely audible over the sobs from many in the crowd. Tuck gave a final reading as Will was lowered into the ground. Then the merry men stepped up one at a time and scattered soil on the coffin below.

Marian was the last to approach the grave. Lifting her veil, she knelt down, closed her eyes and whispered something only she could hear. After the service was over, the grave was filled in and the crowd dissolved into the forest.

Even then, Joe couldn't bring himself to leave the grave, as he stared at the stone headstone that read:

Here lies William Shakelock

Lord of the Forest

Prince of Thieves

King of Englishmen

'Come, Joe,' Uncle Percy said. 'It's time we thought about going home...'

Soon after they returned to the camp where they said their goodbyes to the merry men.

'If there ever be an occasion you need friends, Percy Halifax,' Little John said. 'Then the good men of Sherwood shall be proud to join those ranks.'

'I know that, John,' Uncle Percy replied. 'And thank you.'

Little John turned to Joe. 'The friar deems you would make a fine king. Are you sure that is not your wish? There are many that would support your claim.'

'I'm no king,' Joe replied.

'Only one worthy of the title would ever say such a thing.'

It's still no,' Joe replied, shaking his head. 'Besides, Will gave me a job to do before he died.' He fixed Uncle Percy and Becky with a determined look. 'And I intend to do that.'

'And you will resume your quest for the Holy Sword?' Tuck asked Uncle Percy.

'I'm not sure yet, Angus,' Uncle Percy replied. 'Will was content for Drake to take it so he must've known something we don't. Either way, it's the last thing on my mind at the moment.'

Marian embraced Becky. 'Well, Becky, I bid you a safe journey and pray our paths cross again.'

'I'd like that,' Becky said, returning the hug twofold. 'Will you be okay?'

'Time heals many things,' Marian replied sadly. 'But a love lost can never be truly healed, only mourned. Be that as it may, the true offence would've been if Will and I never voiced our feelings. So I will always have his words to comfort me in the dark years to come …'

A short while later, Uncle Percy, Becky and Joe returned to Will's grave one last time. As they stood there, Joe turned to Uncle Percy and said, 'Uncle Percy, can I ask you something?'

'Of course, Joe.'

'What did Will say to you when he was dying? He whispered something to you, what was it?'

'I can't tell you that at the moment.'

'Why?'

'Because he asked me to show you,' Uncle Percy replied mysteriously. 'I believe he thought it might help us deal with the grief. It might even explain in part why he wanted everything to turn out the way it did.'

'What do you mean?'

'As you well know, with regards to time travel, whatever we do in the past can have a knock on effect and even instigate change in the future - if the Omega Effect doesn't occur, that is. This is something he didn't want to run the risk of changing.'

Becky mulled this over for a moment. 'But what could be so important he'd rather die than risk changing this 'something', whatever it is?'

'Just take my arm and we'll see,' Uncle Percy replied.

Becky and Joe grasped his forearm as he tapped in six digits on his portravella. A moment later, they vanished.

*

As Becky's eyes adjusted to the new environment, she saw trees surrounded them once more. 'Are we still in Sherwood Forest?'

'No,' Uncle Percy replied.

'So where are we?'

'Oh, you'll recognise it soon enough,' Uncle Percy replied. 'Come on.'

They had only advanced a few steps when a familiar building appeared through the branches: Wulvern House.

'What're we doing back here?' Joe asked.

'Hopefully, we're here to see someone,' Uncle Percy replied. 'Well ... two people actually.'

Staring out at Wulvern House, Becky thought it even lovelier than before. Bordered by great beds overflowing with flowers of every colour, the house had been newly painted and the wide lawns freshly shorn. 'How far into the future have we come?'

'Nearly five years from the day of Will's funeral,' Uncle Percy replied.

'Okay,' Becky nodded. 'So who lives here now?'

'Marian.'

Becky looked surprised. 'Marian?'

'Yes,' Uncle Percy replied.

'Can we see her?'

'Let's just stay out of sight ... for today at least,' Uncle Percy said. 'Now we might have to wait some time, but I'm hoping that –'

'Look!' Joe cut in, pointing at the house.

The front door opened. Marian appeared, a large wicker basket crammed with food in her right hand. She was laughing and shouted back to someone to her rear.

At that moment, Becky had the shock of her life. A small boy followed her out, his long wavy brown hair dishevelled and wild. He wielded a fishing pole above his head like a quarterstaff, and thrust it forward as if striking an invisible foe.

'Joe Shakelock,' Marian said. 'You shall break that pole if you are not watchful.'

'Forgive me, Mama,' the boy replied, grinning. 'I just like to fight.'

'I know,' Marian smiled, shaking her head. 'And for that you are truly your father's son.'

Becky glanced at Joe, who had frozen with astonishment. *Joe Shakelock.*

'You asked me what Will said when he was dying, Joe,' Uncle Percy said. 'He told me about this. He knew Marian would have his son.'

Becky's head spiralled. 'But how … what … when?'

'The night we stayed at Wulvern House,' Uncle Percy replied. 'Marian and Will stayed up most of the night talking. Apparently, that wasn't all they did. They made a child … and nine months later, Marian named that child, Joe.'

Joe's face blushed with pride. It took him a few seconds before he could formulate any words. 'Let's go home …' he said quietly.

Uncle Percy coiled his arm round Joe's shoulder. 'Yes, let's …'

Watching Marian and Joe disappear into the distance, Becky found herself flooded with conflicting emotions – sorrow, joy, grief, and to her surprise hope. Will had made the ultimate sacrifice, but he had done it for a reason – a reason he was convinced warranted paying that price. And she had to believe the same. She had to believe he knew something good was around the corner. Yes, they had lost Excalibur, but the war with Drake was far from over, and it was a war she intended to win.

A war they had to win … for Will's sake.

But for now Uncle Percy was right. Emerson Drake should be the last thing on their minds. Now was a time to reflect, to rebuild, and do everything they could to support Joe in the difficult months ahead. And she would willingly do that. After all, he was her brother. She would have it no other way.

Epilogue

Name and Shame

John Mellor was certain he currently inhabited a cell in a Russian Gulag camp. He wasn't exactly sure of where or when, although if pushed he would estimate somewhere between 1936 and 1939. He was also convinced it was a labour camp, not that he was ever let out to work. He would've preferred that. At least he might've seen another human being, other than his brutish prison guard, Olaf, even if he was forced to wear the iron mask so no one could identify him. Instead, he sat here day in, day out in a concrete dungeon with no bed, no chair, and no windows to give any indication there was even a world outside.

The Associates had been clever this time. They made sure Olaf gave him more food than at his former prisons, not enough to increase his strength or weight, but enough to keep the breath in his lungs. He had also been given an extra layer of clothing and a yak-hair blanket to help combat the minus twenty degree temperatures that were a nightly occurrence. Yes, it was clear someone had been given strict instructions to keep him alive. And that was fine by him, because he had no intention of dying.

As he sat huddled in the corner, his cell door opened and a gigantic Associate filled the doorway, blocking whatever light came from the single bulb in the corridor behind.

'On your feet!' the Associate growled. 'It's your lucky day, son.' Striding forward, he kicked Mellor brutally in the ribs.

The kick hurt much more than Mellor would reveal. 'You call that a kick?'

The Associate kicked him again, harder this time. 'I can do this all day.'

'I can take it all day.'

The Associate grasped a handful of Mellor's long matted hair and wrenched him to his feet. 'I don't think so, son. Besides, you're goin' on a little holiday. Mister Drake reckons you need a bit of sun.'

'That's very kind of him,' Mellor replied. 'I fancy a fortnight in the Bahamas –a beach hut, champagne cocktails, swordfish on the barbeque.'

'I don't think that's what Mister Drake's got in mind,' the Associate replied. 'But in a few seconds you can ask him yourself.' He drew his right cuff to reveal a wrist portravella. Keying in six digits, he grabbed Mellor's neck. A moment later, the two men were encased in a glittering sphere of crimson light. In a shattering *boom*, they vanished.

His ears still ringing, John Mellor felt a sudden rise in temperature. Looking round, he knew at once he'd arrived in the atrium of a vast Roman Villa. The high-ceilinged room had frescoed walls, towering marble pillars, a large golden statue of the God, Jupiter, and a lengthy mosaic floor that led to a balcony outside, standing upon which was Emerson Drake.

'Nice to see you again, John,' Drake said, extending his arms. 'And welcome to Ancient Rome.'

Mellor told him precisely what he could do with his welcome.

'Now, now, that's hardly polite,' Drake replied. 'After some of your recent accommodations, I thought you might appreciate a few hours in this beautiful city, particularly on this momentous night.'

'Why?' Mellor replied. 'D'you plan on killing yourself? I would appreciate that.'

'Heavens, no. Why would I do that when I'm so close to realising my ambitions? No, today is the 18th July 64AD. Does that date ring any bells?'

'The Great Fire of Rome?' Mellor replied dryly.

'Quite right,' Drake replied. 'And it's literally just started, why don't you come and take a look? We have excellent seats…'

Mellor didn't move.

Drake gestured to the Associate. 'Mister Denton, would you persuade our friend here to come and join me?'

The Associate pulled out a pistol and pressed it against Mellor's spine, shoving him forward. 'Come on, son, be a nice boy and do as Mister Drake says.'

Reluctantly, Mellor joined Drake on the balcony.

'Now just look at that view,' Drake said, pointing ahead. 'Isn't that the most extraordinary sight?'

Mellor didn't respond immediately. There was no doubt Ancient Rome was one of the most spectacular cities the world had ever seen, but the Great Fire lasted for six days, destroyed seventy per cent of the city and killed thousands of Roman citizens, most from whom were from the poorest sections of the population. 'If you like watching people burn to death, then I suppose it is.'

'Oh, don't be such a killjoy. Seriously, I always find the experience so calming. Actually, this is my sixth time of watching the fire and I always find a different villa to enjoy the show.' He looked back at the Atrium. 'I'm particularly fond of this one. It's the home of the notable politician, Claudius Aelius, and is on Palatine Hill, so we're really quite close to all the action. Exciting, eh?'

'You are a sick monster.'

'Do you think so?' Drake smiled cruelly. 'If I am, then I'm a sick monster with an Eden Relic.'

Mellor struggled to hide the shock on his face.

Drake enjoyed the reaction. 'Yes, I am now in possession of the Sword of Ages – the legendary Excalibur - a particularly important relic if you know the full extent of its powers. But I doubt you will, and I certainly know that fool, Halifax, won't have a clue what it can do.' He chuckled. 'Anyway, I've not brought you here to gloat about the sword, I have others news. Tragically, your old friend, Will Shakelock, is now dead ... and perhaps more significantly to you and your family, your adopted son knows all about his real daddy. Poor Joe, he really didn't take it well. Little tyke.'

Enraged, Mellor was about to launch himself at Drake when he heard the harsh click of a gun being cocked.

The Associate levelled the pistol at Mellor's head. 'Calm it, son.'

'What does Joe know?'

'Everything,' Drake smirked. 'Well ... nearly everything. There are some things very few people know about. For instance, I've been finding out some wonderful tales about you, ones that have led me to the conclusion you and I are not so different after all.'

'We're as different as you can get,' Mellor fired back.

'Really?' Drake replied with mock sincerity. 'And would Edward Timmerson agree with you on that?'

The colour drained from Mellor's face.

'Yes, I know all about poor Mister Timmerson,' Drake replied. 'What a heart-warming story that is. I wonder how Rebecca will feel when she finds out about him?' He snorted. 'Seriously, how can you call me a monster, because if I am - what on earth does that make you?' Then Drake began to laugh - a laughter that settled on the warm night air, before mingling with the screams of terror rising from the inferno below.

Becky, Joe and Uncle Percy will return.

CARL ASHMORE

Carl is a children's writer from Cheshire, England. He has written six books for children: 'The Time Hunters,' 'The Time Hunters and the Box of Eternity,' 'The Time Hunters and the Spear of Fate,' 'The Time Hunters and the Sword of Ages', 'The Night They Nicked Saint Nick,' and 'Bernard and the Bibble.'

He is currently working on the fifth and final book in the Time Hunters series.

He can be contacted at carlashmore@mailcity.com

CPSIA information can be obtained
at www.ICGtesting.com
Printed in the USA
LVOW12s1348270516
490289LV00011B/133/P